The *Spinster Brides*
OF CACTUS CORNER

*Four Women Make Orphans a Priority
and Finally Open Doors to Romance*

**FRANCES DEVINE · LENA NELSON DOOLEY
VICKIE MCDONOUGH · JERI ODELL**

BARBOUR
PUBLISHING

© 2007 *The Spinster and the Cowboy* by Lena Nelson Dooley
© 2007 *The Spinster and the Lawyer* by Jeri Odell
© 2007 *The Spinster and the Doctor* by Frances Devine
© 2007 *The Spinster and the Tycoon* by Vickie McDonough

ISBN 978-1-59789-583-5

All scripture quotations are taken from the King James Version of the Bible.

This book is a work of fiction. Names, characters, places, and incidents are either products of the author's imagination or used fictitiously. Any similarity to actual people, organizations, and/or events is purely coincidental.

Published by Barbour Publishing, Inc., P.O. Box 719, Uhrichsville, OH 44683, www.barbourbooks.com

Our mission is to publish and distribute inspirational products offering exceptional value and biblical encouragement to the masses.

 Member of the
Evangelical Christian
Publishers Association

Printed in the United States of America.
5 4 3 2 1

The Spinster and the Cowboy

by Lena Nelson Dooley

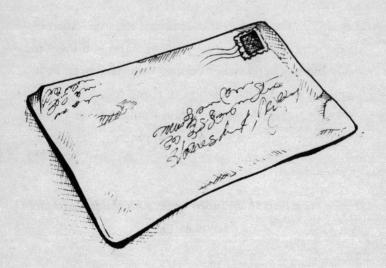

Dedication

This book is dedicated to the new people God has
brought into the critique group that meets in my home—
Saundra Kay, Rhonda Fields, Dawn Morton Nelson,
Lynne Gentry, Joe and Lori May (returned), Khristi Hullett,
Patricia Carroll, Jacqueline (JJ) Overpeck, Mindy Obenhaus,
Kevin Kane, Christy Gibson, Margo Carmichael (finally),
Linda Kozar (online), Jane Thornton, and Kaci Hill.
God just keeps blessing me with wonderful friends.

And as always, this book is also dedicated to James Allen Dooley,
who married me forty-two years ago and still loves me.
My life has been richer because you have been in it.
You are the one person who can come to my office door
and interrupt me when I am writing.
I love you more every day.

A good man leaveth an inheritance to his children's children.
PROVERBS 13:22

Prologue

San Francisco, Spring 1894

W hen the sharp rap on his closed office door roused him, Joshua Dillinger raised his gaze from the legal document he had been studying with intense concentration. He hated distractions, and Charles Ross, his secretary, knew it. Only something of great urgency would cause this interruption.

"Enter." Joshua realized that his command sounded abrupt, but he wanted to get this interruption over with so he could discern any flaws in the contract that had to be ready for signatures in less than an hour.

Brandishing an envelope, the thin man walked briskly across the rug that swallowed the sound of his footsteps. "This was just delivered by messenger, sir. I have a feeling it's important."

He handed the missive to Joshua and hurried out of the room, pulling the door closed behind him. Joshua studied his father's scratchy scrawl on the front of the letter. He wondered how the post office even knew where to send it. The older Father became, the worse his handwriting grew. If Joshua hadn't been used to deciphering the letters he received from his dad, he wouldn't have been able to tell what the address was.

Joshua placed the packet on top of the stack of documents that needed his attention today and turned back to his contract. He returned to the place where he held his finger on the paper, then went back to the beginning of the sentence and started over.

For the next forty-five minutes, he had a hard time keeping his mind on his task. Every few moments, his eyes strayed to the slightly wrinkled envelope. Joshua wondered what it contained, but he had to finish with the contract and send Charles over to the client's office with it.

After his secretary left with the completed document, Joshua stood and stretched. While he concentrated on a hard task, his muscles became more and more knotted. He rubbed his neck with both hands and rotated his shoulders, trying to loosen them, as he stared out across the bay from his perch most of the way up one of San Francisco's many hills. Joshua had chosen this office because of its view of the water. Not only could he keep up with the comings and goings of ships, but watching the bay in all kinds of weather proved soothing. He loved this city and once again thanked the Lord for the opportunities that had led him here.

Finally, Joshua turned around and picked up the letter from

his father. He hoped it wasn't bad news. Using the opener with the beautifully carved scrimshaw handle his grandfather gave him when he first opened the law office, he slit the paper and removed the contents—a sheet of paper and an already-opened envelope with papers inside. Father had forwarded a letter he'd received from his best friend, Fred Cunningham. In his included note, his father added his own request that Joshua do what Fred asked of him.

Now curious, Joshua pulled out the other papers. Before he read the words, his memory revisited a time when he was twelve and his family traveled by coach from Texas to Arizona to visit the Cunninghams. Their ranch spread for hundreds of acres from the base of the Rincon Mountains toward a tiny town, really not much more than a few huddled buildings surrounded by tall cacti with arms that spread toward the sky. What was the name of those plants? Something that started with an *s* and sounded foreign to his young ears.

He had enjoyed that trip. The ranch was larger than the one his father owned in Texas. Much of the time, Joshua had accompanied Mr. Cunningham's nine-year-old daughter on wild rides around the vast acreage. With her brown braids flying in the wind, India could ride better than most of the cowboys. He often wondered about the girl. A few years after that trip, they'd received word that her mother had died. Did her death calm India or make her even wilder? He never heard anything more about them, because soon after that, he left home to study law.

Joshua turned his attention to the message. Fred Cunningham wanted Joshua to go to Arizona and help his daughter run the ranch for a time.

While perusing every piece of paper in the envelope, Joshua discovered that Mr. Cunningham had died almost a year ago. The message shouldn't have taken so long to reach him, but the man's lawyer had forgotten to mail it to Joshua's father until recently. Father had sent it on from Texas.

At first, Joshua decided that he should ignore the appeal. He was a city lawyer, a long way from the young man who grew up on the plains in Texas. He hadn't ridden a horse in years, preferring to use a buggy in the city. However, throughout the long afternoon, his mind kept returning to the request. Mr. Cunningham had been his father's best friend, and he wouldn't have asked something like this if he hadn't believed that India needed help. How could Joshua refuse?

When he finished work for the day, he stood watching the lights flicker on one by one up and down the hills that spread from his office toward the shoreline. Soon many of them reflected in the water of the bay, sending sparkles that looked like stars in the inky liquid.

In the last year, Joshua had taken two partners into the fast-growing firm. Because he worked so hard to build the business, he hadn't taken any time off. With the partners and a couple of junior lawyers to keep things going, maybe he could take an extended leave and fulfill Mr. Cunningham's dying wish.

Chapter 1

Arizona Territory

India Cunningham tried to blow away the curls that fell across her right eye. She didn't want to stain her white-blond tresses with the rich red barbeque sauce concocted by one of her ranch hands, Hector Gonzalez. India had no idea what all Hector put in the mixture, but she knew it left a mark on anything it touched. She would have to rub a lot of lemon juice on her hands before they would return to their natural color. Even then, it might take a day or two for the crimson stain to wear off.

Today should have been a good day for the fund-raiser for the Cactus Corner Orphanage. This time of spring was usually cool and mild. Not today. A blazing sun beat down, bringing a river of sweat that rushed down India's spine. She had worn a brown blouse in case some of the sauce splashed on it while she basted the whole steer her foreman, Nathan Hodges, butchered yesterday. While he slowly turned the spit holding the beef over the fire pit, India painted the side nearest her with sauce, making sure every inch of the carcass would absorb the tantalizing flavor.

Hector's sauce almost guaranteed the success of the event. Cowboys from every ranch for miles around flocked to get their share of the feast and add to the coffers of the orphanage. Today most of the cowhands' pay would be spent to help people instead of wasted in the saloon across from the general store.

The milling crowd kept even a hint of a breeze from reaching India. She had hoped to escape to the hotel and clean up before the festivities began, but the time for that was long past. Maybe no one would notice how terrible she looked since she was by the fire pit at the edge of the crowd. Wrinkling her nose, she shrugged her shoulders, trying to dislodge the fabric that was plastered against the moisture on her back.

"India Cunningham!" Jody McMillan pushed her way through the nearby crowd. "What are you doing still back here?" A frown replaced the questioning expression Jody had worn just a moment ago. "I thought you were going to clean up at the hotel. Didn't you take a room for that very purpose?"

India watched her good friend try to brush away some of the dust that had settled on the skirt of her own dress. Why ever did Jody wear such a light color to a picnic? Didn't she know it would show all the smudges? And all those ruffles would just hold in the heat.

After putting the sauce brush on a plate to catch the drips,

India tried to push her hair back with her forearm. The attempt only dislodged the curls for a moment before they fell again. "I haven't had time to get away."

"Surely you don't want everyone to see you like that." Jody's hands fisted on her hips as she glared at India.

Just what she needed, to be reminded of how awful she looked after toiling over the barbeque most of the morning. If only Martha had been able to help her husband with the beef. Donating the steer should have been enough of a contribution for India to make, but lately, nothing came easy. For some reason, many of the men in the surrounding area didn't believe that a young woman could run a ranch as large as the Circle C. She had to prove her abilities to everyone except the hands on the ranch. They knew that ever since she returned from finishing school back east, she had been more in charge than her father.

"Do you want me to do that while you go clean up?" Even though Jody offered to take over painting the luscious-smelling beef, India could tell that she really didn't want to.

"And get this red stuff all over that dress?" India couldn't help laughing. "You'd never be able to wash it out." She thought about what else Jody had said. *Besides, there's no one I want to clean up for.*

The loud blast of the train's whistle announced the arrival of the eastbound in Cactus Corner, Arizona. Joshua stood and lifted his carpetbag from the seat beside him. He would pick up his larger luggage at the baggage car after he stepped down from the stuffy passenger compartment. He ducked his head and stared out the grimy windows. Cactus Corner was not the tiny village he remembered from the summer when he was twelve, but the mountains in the background held the same purplish cast against the clear blue sky. His family had come about this same time of the year, but he didn't remember it being so hot.

He pulled his attention to the surrounding area. A thoroughfare that intersected the tracks not far from the depot had a sign reading MAIN STREET. People milled around, but many of them seemed to be headed the same direction.

When he stepped down onto the platform, he asked the stationmaster, "Is something special going on today?" Then he noticed the heavenly aroma that made his mouth water and reminded him that it had been too long since he'd eaten.

"Sure is." The man nodded, and his prominent Adam's apple bobbed in tandem with his head. "A big barbeque and auction—to benefit the orphanage." As Joshua approached the baggage car, the man walked right beside him. "You might want to go over there and get something to eat later. It's the best barbeque this side of Fort Worth, Texas."

After retrieving his small trunk and hefting it onto one shoulder, Joshua turned back toward the shorter man. "I have a couple of questions. Where is the hotel, and which way to the barbeque?"

A frown marred the man's face. "You might not be able to get a room tonight. Lots of folks from outlying areas have come in for the festivities. They take every opportunity to get together when one comes along, since they are few and far between." He turned and looked down the street. "The hotel's that way, and a boardinghouse is up there." A thumb thrust over his shoulder accompanied the last comment. "You might get a place there if not at the hotel. If they're full up, I believe there's some rooms over the saloon."

"Thank you." Joshua wasn't sure the information was very helpful, but his mother had taught him to be polite. However, he was certain that he wouldn't take the man's last suggestion. He'd sleep outside under the stars with his trunk for a hard pillow before he would go into that place.

"I could tell you to just follow your nose to the barbeque, but the smell pretty much covers the whole town." The white-haired man laughed at his own joke. "If you go past the hotel and turn right at the next corner, the church is a couple of blocks down that street. Most of the activities will take place in the open field behind the building. I'll probably see you there later."

Getting his name in the hotel registry almost proved the dire prediction of the station agent. After talking until he thought he would lose his voice, Joshua finally procured a room, such as it was. A tiny space the size of a closet in the house he rented in California. The single bed sat beside the wall opposite the door, with both the headboard and the foot almost touching the sides of the room. The space barely allowed the door to open all the way, and a chair sat in one corner. He dropped his trunk on the chair and placed the carpetbag on top. Evidently he would be expected to retire by dark, since the hotel didn't have gaslights on the wall, and no table to hold an oil lamp or candle could be wedged into the meager space. He hoped he would only spend one night here.

Since he'd left his business suits back in San Francisco, getting ready for the festivities didn't take him long. After making a stop in the washroom to get rid of some of the travel grime, Joshua set out to find the church. Stretching his legs after his long journey felt good. He took the indicated street and strode on the wooden sidewalk. Even if the stationmaster hadn't told him how to get there, he would have figured it out. Probably every person who lived within twenty miles of this town headed the same direction he did.

By the time he reached the church grounds, several people had introduced themselves and welcomed him. Maybe they hoped he would contribute to the cause in a big way. . . . Maybe he would.

Cactus Corner must have been built around a spring. Even though he had passed through arid country, this town looked more like an oasis. Trees and sparse grass surrounded the houses he passed, and many of the structures had a few colorful flowers in pots on their porches. He smiled. A pleasant place, for a small town.

A large crowd milled around. People stopped beside several

tables laden with handmade items, such as quilts, hand-carved knickknacks, and even furniture. Many of the women congregated around a display of lacy things and frippery. They chattered and exclaimed over each item they picked up.

Joshua studied the younger ladies, trying to decide if one of them was India Cunningham. When he last saw her, she wore her hair in braids, but strands escaped and curled around her face. Freckles had peppered her nose and cheeks, becoming more pronounced the longer she spent time in the sun. Since she had to be in her twenties now, she might have lost the freckles. He hoped some of them remained. They looked cute on her.

What color were her eyes? He couldn't remember exactly. She had been like a whirlwind, always in motion. Well, it didn't matter. Joshua stood to the side and studied every woman with brown hair who passed him. Somehow, he didn't see anyone he thought was India Cunningham. Should he ask someone if she was here?

Chapter 2

India picked up a long-handled cooking utensil with two thin, pointed tines and thrust it into the hindquarters of the rotating steer. It slid right through and quickly encountered bone. When she pulled out the special fork, bits of the barbequed beef stuck to the metal, and savory-smelling juices seeped out. She picked off a juicy piece and popped it into her mouth, realizing almost too late that she should have let it cool a bit more. But it did taste wonderful.

"Is it ready, Miss India?" Nathan Hodges had added *Miss* to her name when she came back from Mrs. Collier's Finishing School. Even after all this time, it still sounded funny.

The spicy meat almost melted in her mouth. India nodded. "Just right. Do you think you can take care of slicing it?"

The older man reached for a large sharp knife that waited on the table behind him. "Sure thing. Just keep the platters coming."

India wiped her hands on a towel hanging on the waistband

of her voluminous apron. When she had been at the general store last week, Mr. Lawson received a crate of lemons from California. More of the citrus fruit made it, in these modern times, without spoiling since trains delivered them now. India had been tempted to buy the whole box, but she only took half of the fruit, leaving the rest for other shoppers. Her ranch hands liked lemonade, and most of the yellow orbs were gone, even though she was able to store them in the cool springhouse. Four lemons waited for her to return to her hotel room and clean up the mess on her hands. Since Nathan took over slicing the meat, maybe she could finally get away. She motioned Hector to take her place. Giving her a wide smile, the man complied. India knew he took pride in providing the sauce for the beef.

She turned to make her way through the growing crowd, and her gaze connected with that of a man she had never seen before. He wore the same kind of clothes the other cowboys did, but his still looked new and stiff instead of faded and soft, and he moseyed with a similar ambling walk. Something else set him off from the others, but she wasn't sure what. Aside from his good looks, and he had plenty, he towered over most of the people around him. His curls glinted blue-black in the sun as they blew in the gentle breeze and tumbled down on his forehead. From this distance, his eyes looked almost as dark as his hair, but more on the brown side. India's heart skipped a beat, and her hands itched to coax those curls back from his face. *Where did that thought come from?*

Letting out the breath she had held momentarily, India

wished she were anywhere but here looking like some carcass her ranch dog had dragged up from the desert. She pushed an errant curl out of her eyes, then remembered the sauce that stained her hands. Hopefully none of it had transferred to her hair. India didn't want the man, who seemed to be making a beeline toward her, to see how horrible she looked. Why hadn't she listened to Jody earlier? She should have left immediately to freshen up.

India glanced down, made a face at her clothes, which were covered with a fine sprinkling of dust and irregular splatters of red, and raised her chin in a defiant gesture, glancing toward a large tree that shaded the opposite side of the dusty field. What was she doing letting the most handsome man she had ever seen rattle her so? For all she knew, he could be an outlaw.

Out of the corner of her eye, she noticed the stranger stop and start talking to Reverend McCurdy. India knew her pastor would gently ferret out all kinds of information without the man even recognizing what he was doing. Maybe she should plan to spend some time visiting with the clergyman later that day.

While the two men were deep in conversation, India slipped around the other side of the crowd and hurried toward the hotel.

As Joshua made his way through the bustling crowd toward the barbeque pit, a shorter gentleman in a black suit stepped in front of him. How in the world could the man stand to wear a suit in this heat?

"I'm Gavin McCurdy." Gavin's strong voice belied his slight stature. He thrust out a hand, and a smile lit a twinkle in his eyes. "I'm the pastor of this church. Welcome to our community. Are you just passing through?"

Joshua vigorously pumped the outstretched hand. "Glad to meet you, Reverend McCurdy. I just arrived in town about half an hour ago, and the wonderful smells led me straight to the church."

"If you're here Sunday, I'd love to see you in our services." The pastor's hearty welcome brought interested glances from many bystanders in the crowd.

The next few minutes, the clergyman asked many questions that Joshua chose to sidestep. As a lawyer, he was adept at answering without giving any information. He knew what the man was doing, but he didn't resent the questioning interest. He supposed a stranger was somewhat of an oddity in this corner of the world. You had to be looking for Cactus Corner to find it, even though the railroad now connected it to other towns.

When the man of God moved on to greet other people, Joshua's eyes sought the woman he'd glimpsed near the roasting steer. She'd been standing near an older man swathed in an apron. He was now slicing the meat and piling it on large platters held by a wiry Mexican whose smile spread across his face. Joshua's stomach gave a loud rumble, reminding him once again of just how long it had been since he had eaten. He worked his way through the mass of people toward the food, all the time scanning the crowd.

He couldn't find the woman dressed in dark clothing with hair that looked like moonlight shining on a clear lake. He had never seen that color of hair before. She wore it in a careless bun on top of her head with wispy curls forming a halo around her lovely face. Some of the barbecue sauce had smudged her cheeks, but not enough to mask her loveliness. Where could she have disappeared? Oh well, with his luck, she was married to one of the cowhands forming a line at one end of the table loaded with a bounty of food besides the platters of beef.

Past the other end of the long table stood a smaller lady who held a large earthenware crock. Another woman dipped from it and poured the liquid into all manner of drinking vessels—tin cups, heavy mugs, even a few glasses. He was surprised she didn't spill any with all the kids who were darting through the crowd and even ducking their heads to scoot under the table as if it were some kind of tunnel. As Joshua watched, his parched throat felt like the desert the train had traveled through. He probably should try to get a drink before he thought about eating, or he might not be able to swallow any food. He made his way toward the shorter line at the drink table.

With a smile, the woman handed him a heavy mug. He took a long swig. Joshua hadn't expected the sweet, tart taste of lemonade, but it did quench his deep thirst. Too bad there wasn't some ice to cool it more. Living farther north where people experienced winter definitely had added blessings. Some folks cut ice into large chunks and buried them underground surrounded with sawdust. That ice often lasted until the next winter.

Thinking about the coolness only intensified the dry heat he was immersed in, but the lemonade soothed his parched throat. At least he wasn't wearing a business suit.

Joshua took his drink and joined the long line for food, glad that it moved quite fast. Soon he leaned against a scraggly tree on the edge of the open field, shoveling food into his mouth. His mother would be aghast at his lack of manners, but he didn't think anyone here noticed. A lawyer learned to study people, so he enjoyed watching the other people interact. In a small community like this one, everyone seemed to know everyone else. That might be a good thing.

After a while, movement on the street side of the crowd drew his attention. A woman glided through the group almost like Moses parting the Red Sea, and everyone gave her attention. He didn't blame them. She was breathtaking. Although her hair was the same color as that of the woman working with the meat earlier, the resemblance ended there. This woman's hair was arranged in a style that would have been fashionable in San Francisco, and she dressed with understated elegance. Her dark brown skirt didn't have any of the extra ruffles some of the women wore. He imagined her clothing was cooler than theirs. The light-colored blouse wasn't really white, but looked more like the cream he used to skim off the milk back home. It accentuated her smooth complexion, which was more tanned than that of any woman he knew in California. Joshua figured she must spend a lot of time outdoors.

He couldn't pull his attention from her. Then it hit him.

She was the same woman. Evidently she had gone somewhere to clean up.

Joshua would have loved to know who she was, but he didn't want to cause ripples by asking too many questions. He would bide his time and keep his eyes and ears tuned to what was going on around him.

Once again, the parson approached. "Have you seen the desserts on the table by the church?"

Joshua had just sopped up the last of the barbeque sauce with a hunk of bread before he stuffed it in his mouth. It took him a moment to chew it up. Mother would have a conniption if he talked with his mouth full.

"I sure didn't." He took the last swig of lemonade. "I thought this was a fund-raiser for an orphanage or something like that. No one has asked me for any money."

The preacher's laugh had a rich resonation. "Indeed it is. There's a bucket on the corner of the dessert table for people to put in their donations. The women thought that after people enjoyed the wonderful food, they'd be more inclined to be generous."

Joshua nodded. "Good thinking. I've never tasted meat as tender or delicious as this."

The two men headed toward the whitewashed frame building crowned by a steeple.

"They put the desserts in the shadow of the church so they'd be out of the sun." Reverend McCurdy patted his stomach. "I don't really need anything else, but I have to have a piece of

Miss Mabel's buttermilk pie. It's the best I've ever tasted. She always brings it anytime we have a church dinner."

"So did the church start the orphanage?" Joshua shortened his stride to fit the other man's.

"No, but most of the women in the church help the orphanage all they can."

Closer to the building, the ground was covered with sparse grass. Joshua was sure that would keep the dust down. Another reason to put the desserts there.

India had seen the stranger leaning up against a tree when she returned from the hotel. How could she miss him? Even in dungarees and a chambray shirt, he had a commanding presence. Just what was it about the man that made her feel unsettled? Granted, he might be an outlaw, but would a wanted man stay out in the open like that? Hopefully she would get a chance to talk to Reverend McCurdy later.

During the rest of the social, India felt the man's presence, even across the field from her. No matter how she turned or whom she talked to, she knew when he moved from one place to another, almost as if he had some connection to her. For a woman who owned a huge ranch and was the boss of a large crew of cowboys, she didn't understand why she didn't feel in control. Nothing she did could break that nebulous link.

He went with the pastor over to the dessert table and sampled plenty of the sugary sweets. She wondered why he wasn't flabby if he ate like that, but when he walked, his body was poetry in motion. Before she got up the nerve to join the two men in the shade of the church, the newcomer sauntered away, heading back toward Main Street. She took a deep breath and gave a relieved sigh. She was glad he was gone. Wasn't she?

Other strangers had come to town, especially since the railroad tracks were laid. None of them had put her off balance with their presence. He shouldn't have either.

As the crowd thinned, India went to help clean up. She also wanted to see if any of her lemon pound cake was left. She hadn't had time for dessert yet. Only one piece remained. As she slid it onto a saucer, her pastor stepped near the table, perusing the contents.

"We're almost cleaned out, aren't we?" He glanced at the small plate in her hand. "At least you got a piece of something."

She took a bite, savoring the tartness of the lemon mixed with the sweet, buttery flavor of the cake. The morsel tasted wonderful all the way down. "I just love fresh lemons." She turned to face the minister. "So who was the stranger I saw you talking to earlier?"

"Didn't you get a chance to meet him?" The older man's eyes searched her face as though he was looking for something specific. "Nice fellow."

India hoped her expression didn't reveal what she had been feeling. She didn't want him to think she was too interested. "So who is he?"

"You know, come to think of it, he never did tell me his

name." Reverend McCurdy scratched his chin.

"What's he doing in Cactus Corner?" She took another bite.

"He didn't really say." Deep grooves between the man's brows indicated his frustration.

She set the saucer on the table and put her fists on her hips. "He might be an outlaw for all we know."

Her pastor laughed. "I don't think so, India. In my profession, I've had to learn to size up a man pretty well. I don't know his name or why he's here, but he isn't running from the law."

She picked up the cake again and took another bite, frowning as she did.

The man beside her reached into the bucket and pulled out a wad of bills. He unrolled them and riffled through them. "This is the donation he made. It's a goodly amount, India. Don't judge a man before you know anything about him."

After spending a few minutes in the hotel washroom freshening up, Joshua returned to his broom-closet room. He took off his stiff outer clothing and stretched out on top of the covers. At least there was a tiny window that let in a slight breeze. Tomorrow he would see if the livery had any horses for sale. He wanted to ride his own mount out to the Circle C.

Even though he had studied every woman at the social, he didn't see anyone who might be India Cunningham. Maybe he was too late. Since the letter had taken a year to reach him, maybe she had already lost the ranch. Now he wished he had asked the parson about it. He could be going on a wild goose chase. He might have to rethink buying that horse. Perhaps he should rent one and go to check things out first.

After having chased that rabbit, his thoughts returned to the blond he'd seen at the barbeque. For some reason, he'd felt an invisible connection to her, almost as if they'd been tied by strong rope. The feeling didn't release until he started back to the hotel. She was a vision of loveliness, but he didn't know anything about her. He probably wouldn't even see her again. That thought gave his heart a little hitch.

This new obsession would have to stop. After he was sure that India Cunningham didn't need his help, he would board the train for the westward journey back to civilization. He didn't need to leave any complicated ties in this town. He pulled his worn Bible out of his carpetbag. Maybe feeding on the Word would take his mind off her.

When he had finished eating a big breakfast in the hotel restaurant the next morning, Joshua quickly found the livery stable. A beautiful palomino stallion caught his eye. He made a deal to hire the horse for the week, then headed out of town toward the Rincon Mountains. He felt sure he could remember the way to the ranch.

Even though the countryside was mostly desert, splashes of beauty were all around him. Joshua remembered the tall cacti that looked as though they were reaching for the sky. A few of them sported blossoms on their outstretched arms. The ground wasn't bare; it was covered with a different type of vegetation from what he was used to in California. Off in the distance, a line of varying shades of green indicated where the river meandered through the ranch. The two-story ranch house was built on a knoll not far from that river. If Joshua missed the turnoff, he could just ride across country and follow the stream.

The trip took longer than he remembered, but eventually he reached the cluster of buildings. There were more of them than he recalled, though. The house looked much the same. White paint glistened in the bright sunlight, and the shutters and outside trim wore a coat of dark green. Instead of one barn, three stood sentinel far enough behind the house that the barn-yard smells shouldn't reach there. A few smaller houses probably indicated that some of the hands were married, and twice as many bunkhouses as before flanked the barns.

Joshua wondered if all this happened before Mr. Cunningham died or if maybe a new owner had expanded. He rode up to the corral beside the first barn. The man who had turned the steer on the spit yesterday stood with one booted foot hiked up on the bottom rail. He leaned his crossed arms on the top rail and watched a young hand working with a skittish horse.

When Joshua brought his horse to stop by the hitching rail, the man turned around. "You looking for a job?"

Joshua didn't know how to answer that.

"I only put the notice up at the feed store in town yesterday when I went to the barbeque. I didn't expect any takers this soon. Miss India will be glad."

Well, that answered one of his questions. India Cunningham was still here. Maybe he should hire on while he scouted out the lay of the land, so to speak. "Sure, I'd like a job." He stuffed his hands into the front pockets of his dungarees and hunched his shoulders.

The man dropped his foot onto the ground and walked toward him. "I'm Nathan Hodges, the foreman of the Circle C. I do all the hiring and firing, so you don't want to rile me." His laugh took the sting out of the words. "When can you start?"

"Right away. I'll need to go back to town and get my things from the hotel."

"You got much gear?" Nathan held out a hand, and Joshua shook it.

"A trunk and a carpetbag." Joshua was glad the man didn't seem surprised. He knew a cowboy usually traveled with only his horse, a saddlebag, and maybe a bedroll.

Nathan gazed over Joshua's shoulder and called out, "Come over here, Miss India. We already have a taker for the job."

Without turning, Joshua knew whom he would see. He felt *her* approach.

Chapter 3

India had watched the man ride in on the palomino—the handsome stranger who could have been an outlaw but was just a cowboy needing work. Why should she care if the man showed up at her ranch for a job? Twenty or thirty men inhabited the large bunkhouses at any given time. Just because he sparked a special awareness at the barbeque yesterday didn't mean anything.

As she walked toward the two men, the stranger slowly turned and looked straight into her eyes. Her heart took another hitch. This would never do. She had to let him know that she was the boss on this ranch and not give him time to even think about having to work for a woman.

The way his eyes widened was barely perceptible before his face became a stiff mask. She would have missed it if she hadn't been looking straight at him. His flinty gaze seemed to take in everything about her without raking her up and down. She was thankful for that. Maybe having him around wouldn't be so bad, if the man could do the work required of him. The ranch did need another hand in the barn when many of the men went out to round up the heifers with calves that were scattered all over the outlying pastures. She hoped the fact that he was wearing new, instead of well-worn, clothes didn't indicate that he was inexperienced on a ranch.

Joshua studied the woman walking toward them without making it too obvious. Today she wore a no-nonsense split riding skirt and matching long-sleeved shirt. Her hair hung in a braid over one shoulder; wisps framed her face under a well-worn cowboy hat.

He had known of a couple of women whose hair had lightened to blond by the time they reached adulthood, but neither of them had almost snowy hair. Why hadn't he considered that possibility? He wouldn't have wasted so much time looking at every woman with brown hair when he would rather have spent his time getting reacquainted with this beauty.

When she stopped beside the foreman, Joshua noticed a faint sprinkling of the freckles he had wondered about. If he had gotten close enough yesterday, he might have recognized those blue eyes as the ones he remembered from her childhood, but maybe not. Her lashes were thicker and longer than any he had seen on any other woman.

India held out her hand. "I trust Nathan's judgment. Welcome to the Circle C."

Joshua engulfed her hand in his before he shook it. "Thank you. I'm glad to be here."

Before he had a chance to say anything else, she quickly withdrew and turned toward the foreman. Joshua felt as if he had been dismissed—something he wasn't used to—and he hadn't even told her his name.

He stepped back so they wouldn't feel he was eavesdropping. Maybe he should continue to be just a hand until he could see how well she was doing with the ranch. From the way the foreman listened to her, he must respect her and trust her judgment. Did the other men? If he hired on without the other hands knowing why he was really here, perhaps he could learn the truth about how they felt about India.

When the two finished their conversation, India went back into the main house while the foreman turned toward Joshua. "You can take the wagon into town to pick up your gear. When you get back, we'll settle you into one of the bunkhouses." The foreman called over his shoulder to another hand. "Bring the wagon out here, Clint."

In less than half an hour, Joshua headed away from the ranch with the palomino tied to the back of the wagon. He went straight through town to the livery, which was on the other side of the business district, such as it was.

Joshua took off his hat as he walked into the cavernous stable. "I need to talk to you." He wished he had asked the liveryman's name earlier.

The tall, thin man looked up from mucking out one of

the stalls. "You didn't stay away long. You aren't going to turn the horse in, are you?" He stuck the pitchfork in the dirt and leaned both hands on the end of the handle. "I don't give any money back."

"No. Actually, I wanted to know if this horse is for sale." Joshua dusted his Stetson against one leg.

The man leaned the pitchfork against the railing of the stall and pushed back the hair that had fallen over his forehead. "Funny you should ask today. That there horse belongs to Elmer Brody over at the freight line. Just this morning, he said he was thinking about selling him. You'll need to talk to him, though."

Joshua nodded. "Okay, I'll do that. But what about the saddle? I like a saddle that's been broken in, and this one fits me just fine. I'd like to buy it."

After they completed that transaction, with the man offering to make an allowance for some of the money already paid to him, Joshua headed toward the freight office—an unpainted building that had weathered to a smoky gray. When he came back out into the bright sunlight, he owned the stallion. He'd have to rename him, though. The animal seemed smart enough to learn a new name quickly. Goldie sounded more like a mare's name, or even a dog's. King was more masculine.

Joshua walked to the stallion's head and began stroking his forehead and neck while whispering into his ear. "You look really regal, boy, so I'm going to call you King. Before we go back to the ranch, I'll see if the general store has some carrots or apples for you."

Joshua climbed into the wagon seat and looked back toward his new horse. King held his head higher as if he understood every word.

At the hotel, Joshua paid his bill and loaded his trunk and carpetbag in the back of the wagon. Now he was glad he had thought to pack several books. His evenings might be a little lonely out in the bunkhouse. Most of the cowboys his father hired at his ranch in Texas had been rather solitary until they got to know a man. Those books would come in handy.

Before he headed back to the ranch, he stopped by the café for lunch. While he ate, he listened unobtrusively to as many conversations as he could, trying to get a feel for what was going on in the town.

A couple of tables over, two older men talked to the waitress about yesterday's festivities. They made a few comments about India Cunningham, but they were all complimentary. It sounded as if she was well liked in Cactus Corner.

India had turned one of the downstairs rooms in the main house into an office. She liked to see what was happening on the ranch through the windows that wrapped around two sides of the room. While sitting at the desk working on the books, she heard the wagon rumble by on the way to the barn. India had wondered why Nathan sent the newcomer to town in the wagon. Maybe he needed something from the store. She went to the window and leaned close to the glass so she could watch the two men. A large trunk sat in the bed of the wagon, and the same palomino followed the conveyance.

She'd never before known a cowboy to want that much encumbrance. Why did the man have a trunk with him? India wished she could see what he kept in it. Her father always told her that her curiosity would get her into trouble one of these days.

Even though there were things about that cowboy that didn't make sense, India had never found any reason not to trust her foreman. If Nathan thought the man wouldn't make a good hand, he wouldn't have hired him. One of the things she learned when she first started running the ranch without her father was that she needed to be able to trust other people. Since Nathan and Martha had been on the ranch almost as long as India could remember, she knew from their long association that her trust wasn't misplaced.

All this woolgathering wasn't getting the books done. She turned from the window and delved back into the finances of the ranch. She wouldn't relinquish this task to another person. Her father always knew exactly what was going on with the finances. He taught her that a good rancher had to, and she wanted to be a good rancher.

India had ridden across the vast acres and helped with roundups by the time she was a young teenager. That's why she could take over running the ranch when she returned from back east. All through her father's last months, she had kept an eye on everything while letting him feel that he was still in control, making it an easy transition for everyone when he was gone.

Since Joshua had more possessions with him than most cowboys, Nathan Hodges offered one of the empty cabins to him, but he wouldn't be able to get a feeling of what was going on with the cowboys if he moved in there. When he declined, the foreman assigned him an empty bed at one end of a bunkhouse. His trunk would fit in the corner by the wall.

"Since it's Saturday, most of the boys will go into town this evening." Nathan leaned against the wall and crossed his booted feet. "Were you planning on going, too?"

Joshua slid the heavy trunk from his shoulders and put it into place. "I didn't realize this thing weighed so much." He stretched his neck and rotated his shoulders. "I should have let you help me carry it like you offered."

Nathan chuckled. "What's in there? Rocks?"

Joshua gave a sheepish grin. "No, books. I like to read."

The foreman nodded.

"About your first question, I've been in town twice today. That's enough for me."

The other man stood up away from the wall. "Martha told me to ask if you would like to eat supper with us. She didn't feel too good yesterday, so she didn't go to the shindig in town, and she'd like to meet you."

Joshua stuffed one hand into the front pocket of his dungarees. "I wouldn't want to be any trouble."

Nathan hooted a loud laugh. "Trouble for Martha would be if she didn't get to meet you today. Besides, she likes to cook."

Joshua pulled out a pocket watch. "It's already four thirty. Do you have any work for me this afternoon?"

The foreman shook his head. "Naw. Everyone's off on Saturday afternoons."

"What time do you want me to come, and you'll have to tell me which house." Joshua slipped the timepiece back into the small opening just below one of his belt loops.

Nathan started toward the front door. "We usually eat at six."

Joshua followed the foreman. "I won't be late."

When they reached the porch, Nathan pointed toward the largest of the cabins behind the main house. "India's father built that house for Martha and me when he hired me to be his foreman."

After Joshua watched the man amble toward his home, he went to the wagon and retrieved his carpetbag. He stowed it on top of his trunk, then drove the wagon and King to the wagon yard beside the main stable. First, he took King to the stall Nathan had told him to use. He soothed the stallion and filled his trough with feed. He rubbed down the two horses that pulled the wagon and returned them to their stalls.

A flurry of activity around the bunkhouses indicated that the other cowboys were cleaning up. A few even made use of the outdoor shower. Joshua hoped they didn't use all the water in the tank, because he wanted to get rid of some grime before he went to eat with Nathan and Martha. Of course, it was a large tank, and probably the men knew how to conserve water so everyone could have a turn.

By five thirty, all the cowboys had ridden out in groups of three or four toward town. He took a quick shower, wishing he had asked Nathan about how to get hot water for shaving. He'd just have to go to supper with stubble on his face, something he never would have done in San Francisco, but he really didn't like a cold shave.

When he left the bunkhouse to start toward the foreman's home, he noticed India step from her porch. He stopped and waited to see if she was headed toward him, but she didn't even look his way. She did, however, go straight toward Nathan and Martha's. Evidently she hadn't recognized him, and he'd told Nathan his name out of her hearing. Maybe Joshua could keep it a secret from her until he knew the lay of the land. Tonight could be interesting.

Nathan answered his knock. "Since all the other hands are gone, Martha invited Miss India to eat with us, too."

The older man stepped back, opening the door wider. Joshua searched the room until he saw India standing in the archway between the kitchen—where another woman bustled around—and the dining room.

Her startled gaze collided with his, and a slight blush colored her cheeks. "I thought you went to town. . .with the other hands." The last phrase was almost a whisper.

She glanced at Nathan before looking at Martha.

The other woman wiped her hands on her apron. "I told Nate to ask him for supper. I didn't get to meet him yesterday." She smiled at her husband. "He didn't tell me how handsome the new hand is."

The blush on India's cheeks deepened and bled across her neck. Joshua almost laughed. So she wasn't the self-possessed woman she seemed to be yesterday at the barbeque.

"I don't know any of the men yet, so I decided to stay on the ranch tonight." He wasn't ready to tell her that he wouldn't be caught dead in a saloon.

Maybe he was being too harsh in his judgment. Perhaps the hands had other things in mind for their evening entertainment, but he doubted it.

Nathan laughed. "Some of them won't ever want you trailing along with them. I believe they've gone courting."

Okay, so he *was* being too harsh about some of them. Time would tell about the others.

"Come on. Let's be seated." Martha set a couple of bowls on the almost full round table. "Don't want the food to get cold."

Joshua planned to pull out India's chair for her, but she slipped into the nearest seat before he reached the table. After they were all sitting down, Nathan pronounced a word of thanks to the Lord. Joshua was glad the foreman shared his faith. He wondered about India. He couldn't remember them going to church when he was here as a boy.

While they passed the food, Nathan started the conversation.

"I haven't seen any of the other hands carry timepieces, and that's a really fine watch you have."

Joshua pulled it out of his pocket and stared at the etching on the cover. He opened it and peered at the face. "This was my father's watch. It belonged to my grandfather before him. He gave it to me for my eighteenth birthday."

"May I see it?" India reached her hand toward him, and he snapped the timepiece shut and unhooked it from his belt loop before giving it to her.

She studied it on one side, then turned it over. "The workmanship is beautiful. It reminds me of something I've seen before, but I can't remember when or where."

When she returned it to him, the gold felt warm. Joshua was sure her hand would feel just as warm, only much softer. For a rancher, her hands were exceptionally smooth with no calluses. Either she wore gloves, or she didn't do much of the heavy work.

The next morning, India hurried to dress for church. She hoped she would see the new hand riding to town for services, too. But when she harnessed one of the horses to the surrey, no one besides Nathan and Martha headed the same way.

Jody had invited Anika, Elaine, and her for dinner after church. She hoped being with her best friends would take her mind off that man. Unfortunately, during the service, her thoughts often wandered. She was sure Pastor Gavin preached a wonderful sermon as usual, but she hoped no one asked her what he said.

Soon the four women sat around the small kitchen table. Jody's cooking was legendary, and today was no exception. While they partook of the bounty, the friends talked about inconsequential things. All too soon, someone asked the question India didn't want to hear.

"So did you see the stranger who came to the barbeque on Friday?" Jody made eye contact with India.

After swallowing what she was chewing so she wouldn't choke, India nodded. "He was hard to miss."

"Aren't you glad you went back to the hotel and changed clothes?" Elaine's auburn hair was pulled up into its usual bun on top of her head, and it wobbled when she turned her head quickly.

"Of course." India tried to make light of her answer. "I wasn't really wanting anyone to notice me while I took care of the meat." She shoved another bite into her mouth, hoping the other women would change the subject.

Jody picked up on what she said. "Did the man notice you?"

"He'd be crazy if he didn't." Anika scooped some mashed potatoes onto her fork.

Jody stared at her. "So you noticed him, too."

"Just because I believe in women's suffrage doesn't mean I can't appreciate a good-looking man, does it?" With a dainty motion, Anika placed the food in her mouth.

"I didn't mean anything by what I said." A look of contrition wrinkled Jody's brows.

India decided she might as well tell them the rest of the story. "He came to the ranch yesterday looking for a job. . .and Nathan hired him."

Three pairs of eyes stared at her.

"I suppose Nathan knows what he's doing, but that man has secrets." By their raised eyebrows, India could see that her statement surprised her friends.

Jody clasped her hands in her lap. "What do you mean?"

India thought a minute so she would get all the details right. "For one thing, his clothes are too new. If he's been working as a cowboy, why aren't his clothes broken in?" Jody looked as if she might defend the man, so India rushed on. "And he travels with a trunk and a carpetbag. How many cowboys have you seen carry more than just their saddlebags?"

With a deflated look, Jody leaned back. "He came into the freight office yesterday and bought Goldie from Mr. Brody. It seems odd that he didn't already own a horse. If he's a cowboy, why didn't he ride his horse to town?"

"Martha invited both of us for supper last night. I had hoped to learn more about him, but even though we talked a lot, and Nathan asked him a lot of questions, he didn't give us any information in his answers." Each time India said something else about the man, she felt worse and worse. "He even carries a pocket watch. A very elaborate gold one. Have you ever seen a cowhand do that? I just know I'll have to keep an eye on him to make sure he's who he says he is."

Anika, ever the lawyer, stood and took her plate to the dry sink. "I could have him checked out for you. What's his name?"

India stared at each of her friends before she answered. "I don't know," she whispered with a sinking heart.

Chapter 4

*J*oshua Dillinger. His name was Joshua Dillinger. For some reason that sounded vaguely familiar, but India couldn't remember why. That vagueness only added to her discomfort with the man. When he was around, all her old insecurities flooded back. Because her father never had a son, she had done all she could to prove to him that she was just as good, but Daddy had never recognized that fact.

Then after he was gone, India had to prove herself all over again. The regular hands who stayed on the ranch year-round knew her abilities, but every time they had to hire extra hands, the discrimination happened again. No one wanted to work for a woman. If Nathan hadn't been so loyal, she never would have been able to run this ranch. He gave her the respect she needed, and the other men finally followed his lead.

India looked down at the ledger spread open on the desk in front of her. She should work on the books, but that new man distracted all her thoughts. She huffed out a deep breath and picked up her last stubby pencil. The next time Nathan went to town, he would have to buy her some more.

A knock sounded at her open office door, and she looked up. "Come in, Nathan. I was just thinking about you."

The man crossed the waxed hardwood floor in a few long strides. "I hope I didn't put those frown lines on your forehead."

India laughed. "No, you didn't." She held up the flat wooden pencil. "I need you to get more of these when you go into town for supplies."

Nathan sat with one hip on the front corner of her desk. "I'm thinking about sending Joshua for the supplies."

She leaned back in her wooden swivel chair. "Do you think that's a good idea?"

He crossed his arms. "I've seen you watching him like a hawk. Almost as though you're waiting for him to make a mistake. You're not usually like this. How long has he been here now?"

"Two weeks and four days." After she said the words, she regretted them. She didn't want her foreman to know how often she thought of Joshua, and that answer made it sound as if she had counted every day. So what if she had?

"Right, and he's a hard worker." The grooves between Nathan's eyes indicated his seriousness. "When are you going to give him a break?"

India rubbed the ache in both sides of her forehead with the thumb and middle finger of one hand, then looked straight at her foreman. "Okay. You've told me more than once that you trust him. I promise I'll take your word for it."

Nathan stood up. "Good. I'll send him to town right away."

After the foreman exited the house, India went to the window and watched him walk across to the corral. Joshua was helping one of the younger hands practice roping the cows that milled around inside. When Nathan reached him, they started talking. She knew exactly when Nathan told him that he was going to town, because Joshua's gaze turned toward the house as if he questioned whether she agreed.

Before Joshua made it to the barn to hitch up the wagon, India opened the ranch house door. He hoped she wasn't coming to tell him that she didn't want him to run this errand. He planned to check if there was anything in the mail for him, especially from his partner telling him how everything in San Francisco was going.

Joshua turned toward India and smiled. She hadn't said anything about remembering who he was, and he hadn't brought it up yet. Perhaps it was time, but he didn't want to rush the moment. He hadn't found out as much as he wanted about how well she was doing with the ranch. When his anonymity was destroyed, he felt sure the other hands would clam up around him.

India stopped in front of him. Remnants of the girl he remembered still lingered, but the woman had almost over-taken them. She shaded her eyes with one hand. "I have a few more things I'd like you to pick up for me." She thrust a list toward him.

When he took it from her, he nodded, tempted to grasp her fingers in his. All kinds of feelings ran through him, but he couldn't pursue them until he finished the job he'd come to do. Joshua stuffed the paper into his shirt pocket before climbing up on the wagon seat. He could feel her gaze boring into his back as he rode away.

After Joshua picked up all the things on both lists and left them on the counter for the clerk to add up, he headed toward the post office in the back corner of the general store. "Got anything for the Cunningham ranch?" He couldn't believe how quickly he'd slipped into the vernacular of a cowhand. No one in his law office would believe it if they heard it. He was known all over northern California for his oratory skills.

"Sure do." The sandy-haired man reached for a packet tied with twine. "It's been awhile since anyone from the ranch came to town. Miss India usually helps at the orphanage a couple days a week."

As Joshua walked back toward the counter in the store, he pondered that information. Why had she stopped? Was something wrong with the ranch? Or did she not trust him and want to keep an eye on what he was doing? He chuckled at that thought. If she only knew.

On the ride back to the ranch, Joshua stopped the wagon when he was far enough from town for no one to see what he was doing. He picked up the mail and carefully untied the package.

Sure enough, a fat envelope was addressed to him. He stuck it inside his shirt and retied the packet. He would take time to study the papers later.

India must have been watching for him, because she came out on the porch before he reached the house. "Did we get any mail?"

Joshua held it up before stepping over the side of the wagon. She met him halfway with her hand outstretched. After he placed the bundle in her hand, she quickly untied it and began to shuffle through the pieces of mail before looking up.

"Do you know where Nathan is?"

"When I left, he was going to help the hands get ready to ride out for the calf roundup in the morning." Joshua waited to see if she wanted anything else from him.

Instead, she turned and strode toward the large bunkhouse.

India forced herself not to look back as she walked away from Joshua. She tried to force him from her thoughts, too, but had less success with that. She almost regretted her last trip to town, but she hadn't been in a while.

She hadn't wanted to talk about Joshua. But her friends had asked about him the whole time she was with them. She had attempted to avoid all that questioning. When she had answered, the three of them seemed greatly amused about something that completely eluded her.

She didn't know what she felt. On the one hand, he worked

hard, but she still didn't truly trust him. He was keeping some secret from her. And that bothered her. . .more than she wanted to admit.

Another thing India didn't want to admit to anyone was her attraction to the man. Not just to his good looks, and he had plenty. Something about him tugged at her heart, while her mind wanted to push him away because of his air of mystery.

Her boots kicked up dust as she stomped toward the bunkhouse. Nathan had a letter, and she needed to give it to him, but sometimes she felt that he could see what was going on inside her. That would never do. How would she keep control of the ranch if he knew that she was so double-minded about Joshua? All the men, including Nathan, needed to see her strength and leadership, not some dreamy-eyed woman. India didn't even notice Nathan coming toward her until he stopped right in front of her.

"Did you want to see me for something?" He hooked his thumbs through his front belt loops and studied her face from under the brim of his hat.

She nodded and shuffled through the envelopes again before pulling out one of them. "This letter came for you. I thought you might like to see it."

He took it and smiled. "It probably could have waited until I came to the office." However, Nathan quickly tore the end off of the letter, blew into it, and slid out the paper.

India watched him a moment before turning toward the house.

"Wait a minute, Miss India." Something in his voice stopped her. "This here has some bad news in it."

She whirled around. "I'm sorry, Nathan. Who is it from?"

The paper in his hand shook. "My brother." He gulped, and his Adam's apple bobbed up and down. "He says Dad's dying. He says I need to come home quickly, or I might not see him again."

India put a comforting hand on his arm. "Then you and Martha must go."

A lone tear made its way down his wrinkled cheek. "It's time for calf roundup. I can't go."

India could take over the complete running of the ranch if she had to. She could be the foreman in his place. "I can do it."

"You shouldn't have to." He covered her fingers with his calloused hand. "You're the ranch owner, and there are plenty of men who can do the work."

"And I can ride and rope with the best of them."

Nathan stood in thought for a long moment. "Joshua could fill in for me while I'm gone."

India's heart thumped out of rhythm. She worked very closely with her foreman. Could she work that closely with Joshua? "Isn't there anyone else who could do it?"

He shook his head. "None of the rest of these yahoos could handle it. They're good wranglers, but none of them can see the big picture like Joshua can."

She stepped away from him, but she had to try one more time, so she turned back. "But won't the other men resent a new man bossing them around?"

"I don't think so. He has a good relationship with every one of them."

Joshua stood beside India while Nathan told the hands that he was leaving for a while. When he announced that Joshua would be the foreman while he was gone, not a single man blinked an eye. Joshua was thankful that Nathan had made it easy for him to fit into his boots. The man had everything planned for him.

After driving Nathan and Martha to the train station in Cactus Corner, Joshua quickly settled into his new job. He followed Nathan's suggestions when he assigned men to teams and sent them to different parts of the ranch.

The next morning, he watched the hands leave at early light, wishing he could go with them but understanding the reason Nathan didn't want India left alone. Then he strode toward the main house. India had told him she would fix his meals while the cook was out with the chuck wagon for roundup.

He stepped up on the porch, and the tantalizing aroma of sizzling bacon mixed with the fragrance of biscuits made his stomach rumble. Although the grub he'd been eating had been filling, this breakfast held more promise. Before his knuckles connected with the door, it swung open.

"Come in, Joshua."

He hadn't heard India say his name very many times since he'd come. The throaty musical quality of her voice gave it a special sound that went straight to his heart. "Something sure smells good."

She hurried into the kitchen and grabbed a bundle of toweling before lifting the pan of biscuits from the stove. "I'm not as good a cook as Martha is, but I get by."

Joshua watched her for a moment. Stray curls fluffed around her face, which held a becoming blush. A longer lock of hair lay down the back of her slender neck. For a moment, he wished he could plant a kiss in that exact spot. He shook his head to clear his thoughts and walked over to the sink. "May I wash up here?"

After her nod, he lifted the handle and pumped vigorously to fill the pan. If they were going to work closely until Nathan got back, Joshua would have to curb his growing fascination with everything about India. A moist bar of soap sat in a bowl in the window. He used it to lather his hands before plunging them into the water for a rinse. Although he didn't look toward her, he knew she watched his every move.

He turned while drying his hands. "Thank you for allowing me to take Nathan's place while he's gone."

Her eyes widened. She probably hadn't expected him to bring that up. "You're welcome."

"I won't do everything exactly as he does, but I'll do a good job."

She lifted her chin. "So Nathan told me."

Joshua couldn't tell if she agreed with her foreman or not. With nothing else to say, he pulled out the chair across from where she stood. Everything within him wanted to pull out her chair first, but he wasn't sure what she would think about that. He didn't want to upset her at this juncture.

Surprisingly, the meal went well. Soon they were exchanging pleasant conversation about the workings of the ranch and what was going on in town. Even though India only went on Sundays lately, she kept up with what was happening.

About the time Joshua decided to tell her why he was here, she stood and picked up her dishes. "If you have everything under control here, I'm going into town today. It's been awhile since I helped at the orphanage."

He quickly stood, too. "That's fine. Nathan left me with lots of written instructions. It will give me time to study them again." And also give him time to read all the papers his partner had sent him.

India couldn't get out of the room quickly enough. She hadn't realized that having Joshua share her meals would upset her equilibrium. She enjoyed watching him so much she almost forgot to eat. What was it that pulled her heart toward him while her mind told her to be careful?

On the way into town, India was glad the horses knew the way without being driven. She spent most of her time going over the breakfast with Joshua. Since he'd been at the ranch, Joshua's hands had grown some calluses, but he kept them well groomed. *Graceful.* His hands were graceful as they pulled apart a biscuit and slathered it with butter and mesquite bean jelly at breakfast. And he had perfect table manners, much better than those of most of the cowhands. Perhaps when she returned she should ask him where he came from and why he looked for a job at her ranch. With that resolution, she raised the reins and urged the horses a little faster.

"India, there you are." Jody arrived at the orphanage at the same time. "We've been missing you." She glanced in the back of the wagon. "What did you bring today?"

"Martha has been making beef jerky. The older kids like to chew on it while they do their lessons." India went around to the back and picked up a small barrel.

Jody looked in a wooden crate that sat beside it. "Has she been making more clothes for the babies?"

India nodded. "You know Martha. She doesn't waste a minute." She hoped maybe she and Jody would be the only ones to help today.

When they walked into the large main room of the orphanage, her hopes were dashed. Anika leaned over the top of a large wooden barrel. Elaine watched her, jiggling a baby on her hip.

Anika rose, bringing a pretty frock with her. "This mission barrel has some nice things in it." She held the dress up to Elaine. "I believe this would fit you."

Elaine's face turned red. "I don't usually take anything from the mission barrels."

Anika placed her hands on her hips, one of them still holding the garment. "And why not? These things are for the orphanage, and you work here. It's way too large for any of the girls and too grown-up of a style, as well."

India set the small barrel on the table and joined them. "I agree. Its color would look good with your hair."

She reached out and took the baby and pulled her into a hug. "Aren't you just growing so much?" She planted a kiss on a chubby cheek, and the little girl laughed out loud.

While they worked, the four women took turns holding the youngest orphan, tickling her and cooing to her. Just as India feared, it didn't take long for the questions to start.

Anika stood folding the clothes from the barrel and separating them by size on one of the tables. "So how is your new ranch hand working out?"

Before India could think of how to answer, Jody added, "Have you found out his name yet?"

"Joshua." At least that was an easy question. "Joshua Dillinger."

Even Elaine was curious. "He's still there, isn't he? I thought I saw him in town yesterday."

India took a deep breath, willing her body not to betray her, but it did. "Yes, he came to town for supplies." She could feel a flush creeping up her neck and cheeks.

All pretense of working stopped as they crowded around her, bombarding her with questions and comments. Maybe staying on the ranch might have been a good idea. As soon as she could do so gracefully, she'd leave.

After Joshua read all of Nathan's instructions and the papers from the law firm, he decided that now would be a good time to check on the finances of the ranch. All the other hands were out on roundup, and India should be gone most of the day. He stowed his personal papers in his trunk and hurried to the house.

India kept the ledger in the top right drawer of her desk. Joshua pulled it out and started making his way through the entries for last year. Although he used an accountant for the law firm, he had helped his father keep the books for the ranch in Texas. It didn't take him long to figure out exactly how they did their accounting.

When he reached January of this year, Joshua heard the wagon stop in front of the house. He should have noticed it sooner, but when he was concentrating on something, he had learned to block out distractions. In all the noise of a city, that was important.

Joshua looked out the window to discover India stepping up on the porch. He quickly shut the ledger and pushed it into the drawer. By the time she entered the front door, he was halfway across the office, trying to walk quietly. Maybe he could slip out if she went upstairs or toward the kitchen.

She must have heard him, because she jerked open the office door. "Joshua Dillinger, what are you doing in here?"

Her question hung in the air like a diamondback rattlesnake about to strike.

Chapter 5

The air in the office tingled with suppressed tension, making it hard to breathe. India stared at Joshua. Why had she trusted him? *Because Nathan does.* She ignored the quiet voice that whispered in her mind.

"I asked you a question." She bit out the words, then hesitated only a split second. "But I have another one for you. Why aren't you out with the roundup?"

Joshua shifted position, almost as if he relaxed. He took so long answering, she figured he was formulating something believable without revealing his true colors.

"Aren't you going to answer me?" She thrust fisted hands against her hips and added heat to her glare.

"India"—he left off the usual *Miss*—"Nathan didn't want me to leave you unguarded while all the men are gone. He told me that he stays here during most of the roundup, too."

Well, that much was true, but India hadn't realized Nathan thought she needed guarding. "I can take care of myself." She stretched as tall as she could and took a deep breath.

"Of course you can." A tentative smile lit his face. "I'm not trying to say you can't, but you have to admit the ranch headquarters are rather isolated. Plenty of outlaws might take advantage of that fact. The success of the Circle C is well-known in this part of the country, which could make you a target."

"We're getting away from the subject of my first question." India crossed her arms and gave him her fiercest stare.

Joshua strode toward two leather chairs that sat near the windows. He pointed at one. "Sit down and we'll talk. I've been needing to tell you some things anyway."

The man sure was bossy. She didn't want to give him the impression that he was in control, but she did perch on the edge of the chair, without uncrossing her arms. "Go ahead." A nod accompanied her terse order.

When he dropped into the other chair, he relaxed against the back. "You don't remember who I am, do you?"

Where is he going with this discussion? "Should I?"

Joshua leaned forward with his forearms on his thighs and clasped his hands. "I visited the ranch when you were nine and I was twelve."

What he said triggered a long-forgotten scene. "Joshua. . . Dillinger." The words came out in a whisper.

India dropped her hands to her lap and closed her eyes to bring up the memory she had often revisited for a few years after his family left. When had she stopped dreaming about the boy who joined her when she rode like the wind across the dusty plains of the ranch? His high spirits almost matched hers.

"No wonder the name sounded familiar." She opened her eyes and looked at him in a new way, studying the black curls that now fell across his forehead.

Her attention moved to his eyes. India should have recognized those eyes that had shared in her fun so long ago. Maybe it was because Joshua was now so serious. She remembered him as a happy boy, who laughed a lot. Where had that daring boy gone?

"So why did you come to my ranch looking for work?" She needed to get to the bottom of why he was here. . .in this room.

Her gaze traveled around, trying to see if anything was out of place. She couldn't find anything that looked disturbed. She hoped he would have an explanation she could accept.

Joshua stood and shoved his hands into the back pockets of his dungarees. She'd seen him do that several times since he'd been on the ranch.

"I didn't really come looking for a job, but when Nathan assumed I did, I took the opportunity."

Why did he need an opportunity? India wasn't sure she liked the sound of this, and she didn't like him hovering above her or nosing through her business. She needed to let him know that she was still boss of this ranch. She stood and crossed her arms again.

He cleared his throat. "I received a letter from your father's lawyer."

"Daddy has been dead for over a year."

He nodded. "I know. His lawyer forgot to mail it any sooner, and it went to my dad in Texas. He forwarded it to my law offices in San Francisco."

"You're a lawyer?" This was getting complicated. "Then why would you want to work on a ranch?"

Joshua raked one hand through his hair, forcing his curls away from his face. "Your father wanted me to make sure you could run the ranch on your own. Besides, I've enjoyed revisiting the things I grew up doing."

"You didn't think I could run the ranch!" India stomped over to her desk and leaned against the front of it. "What were you looking for in this office?"

Almost as if he were mimicking her, he crossed his arms. "I wanted to see if you were in any financial trouble."

She stood up in his face. "How were you going to find out?" When he didn't say anything, the answer slid into her mind. "You looked at my books, didn't you?"

India knew she was almost screeching, but she didn't remember when she had been so angry. The look on his face was all the answer she needed. "Let me tell you something, Joshua Dillinger." She thumped her forefinger against his muscled chest. "I do not need a cowboy—lawyer—or whatever you are sashaying in here trying to take over my ranch. I was running it before my father died, and I can run it now."

Her throat clogged with tears of frustration, but she didn't want him to see them. He might think she was weak. She whirled and started toward the door.

Joshua's strong hands closed around her shoulders, halting her progress. "Please, India, listen to me." When she stopped her headlong plunge away from him, he moved around in front of her. With one finger, he lifted her chin until she was staring into his eyes, which held a look of tenderness. "I'm not trying to take over your ranch. I just wanted to know if you needed my help. Because of the close ties our dads shared, I thought I owed your dad that much."

India couldn't stop the two tears trailing slowly down her cheeks.

"Oh, India, I didn't mean to hurt you." Without thinking, Joshua pulled her against his chest, enclosing her in his arms. "I really only wanted to help."

He felt her relax against him, and more tears stained his shirt, but he didn't care. He stroked her back and murmured soothing words against her hair. Why didn't he tell her sooner who he was and why he was here? Maybe she would have been able to accept his presence. He whispered prayers for her while she continued to sob in his arms.

A long time later, she finally stopped crying and pulled away, mopping her face with both hands. "I'm sorry I broke down." She moved toward the front windows and stared out.

"I've had to be strong ever since Daddy died. I haven't really cried." She turned a rueful expression toward him that arrowed straight to his heart.

Joshua leaned against the front of her desk and crossed his ankles. "I didn't want to add to your pain, but I'm glad you finally cried. That's the only way to release your grief."

She swiped at her eyes. "I imagine I look a mess. Sorry your shirt's wet."

"You could never look a mess." He wasn't sure he uttered the words out loud until her eyes widened. "You're a very beautiful woman, not at all like the pigtailed hellion who rode like the wind. I just miss all your freckles."

India burst out laughing. "I don't. . . . What do we do now?"

He stood up and walked toward her. "What do you want to do?"

This time when she crossed her arms, the gesture looked defensive, not defiant as she had been earlier. "I'm not sure. I suppose you looked at the ledger."

He wished he could take her in his arms again. "I'm not going to lie to you. I did go over all of last year's pages. I was just getting to this year when you arrived. So far everything looked good to me. Has this year been good, too?"

She nodded. "We're doing fine."

"If you want me to leave, I will." *But I don't want to.* "Will you let me stay until Nathan comes back? I'd feel better if you would."

He could think of other things that would make him feel

better, too, not the least of which was tasting her trembling lips. When had he moved from being fascinated by her to longing to make their relationship something permanent? How could that ever work out with her in Arizona and him in San Francisco?

Chapter 6

Joshua finished cleaning up and headed out of the bunkhouse. With the men coming back from roundup today, he had expected Cook to prepare the evening meal, but India insisted on taking over for him. She said that Martha usually did supper after roundup to give Cook time to clean out the chuck wagon. Joshua would miss his evening meals alone with India. Over the last two days, they had spent a lot of time catching up on each other's lives. All he learned about her fascinated him, except the side of her that had to be in control of everything. She sounded as if she feared losing everyone's respect if she let down her guard even a bit. This troubled him.

He knew she went to church regularly, but where was her trust in God if she had to have such tight control of everything—the ranch, her emotions, her grief? Maybe they would have to have a serious talk about spiritual matters. Joshua wasn't looking forward to upsetting her, but he feared that kind of discussion would.

After stepping up on the porch of the cookhouse, Joshua reached for the handle but didn't need it. The door swung inward of its own accord, and the tantalizing aroma of rich beef stew wafted around him, causing his mouth to water. India was a woman of many talents.

He spied her in the other end of the large room, just outside the kitchen, and hurried toward her. "I'll help you serve the men."

The look she gave him would have been comical if it wasn't so serious. "Now why would you do that?"

"It will give me a chance to thank each of them." He even tied one of the large utilitarian aprons around his waist. "I'll dish up the stew while you take care of the biscuits."

The first of the hands sauntered in, followed by several more in quick succession. The men picked up a bowl and a plate. Tin cans scattered along the length of the two tables held eating utensils.

Joshua ladled a big scoop of the savory soup. "Good job on the roundup, Hankins. Thank you."

The man studied him through squinted eyes, then gave a nod.

The next few minutes passed in the same manner. After getting a serving of stew, each man went to India for two or three of the fluffy biscuits. Joshua had eaten enough of them the last few days to know how good they tasted.

When all the men were seated, Joshua filled a bowl for himself and one for India and set each in front of one of the two empty chairs at the end of the table. India started a heaping plate of biscuits down each table before bringing some more to share with him. While the men ate and talked to each other, Joshua enjoyed his own food.

"So when are you going back into town to work at the orphanage, India?"

She looked up from her plate and gave him a questioning look. "I told you why I haven't been going so much. I'm really tired of all the questions and insinuations."

Joshua took a drink of the cool well water. "How about if I go help you and your friends tomorrow? Then they can get to know me, too. That way I won't be such a mystery to them."

India studied him thoughtfully before answering. "Don't you need to stay here with the men?"

"I'll give them assignments before we leave. None of these men are slackers."

She studied him for a moment. "If you're sure you want to do that."

"I'd like to get a look at this orphanage, since I contributed to it the day of the barbeque."

India had a hard time deciding what to wear to town. On any other day, she would have just slipped into the first skirt and blouse she picked up. For some reason, knowing that Joshua was accompanying her made her pause and consider before she chose something. She stared into the looking glass above the bureau. What did he think about her nearly white blond hair? He had told her he missed her freckles, but when she leaned closer to the mirror, she saw plenty of them. Maybe he hadn't been close enough. Just the thought caused heat to start in her midsection and make its way into her cheeks, leaving a blazing path on her skin. She pulled the neck of her unmentionables away from her chest and used it as a fan. She shouldn't be thinking about the man as anything but an old friend who would leave when Nathan came back. Didn't most people consider her a spinster? He probably did, too. Although she was only in her early twenties, most young women around here wed in their late teens.

After giving her head a quick shake to dislodge these thoughts, she picked up a navy blue skirt, sprigged with tiny white flowers. The light blue lawn blouse brought out the color of her eyes. After turning the long braid that hung across one shoulder into a figure-eight bun at the nape of her neck so it wouldn't interfere with her Stetson, she took a deep breath and ventured out on the porch.

Joshua was hitching the horses to the wagon. For a moment, India watched the sun play across his muscles, bunching and releasing as he worked. The man was strong. . .and good-looking. The fluttering that settled in her stomach brought a sigh to her lips. Why couldn't she control these feelings as well as she took care of everything else?

When he finished his task, Joshua looked toward the house and gave a wave of his strong, tanned hand. "I'll be right there."

India picked up the wooden crate she had filled earlier with things for the orphanage. The wagon stopped in front of the house as she made her way carefully down the three steps. Joshua's long stride brought him quickly up the line of flat stones that led from the house to the gate.

"Here, let me carry that."

He took it from her arms before India could tell him that she was doing fine. He even crooked the arm closest to her as if he wanted to escort her. She started to tell him just what she thought about that but decided not to. Instead, she slipped her hand into the space beside his elbow. The muscles of his forearm felt hard as rock. How could a man who worked behind a desk most of the time develop these kinds of muscles?

The man was an enigma.

Joshua enjoyed the ride into town. Since he shared the wagon seat with India, he made sure he sat close enough that when they hit a bump, their arms touched. The first time, she flinched, almost as if it hurt. He glanced at her out of the corner of his eye. She tightened the muscles in her jaw and turned her attention to something off in the distance ahead. This gave him the opportunity to study her. With skin that looked soft and smooth despite the fact that she was often out in the sun, India was by far the most beautiful woman he'd ever seen. He could imagine her holding her own in any society gathering in San Francisco.

But did he want to see her there? This wild, sometimes

desolate land was part of who she was. Could he take her away from all of this?

Did he want to stay here with her? The more he thought about it, the more feasible it sounded.

"So what's so interesting out there?"

She turned startled eyes toward him. "I was just watching the green trees that line the river bordering the ranch. We really need its water in the late summer."

Always the ranch. Did she ever think about anything else?

Before he could decide how to bring up her need to control everything, he noticed four men riding toward them. As a precaution, he had strapped a pistol on his hip before they left the ranch. He never knew when he would need it for protection from snakes—of many kinds.

"Do you know those men?"

India studied them as they got closer. "That's another rancher with some of his men."

When the men drew close enough, Joshua raised a hand in a friendly salute. The cowboys pulled close to the wagon and stopped their horses, raising a large cloud of dust. If it had been Joshua, he would have slowed his horse gradually in consideration of the other travelers.

"Have you been to town?" India gave the first greeting.

The taller man took off his hat and fanned himself with it. "Yes, my wife had several things she wanted us to take to the orphanage today, and the boys had a little business they needed to take care of."

Joshua could smell what kind of business they had been participating in. The fumes of alcohol wafted toward the wagon. He was glad India wasn't alone. Maybe he should make sure she didn't ride into town alone again.

After India told the rancher to greet his wife for her, the men rode on, and Joshua clicked his tongue as he picked up the reins. The rest of the way to Cactus Corner, he tried to figure out how he would broach the subject with India. He knew she wouldn't welcome his interference.

India felt relieved when they arrived at their destination. The ride hadn't been comfortable. The attempts at conversation during the ride had fallen as flat as her first pancakes. Where had their easy comradery gone?

Every time their arms brushed against each other, that silly sensation once again rushed through her. If she didn't know better, she would think she was a young teenager just becoming aware of the masculine gender. Then she realized that it was the first time she had ever been interested in a specific man.

When she came home from back east, none of the young men sought her out. Although her father did what he thought was best for her, he couldn't have been more wrong. No one in this area of Arizona Territory wanted someone from Mrs. Collier's Finishing School. They wanted a woman who knew how to thrive in this part of the country. That might have been one of the reasons India tried so hard to prove she could run the ranch—even before Daddy died.

After stopping the horses, Joshua rushed around the back of the wagon to help her alight. The gold flecks in his dark brown eyes glistened in the bright sunlight, and his fingers splayed around her waist made her feel breathless.

Unfortunately, Anika, Elaine, and Jody came through the open door of the orphanage and witnessed her exit from the vehicle. Hopefully they would think her cheeks were red from being in the sun, but she knew different. His touch sent a blush to her cheeks as quickly as the bumps on the ride made her stomach jumpy.

"So"—Anika stood arms akimbo—"this is *the* Joshua Dillinger that I've been hearing so much about."

Joshua released his hold on India and turned around, but not before she heard his soft chuckle. "Just what have you been hearing about me? You're Anika, aren't you? India described you exactly."

He held out his hand, and Anika gave him the firm handshake she always used, almost like a man's. "Yes. I'm a lawyer, also. Maybe we can compare the differences in practicing law in a small place like Cactus Corner as opposed to a city like San Francisco."

His questioning gaze targeted India. "So what have you been telling her about me?"

Thankfully Jody intervened. "Oh, she's not the only one in town talking about you."

Joshua pulled his Stetson from his head and brushed it

against his leg as he often did. "Don't you work in the office of the freight company?" After Jody nodded, he continued, "I remember seeing you there when I bought King."

"King?" Jody wrinkled her brows. "I thought Elmer sold you Goldie. I don't remember him having a horse named King."

Joshua's rich laugh pealed forth. "Goldie isn't a very good name for a stallion, so I renamed him King. He took to it pretty quickly."

The group moved around to the back of the wagon and started carrying in the things India and Joshua brought from the ranch. Cook had sent a few cuts of the steer he butchered yesterday, which they kept in the springhouse over night. Elaine took it to the kitchen so Carla, the cook at the orphanage, could start chopping it into smaller pieces for the stew they would eat at noon.

India couldn't believe how much they accomplished that day. With Joshua helping, they completed many of the needed repairs. He promised to come on his next day off and give the building a new coat of paint.

She and Joshua started home in plenty of time to reach the ranch before dark.

When they were away from town, India turned toward him. "I didn't want to say anything back at the orphanage, but we don't have enough extra money to buy paint." When he turned to face her, she read the surprise in his eyes.

"I gave a pretty substantial amount at the barbeque." He cleared his throat as if the admission had a hard time coming out.

She nodded. "Pastor Gavin showed me the wad of bills you dropped in, and we are thankful."

"Then what's the problem?" He looked back toward the road.

"Well, the fund-raiser wasn't for the day-to-day running of the orphanage. Didn't you notice how crowded it is?"

"It did seem so." He certainly wasn't wasting any words. "So what was the money for?"

"We're saving to buy the empty mercantile building next door." Just the thought made India happy. "We'll have more room for the kids we have now, and we can even take in more, if we need to."

They rode along in silence for a while. India spent the time thinking about what needed to be done at the ranch when they got back. She almost missed his next softly spoken sentence.

"Then I'll pay for the paint myself."

Chapter 7

Over the next two weeks, whenever India went to town, Joshua accompanied her. Soon everyone she knew seemed to be in cahoots, figuring out ways that she and Joshua would have to spend time together. Pastor Gavin along with the rest of them. Not that she minded, but the time would come when he would go back to his law practice in San Francisco. She tried not to think about that.

Anika, Elaine, and Jody each found a chance to talk to her alone. Every single one of them told her not to let him get away, as if she were trying to snag him for a husband. She didn't want to think about that either. Sorting out her jumbled emotions would take more time than she had to give to it.

All too soon, India received the letter she had been dreading. Nathan and Martha would be home today. As she read the words, her heart pounded in panic. What would she do now?

India took a deep breath and squared her shoulders. She

would run the ranch just as she did before that man rode back into her life. That's exactly what she would do. Unfortunately, the thought settled like a huge stone in the pit of her stomach.

Pasting a smile on her face, she went out to the barn to give the news to Joshua. Within half an hour, they were headed toward town in the wagon with their horses tied to the back. She hadn't wanted to ride in the back of the wagon on the way from Cactus Corner to the ranch, and she wouldn't think of asking Nathan and Martha to do it either.

Evidently Joshua was affected by the news, too. Neither of them talked on the way to town. They arrived just in time to hear the train whistle as it approached the depot. To India's heart, it sounded mournful, a death knell to hopes she hadn't even admitted she harbored.

After all the greetings, Joshua helped Nathan load the baggage into the wagon. Then he invited them to go to the café with him and India. He would buy everyone a meal before they returned to the ranch.

Nathan looked rested. As a matter of fact, so did Martha. Even though he'd lost his father, the trip must have been good for them. Over a meal of smothered steak and mashed potatoes, Nathan told all about his family. Martha inserted that they were glad to be back home.

India was just as quiet as Joshua during the delicious meal

that went down like sawdust in his throat. The time for a decision was here, and he wasn't sure what India would think of his ideas.

After getting Nathan and Martha situated in the wagon and started toward the ranch, Joshua turned to India. "Let's take a detour by the river on our way back." He stuck his fingers in the hip pockets on his dungarees. "Maybe we could sit on that big rock that juts out over the water and talk awhile."

For some reason, her eyes held a wary expression, but she agreed.

The summer sun beat down on them as they rode across the arid land, but their speed whipped up a wind that cooled them. When they slowed near the river, the canopy of sheltering branches gave comforting shade. After walking the horses to the span of grass that lined the riverbank, Joshua quickly dismounted. How he wanted to help India down and encircle her with his arms, but that would have to wait. . .hopefully not forever.

India sat on the rock and arranged the split skirt to cover her legs completely. She stared across the water that shimmered with reflected sunlight. Joshua lowered himself beside her.

He waited a minute or two before he broached the subject on his mind. "We need to talk, India." She turned her gaze toward him, and he found it unreadable.

"Okay. What do you want to talk about?"

"You. . .me. . .the future." He felt like a stammering schoolboy.

The wall of her defenses strengthened visibly. "So what about me?"

He took her hand, and she didn't pull away. "Can we pray together first?"

She nodded her assent and bowed her head.

Lord, help me. Joshua cleared his throat. "Lord, we're at a crossroads here. We need Your wisdom to help us see the way You've set before us. We ask for that wisdom, in Jesus' name. Amen."

When she raised her head, she still didn't take her hand from his. That was a good sign, wasn't it?

He might as well plunge right in. "I've noticed that you always have to be in control."

India clenched her other hand but still didn't remove the one he held. "And?"

"Maybe you're not trusting God enough." The expression in her eyes hardened a little. "I know you're a Christian. I'm just saying that maybe you should trust Him to fight your battles for you." What else could he say to get her to understand? Maybe he should just let her think about it for a bit.

They sat in silence with India staring across the river for quite a while before she spoke. "Maybe you're right." She turned to look at him. "I understand that He knows best, but it took a long time for the men around here to accept me as a ranch owner—not only because I'm young, but also because I'm a woman."

He smiled into her eyes. "Yes, you are."

A blush stole over her cheeks, giving her a special glow.

"When I was a boy, my father had me memorize a Bible verse that has carried me through many hard times. It tells us to trust in the Lord with all our hearts, instead of leaning on our own understanding. If we acknowledge Him in all our ways, He will direct our paths. I believe that's one of the reasons that I've been so successful."

India glanced down at their hands and gently pulled hers away before clasping both hands around her upraised knees. She stared into the water flowing below them. "Do you think God brought you here, Joshua?"

He liked the sound of his name on her lips. "Yes, I do."

"You know I thought you came here to try to take over the ranch, don't you?"

He needed to be totally honest with her. "I guessed as much. Do you still believe that?"

"No." The soft word floated toward him on the breeze. "What are you going to do now? Go back to San Francisco?"

"Is that what you want?" He watched her intently, trying to discern her thoughts.

Finally, she turned to look back at him. "I'll really hate to see you go."

That's all he needed. "I don't have to."

She stood and walked to the back edge of the large rock before she turned around. "What are you saying?"

He scrambled to his feet but stood where he was, afraid to approach her yet. He'd be tempted to pull her into his arms and smother her with kisses.

"That I love you, India."

A spark lit her eyes. "But you live in San Francisco, and I own a ranch in Arizona Territory."

And never the twain shall meet. He'd see about that. "Would you be willing to go to San Francisco with me?"

Their gazes locked, and it almost felt like an embrace.

"What would we do with the ranch?"

India said *we,* as if they were a couple. Hope sprang forth full-blown in his heart. "*We* can decide that together."

Mischief colored her expression. "Are you asking me to marry you, Joshua, or are your intentions dishonorable?"

He took a step in her direction. "I offer nothing but marriage."

"Yes." She flung herself toward him, and he enclosed her in his embrace.

"India." Joshua was so full of emotion, he couldn't say anything else for a moment. "You won't have to give up your beloved ranch. In my Bible reading this morning, I came across a proverb that said a good man leaves an inheritance to his children's children. When I look into your smiling face, I see the foreshadowing of our children, and they need to grow up on their grandfather's ranch."

Her bright eyes trembled with unshed tears. He hoped they were tears of happiness. Gently he kissed her forehead, and her eyes drifted shut, spilling a tear on each cheek. He dried each of them with his mouth on the way to her luscious lips. They tasted of honey and sunshine and ignited a depth of love he'd never imagined.

He had only planned to give her a gentle kiss to seal their engagement. When India's arms crept across his shoulders and she relaxed against his chest, he deepened the kiss. She responded with passion. Joshua felt as if heaven opened and God placed His seal on their promise to each other.

Epilogue

India stood in a bedroom on the upper floor of the board-inghouse. So much had happened in such a short time. Today was her wedding day. In only three weeks, her best friends had helped her make a wedding dress and a trousseau to take on a honeymoon to San Francisco. They would soon be here to help her prepare for the ceremony.

Joshua had spent last night at the hotel so he wouldn't see her until she arrived at the church. His parents arrived last night, too. She was sure they were having a good time with their son.

Probably everyone for miles around Cactus Corner would attend the celebration today. India's head swam from the speed with which everything was accomplished. She thought about the land that she had inherited from her father—her heritage.

Those musings were interrupted when she noticed her help-ers driving down the street in a carriage. She quickly finished her ablutions so she would be ready when they came upstairs.

The first one through the door was Jody, who rushed to

give India a hug as if they hadn't spent the last twenty-one days working together. "So are you excited?"

India placed a hand on her stomach to try to stop the flutters there. "Of course."

Anika and Elaine came in carrying the dress, being careful to protect it from being soiled. When India was back east, many of the women had taken up the tradition started by Queen Victoria of England of wearing a white wedding dress. The practice hadn't really made its way this far west, but she had decided that if she ever married, she'd wear white. She had been pleasantly surprised when the general store had a bolt of white silk in its dry goods department.

The women bustled around helping India. Jody arranged her hair in an elaborate upswept style with long curls falling over one shoulder.

As she finished India's hair, Jody asked, "So you're going to San Francisco? Will you go today or tomorrow?"

India felt a blush move across her cheeks. "Joshua didn't want to spend our wedding night riding the train, so we'll go tomorrow."

"A wise move." Elaine helped Anika drape the dress carefully across the bed. "But are you moving there? You haven't really shared any of your plans with us."

Joshua's wise decisions under the leadership of the Lord had brought a satisfying answer to their dilemma. "No, we'll live on the ranch most of the time, but we'll go to San Francisco from time to time. And when we're gone, if Nathan needs to get in touch with us, there's always the telegraph. Joshua is still the senior partner in the law firm."

Anika raised her eyebrows at that statement. "Is Joshua planning to practice law here?"

India laughed. "Of course not. There's not enough business to keep both of you busy. His legal expertise will help with things at the ranch, though."

While her friends held the dress, she stepped into it before they pulled it up over her hips. After slipping her arms into the sleeves, they started fastening the long line of buttons that went up the back. How would she ever get out of the dress? A vision of Joshua standing behind her, carefully unfastening it, sent heat rushing all through her. She needed to keep her thoughts on the next few minutes, not the wedding night.

Joshua waited at the front of the church with Pastor Gavin McCurdy. He never dreamed when he decided to fulfill Mr. Cunningham's request just how much it would change his life. . .for the better. He knew God had sent him to this place, and he was glad he had listened to the Lord's direction. The most wonderful woman in the world was soon to be his wife. *His wife*. The words still felt strange, but wonderful.

Mrs. McCurdy came in the back door and walked down the side of the room toward the piano. After she sat down, she began to play the "Wedding March." India had chosen the music because she came to love it when she was in finishing school. However, Joshua wondered if the woman at the piano had ever played it before. It didn't matter, because the back door opened and Nathan escorted India down the aisle toward him. Everything else faded from his consciousness. He couldn't take his eyes off his bride—looking like an angel as she slowly walked toward him. *Thank You, Lord, for the gift of this woman.*

LENA NELSON DOOLEY

Lena loves to write stories. She's blessed that this is her full-time job. Another of her favorite activities is mentoring other authors and helping them move toward to publication. Because of this, she was awarded the American Christian Fiction Writers Mentor of the Year award in 2006. Several times a year, Lena is a speaker at writers' meetings and women's meetings across the country.

Lena has written nine Heartsongs and has stories in five Barbour novella collections. She has had books on one of the top ten favorite lists in the Heartsong Readers' Poll for four years. Last year one of her books hit #1 on a Christian fiction best-seller list in the UK.

Married more than forty-two years, Lena and her husband spend a lot of time with their children and grandchildren. They're active in church and love to travel. Some of the places they visit become settings in her novels.

She enjoys hearing from her readers. You can find out more about her on her Web site, www.LenaNelsonDooley.com, or on her blog: http://lenanelsondooley.blogspot.com.

The Spinster
and the Lawyer

by Jeri Odell

Dedication

This book is dedicated to the love of my life.
Thank you, Dean, for the past thirty-four years.
You are a good man and have filled my life beyond measure.
I'm so grateful we've made the journey together.

And to You, Lord, without whom I wouldn't
even have the privilege of writing.
Blessed be Your name.

And the King shall answer and say unto them,
Verily I say unto you, Inasmuch as ye have done it
unto one of the least of these my brethren,
ye have done it unto me.
MATTHEW 25:40

Prologue

Chicago, Autumn 1884

I asked Anika Windsor to marry me last night," Tucker Truesdale informed his roommate.

Edward's bushy brows shot up. "Marry? Are you certain? You haven't known her exceptionally long."

Tucker grinned. Edward was far more cautious than most. "I'm certain. She's wonderful. I wish you'd take the time to become better acquainted."

"Time? Who has time for anything except studying those law books?" Edward pointed to the stack perched on their tiny table. "How ever did you find time to court her?"

"We haven't exactly courted." Tucker's heart sped up a notch as he pictured Anika with her chestnut hair and hazel eyes. "We study together and share supper. But almost immediately, I realized she was different. There is no girlish silliness in her, yet she understands joy and laughter."

Edward only shook his head.

"She's beautiful, with a nimble mind and a heart that truly loves God. She wants to make the world a better place. We'll marry next spring, as soon as we finish law school."

"I wish you well." Tucker knew from Edward's expression that he doubted the wisdom of their decision. "It has certainly happened quickly."

"Yes," Tucker agreed. "We plummeted hard and fast, but we truly love each other and can't imagine our lives lived separately."

No man could truly understand this journey called love until he walked the path. A few months ago, Tucker would have been just as skeptical. But not now. Not after they'd whispered words of affection to one another, not after last night when they'd promised each other forever. Theirs was the perfect romance, and he continually thanked God for this incredible woman.

"Are you ready to walk to class?" Edward asked as he picked through the stack of books, finding the ones he needed.

"Sure." Tucker grabbed his coat and followed Edward out into the brisk morning. "If the weather continues this direction, we may have snow early this year."

They passed a suffrage rally on their walk to their first class of the day. Edward waved to the protestors. "Of course it's 90 percent women."

"How can they not understand the plan God has laid out for the family?" Tucker asked. "The man is the umbrella over his wife and children. His job is to provide for them and protect them from the harsh realities of the world."

"Apparently some of them wish to gain their own rights to provide for and protect themselves—harsh realities to boot."

Though Edward scanned the crowd, Tucker couldn't even look at them. How could they say they love God, family, and country and yet rebel against Him like this?

"Isn't that Anika?" Edward pointed in her direction.

Tucker stopped dead in his tracks. His heart pounded, and the noise echoed in his ears. He longed to deny the truth before him, but Anika marched in plain sight for all to see, carrying a sign not only proclaiming a woman's need to vote but insisting it was her God-given right.

Tucker strode toward her, his anger increasing with each step. "What, may I ask, do you think you're doing?"

Startled, Anika turned. Tucker approached, and her heart bubbled with joy at seeing him. Then she noticed the anger etched across his features. He grabbed her sign from her and threw it on the ground. That was all it took for her ire to flare.

"The better question—what do you think you're doing?" Anika retrieved her bent sign.

The crowd milled around them, people whispering and staring.

"I can't abide a suffragist." His eyes blazed.

Anika realized she'd never seen him like this—angry and

unbending. "What are you saying?"

"No wife of mine will march around with some silly sign or support this disagreeable cause."

Now he'd really made her mad. Speaking very softly, she said, "And no husband of mine would oppose the need for women to be treated with respect, as any intelligent, thinking person deserves."

"Have I ever shown you disrespect?" he demanded.

"You just did when you took my sign from me and tossed it on the ground like common trash." She studied his handsome face—the face she'd grown to love—but maybe she didn't really know the man behind it at all. "How did we miss discussing our views on suffrage?"

"I just assumed—"

"That my views were exactly as yours?" She shook her head. "I'm shocked, Tucker—not only by your response today but by your narrow-minded thinking."

"I have never been accused of being narrow-minded."

"I'm not accusing you. I'm stating it as fact. You, Tucker Truesdale, are narrow-minded." She punctuated her words with her pointer finger against his chest. "It is not a crime to be a woman, nor is it a crime to want to make life better for other women. If you cannot see this, then you are not the man I thought you were. Nor are you a man I would *ever* marry." She stomped her foot, raised her sign, and marched back into line.

Her next time around the square, she noted that Tucker

had left. She knew they'd just ended the shortest engagement in history, and a plethora of emotions stirred inside her heart. For two lawyers, they'd done a poor job of conflict resolution.

Chapter 1

Arizona Territory, September 1894

The conductor announced they'd arrive in Cactus Corner in approximately thirty minutes. Tucker removed the letter from his satchel that summoned him here to this—he glanced out the window of the train car—godforsaken part of the world. He had traveled extensively, but this was his first trip so far west, and the desert was ugly at best—dry, brown, and desolate.

He read the letter one last time, wanting to be clear on his instructions.

> *Mr. Truesdale,*
>
> *Thank you for responding to the men of this community and our plea for fair representation. You came highly recommended as an expert on land issues, and we feel confident that you can resolve this injustice that took*

place in our area. We look forward to your coming in a few weeks.

Upon your arrival, you'll find the opposing attorney in the office directly across the street from the depot. She's not expecting you, as we believe surprise will give us an edge.

Sincerely,
John Turner

Following Mr. Turner's signature were about a dozen others. *No surprise that the other attorney is a woman—surely a suffragist, too.* The thought left a bitter taste in his mouth and brought Anika to mind. Though they had never spoken again, he'd spent that last year of law school as an avid spokesman against suffrage. Always at odds, he fought her every attempt to promote women's right to vote.

Tucker focused his attention on the present—no point dwelling on the unpleasant dregs of the past. He had used his good name and reputation to slow down the process in the Pima County Land Agent's office in Tucson until he could get here. Once he gained a feel for the situation, he'd file the necessary appeals with the courts in order to stop the entire process. He hadn't lost a case in almost six years and wouldn't lose this one to some woman lawyer.

Tucker climbed down from the train car and stretched cramped muscles. As he scanned the horizon, the mountains off in the distance to the east drew his gaze. They stood gallant and fairly close. Cactus Corner sat in a valley, and on the far horizon in every direction were mountains. Nothing like his home state of Nebraska.

Tucker boosted his trunk up on his right shoulder and made a beeline to the boardinghouse across the street—the quaint two-story, wood-sided building with rockers on the porch—sitting right next to the lady lawyer's office. He rented a room for the next month, guessing he'd be there at least that long, grabbed his satchel, and headed next door. He preferred boardinghouses to hotels—family-style meals made the stay feel more like home.

Home. That single word brought an ache of loneliness upon him. He'd never planned to become a land expert, traveling from here to there, never really having a place to hang his hat. Sure, he'd seen more of the country than most people even dreamed of, but other than his family back on the old homestead, he had nobody. No friends. No one. He shook off the dark feeling assaulting him, raised his chin, and entered the attorney's office.

The room was empty, but the door squeaked loudly enough that his presence had been announced to everyone in town. He glanced around the stark office—nothing like most of the lawyers' offices he'd visited around the country. Small, cramped, and simple. Hard wooden chairs, a beat-up old desk in the corner, and the counter he now leaned on.

"Hello. May I—"

Anika. His heart tripped over itself. He'd not expected to see her again or feel all the emotions churning inside him. She'd waltzed out of a back room, that smile he remembered too well lighting her face—until she obviously recognized him. The smile faded, and she stopped halfway to the counter. Her face paled. She sucked in a deep breath, stood tall, and moved with her usual regal grace toward him.

"Help you, Mr. Truesdale?" She attempted a smile, but it fell short of the one he'd seen on her face seconds ago.

Anika grasped the counter, not certain she could stand on her own. Tucker, the man she'd never forgotten, stood barely two feet from her in this rural office, looking better than she'd remembered. He'd matured. His face revealed signs of wear, and gray hairs were sprinkled through his dark beard, which surprised her for his thirty-four years. But those deep blue eyes that resembled the purplish mountain off in the distance still caused her heart to thud.

He appeared as overwhelmed as she felt by this unexpected encounter. Never in her wildest dreams or worst nightmares had she imagined meeting him again. She had no idea what to say or why he'd shown up here. Suddenly, she did know. Like the dawn breaking through a starless night, she knew. He was the reason the land claims she'd helped file were tied up with red tape.

Squaring her shoulders, she prepared for a battle. Sadly, she and Tucker didn't fight well. Their last one still brought remnants of hurt and pain. "Is there something I can help you with?"

she repeated. Her words were frosty and curt.

Tucker raised his chin a fraction of an inch. His eyes met hers, and they contained no warmth, nor did they gaze upon her with respect and admiration as they once had. He laid his satchel on the wooden counter and pulled out some paperwork.

"This appears to be an official visit. And here I'd hoped you'd come to your senses about suffrage and had come to apologize." She meant for her words to provoke, to place him on the defensive. She needed every advantage. Attorneys everywhere knew Tucker Truesdale was a respected and formidable opponent—one who always won.

He only smiled. Her words seemed to have had the opposite effect than she'd hoped for. They apparently reminded him why he was here and cut any ties he felt to her or their past.

"Yes, Miss Windsor, I'm here representing Mr. Turner and a dozen of the other men living in this community who are appealing the land claims you helped file."

Her heart dipped, and she knew she was in for the war of her life. "Everything was legal and aboveboard. I assure you I followed the laws to the fullest measure."

He rubbed his beard with his thumb and index finger while he studied her through narrowed eyes. "I find it fascinating that thirty single women all over Pima County knew the exact date the Carey Land Act was signed into law and had their money and paperwork ready on said date. Not only that—there wasn't one man in the entire pile who claimed a 160-acre parcel. Why is that, Miss Windsor?"

His attitude infuriated her. "First, Mr. Truesdale, I'd like to remind you that I am not responsible for what the men in this town do or do not do. If they are uninformed, that is not my problem. Second, I am not on trial here, but if I were, a judge would speak to you about badgering the witness. Now if you'll excuse me, I have work to do." She turned to walk away.

"I'd hoped we could reach a reasonable compromise."

His words stopped her retreat to the small space in the back where she stored all her files, briefs, and law books. "What, in your opinion, is a reasonable compromise?"

"You convince twelve of those thirty women to give up their claims so these men have a fair chance."

"A fair chance!" The nerve of this man. "They had the same chance these ladies had. I'm sorry if they didn't pursue it in a timely manner, but I will not ask anyone to give up her claim."

"How will these women run ranches, Miss Windsor? What do you possibly know about raising cattle, breeding, or building fences, for that matter?" A frown creased the spot between his brows.

"They can hire your men to work for them." She nearly spat the words at him.

"These men aren't willing to work for women bosses who had whims to try their hands at ranching." His gaze held disappointment, maybe even disgust.

"Whims?" Her voice had risen and gained volume. "Whims, you say? These women worked, planned, and saved for this opportunity. How dare you imply it was a silly impulse? I will not ask one of them to give up her dreams and hard work for some man who had no sense to plan for the future!"

"Then, Miss Windsor, I will see you in court. And I don't lose in front of a judge."

Anika's heart pounded, but she stood her ground. "There is a first time for everything, Mr. Truesdale. Good day." Turning, she made a straight path to the back room, and when she got there, her entire being shook. Leaning against the wall, she took in a deep breath, and her eyes burned with unshed tears. *How did I ever love him? He is the most arrogant, pompous man.*

The front door squeaked loudly, and Anika rushed to lock it, pulling the shade over the window, needing some time to recover. She'd walk over to the orphanage, and hopefully her friends would be there. Scribbling a quick note to hang on the front window, she informed whoever might inquire that she'd return after the noon meal.

As she hurried south on Main Street, across the railroad tracks, the hot, still air caused a stifling heat. Thank heaven the orphanage and her office were neighbors; only the tracks lay between them. She hated to walk far in this heat and normally avoided going outside most days, until the sun settled low in the western sky.

When Anika entered the orphanage, Jane, Charlene, and Rainsong all ran to her. She hugged Jane first. With her rare combination of blond hair and brown eyes, she was growing into a real beauty.

"How are Grace and the toddlers today?" Anika asked Jane as she bent to embrace Charlene and Rainsong.

"I love helping her with the little ones. We just finished bathing them, and they all smell heavenly." Jane's eyes took on the dreamy look of a fifteen-year-old girl. "Did you see that new boy in church Sunday? Maybe someday he'll court me, and we could have a passel of young'uns of our own."

Anika smiled at Jane's naive, romantic ideals. She'd had those, too—once. An ache settled in her heart. Now she and Tucker were bitter enemies. Shaking the sadness, she rose.

"Maybe that's God's plan for you, but could be He has something entirely different." God had something unequivocally different for her than she'd imagined. Somewhere along the way she'd dreamed the same dream as Jane, but that wasn't to be. "That's why I want you to keep up with your schooling, so you can be ready for anything."

Anika turned to Charlene. "Honey, run and fetch me the brush, and I'll help you with your hair." Anika brushed the child's stringy hair every chance she got.

"I am workin' hard on my studies," Jane assured her. "Now I'd better run, or Grace will have my hide." Jane hugged her again. "I want you to teach me everything you know about boys." And she was gone.

Anika sighed. She knew nothing about boys, absolutely nothing. Lifting Rainsong into her arms, she asked, "How is my favorite six-year-old today?" Anika stroked Rainsong's beautiful long black hair. God had given her black eyes to match.

Rainsong placed both of her pudgy, bronzed hands on Anika's cheeks.

"I love you, Miss Anika."

"Oh, I love you, too, sweetheart." She hugged the child close, maternal feelings filling each pore of her being.

"I thought I heard your voice." India breezed into the room. "Your timing is impeccable. Carla is sick today, and we need help in the kitchen. The sad truth is it may take all four of us to feed this crew—a task Carla manages three times a day by herself."

Anika giggled, picturing the four of them with flour strewn from here to there. "I'll be but a moment. First, I have a most important hair-brushing engagement."

Charlene had returned, so Anika lowered Rainsong to the floor and settled into a rocker in the parlor. The ten-year-old knelt in front of her, and Anika spent about five minutes brushing the blond locks. Too bad Rainsong couldn't share her well-endowed head of hair and replace Charlene's thin, wispy locks.

"All right, honey, your hair looks lovely. I'm going to help in the kitchen." Anika kissed the top of her head, thinking how just being here at the orphanage always made her feel better.

Entering the kitchen and washing her hands, she asked, "What can I do?"

"Peel about a hundred potatoes," Jody joked.

"What brought you our way in the middle of the day?" Elaine questioned as Anika seated herself on a stool and picked up the first potato. "Are you taking an early lunch break as Jody is?"

"I longed for a friendly face. You'll not believe who paid me a visit this morning."

Her three closest friends all took turns speculating, but of course no one guessed correctly.

"Tucker Truesdale." Anika stated the name matter-of-factly.

"Tucker Truesdale!" they all repeated, astonishment echoing through their voices.

"The old beau, Tucker Truesdale?" Elaine questioned.

"One and the same," Anika assured them.

India grinned. "Did he come to right his wrongs, beg your forgiveness, and carry you off into the sunset?"

Anika rolled her eyes. "Hardly. Just because that happened for you doesn't mean the rest of us will ever marry. At thirty, it's highly unlikely for me." Anika failed to sound as carefree as she'd hoped. Then she proceeded to share this morning's confrontation, surprised by the quiver in her voice. She prided herself in her ability to remain composed. Tucker's intrusion into her well-ordered world had affected her more than she wanted to admit—even to herself.

Then Mrs. Jacobson entered the kitchen with none other than Tucker Truesdale on her heals. Anika nearly toppled off her stool. Their gazes locked. She felt certain her mouth gaped, but she had no power to pull it shut. Must he invade her personal world as well as her professional one?

Chapter 2

*A*nika. *Oh great, another run-in with the woman whose tenacity matches that of a raging bull!* It seemed with every meeting their exchanges only grew worse.

Mrs. Jacobson said, "This gentleman is here to help. He's staying in our little town for a month or so on business, and when he travels, he always volunteers at the local orphanage. Gives him a connection. This is Mr. Tucker Truesdale—"

A clanging rang out from the sink area. The woman with the curly auburn hair pulled into a tight knot bent and rescued the knife from the floor. Each woman's face was aghast. They'd obviously heard his name a time or two, and not in a good light.

Mrs. Jacobson continued with the introductions. "This is Mrs. India Dillinger, Miss Anika Windsor, and Miss Jody McMillan. They also volunteer here—almost every day. And this is Miss Elaine Daly. She is one of our staff."

"Ladies, it's a pleasure." However, he knew none of them considered it so.

No one moved. They all just stared. Finally, Mrs. Dillinger acknowledged him. "Yes, well, we must get lunch finished. Why don't you prepare these string beans? We'll put you over there." She pointed to a corner of the large kitchen—a place as far away from Anika as the room allowed.

Mrs. Dillinger provided a stool for him, then placed a large bowl of beans and a pan of water in front of him. The room that was filled with chatter upon his arrival now rang out in stone-cold and uncomfortable silence. He popped the ends off the beans and tossed them into the pan of water.

After five minutes or so, he could no longer stand the discomfort. He approached Anika. "I'm truly sorry for our scuffle this morning. I had no idea you'd be here, or I wouldn't have come."

For a brief second he spotted the hurt in her hazel eyes before the coolness replaced it. Guilt assaulted him. He'd never intended to hurt her, but somehow it had become a pattern woven into the fiber of their encounters. "I'll leave. Ladies, I'm sorry to have intruded upon your day." He made eye contact with each of them. "I promise, in the future, this will be one orphanage I shall avoid. My apologies again."

He strode toward the door. Much of the anger he'd felt toward Anika had dissipated, leaving in its place an ache for all they'd once shared. For the first time he realized he had missed her, and he'd never even acknowledged the loss he withstood when they had parted ways. Sure, he'd thought about her occasionally over the years, wondering if she'd gotten her faith and causes to coincide, and now he knew.

"Wait." Her voice was quiet and hesitant.

He turned to face her. She bit her bottom lip, and a gamut of emotions played across her features. He studied her—the velvet skin of her face, the ringlets curling around her temples, the silky chestnut hair wadded into a bun. She apparently struggled to find the right words, and he fought an overwhelming longing to pull her into his arms and find a route around this whole mess.

"Please don't leave—" Anika paused.

How he wished she'd said that on their fateful day a decade ago.

"What I mean is, we are both adults, and there is no reason we can't each help here at the orphanage. Heaven knows there is always more work than time or people to get it done." She smiled. Sincerity filled her tone and her eyes. Walking toward him, she reached out her hand to shake in agreement. "Truce? At least when we're at the orphanage?"

Her touch was warm. How he'd unknowingly missed it. "Agreed." His voice betrayed him, sounding husky and almost tender. What was wrong with him? He was a trained professional who read every nuance of tone and expression and disciplined his to reveal nothing.

"It's my fault my friends are uncomfortable around you. They are all really lovely ladies, I assure you." She gazed with affection at each woman.

"I'm certain they are," Tucker agreed.

"Please accept our regrets as well." Mrs. Dillinger smiled for the first time.

"Yes, we weren't welcoming to you at all," Miss McMillan added. "Normally we embrace all volunteers."

"We'll forget you're the man who broke Anika's heart, if you'll forget our rude behavior," Miss Daly bargained.

Broke Anika's heart? Glancing at Anika, her cheeks reflected every shade of pink. She ducked her head. How foolish of him. He'd not realized he'd broken her heart or that his had been broken, as well. It seemed to him she went along fine without him. They'd both been so young, idealistic, and prideful. Maybe God had brought them back together for another chance. No, couldn't be. She still fought the good fight of suffrage for the wrong team.

He cleared his throat. "Back to the beans, then."

Anika smiled. "Thank you," she whispered, laying her hand on his arm.

Her eyes glistened, and his heart bubbled over with feelings for her. Feelings he'd buried before they'd apparently died. Now they popped up like wildflowers in the spring, invading his very being, just as the colorful blossoms invaded his father's pastures back in Nebraska. Shaking his head to clear the thoughts, he knew he must stop all this nonsense. He was here in Cactus Corner for a war, and the war was against Anika Windsor. There could be no fondness or affection between them. He must keep his wits about him.

As Anika rocked on the front porch of the boardinghouse late that afternoon, she watched God paint the sky with another beautiful Arizona sunset and questioned her own sanity. Today Tucker felt like a friend, but in reality he was her foe. He was the only man she'd ever loved, and the only person she'd also disliked with such intensity.

Elaine claimed the rocker next to her. "You look a million miles away. Today was hard for you, wasn't it?"

Anika sighed and nodded. "Tucker confuses me." She stared off at nothing in particular. "I grew up believing I could make a difference. From the time I was a little girl, my father said, 'You can change the world one person at a time.' He said that to me almost daily my entire life. That's why he became a judge, to make the world a better place. And that's why I became a lawyer."

Elaine's expression was compassionate. "You do make a difference. Look at the lives you've touched at the orphanage. You always embrace the downtrodden and the weak. You'd help anyone who needed it—man, woman, or child."

"I suppose, but my heart goes out to women and children. Most men can take care of themselves and their families, but our society makes it more difficult for women who don't have a husband. That doesn't seem right to me." Anika stood and paced to the edge of the wooden porch.

"Do you think I'm wrong to fight fiercely for the causes that will make the world better for women and children?" She leaned her back against a post, facing Elaine. "I feel as if I've found a balance between my faith and suffrage, but maybe I'm only fooling myself. I mean, I love the Lord and am committed to Him, but so does Tucker. His relationship with the Lord is of the utmost importance to him, too." Anika stared at the rainbow of colors highlighting the sky—pinks, oranges, purples. "How can there be one God we both love, yet our views be so contradictory? Which one of us is wrong?"

"I don't know, Anika." Elaine rose. "Maybe you're both right and both wrong. The first commandment is to love God and the second to love others. Are you loving Tucker, and he you?" Elaine shrugged. "Seems he's a man with strong opinions, and yours are equally as strong."

Anika nodded. "I know. Never the twain shall meet." She knew her tone sounded dejected. "Now you understand why we were completely unsuited for marriage."

"I think what I understand is your need to convince yourself this is an insurmountable, irresolvable issue. . .but what I really understand is that yours and Tucker's feelings still run deep. You still love him, Anika." Elaine, as always, spoke matter-of-factly.

"How can I love a man who makes my blood boil? A man who can't agree with me on this most important matter? A man who spent the last year of law school opposing me at every turn? No, I once loved him, but those days are long gone."

"They may be gone, but they are not forgotten—not by either of you. I was there this morning, remember?"

What Anika remembered about this morning was that for one brief moment, all the causes vanished. She and Tucker stood face-to-face, her hand shaking his, and all she wanted—longed for—was his strong arms to once again enfold her into the safe harbor of his chest. But of course there would be no tenderness between them—only more conflict, in a courtroom, before a judge. And one of them would lose. Then he'd move on to the next case, in the next town. Anika would be left behind with more memories to reconcile and more pain to survive.

"No, Elaine, you're wrong." Anika smiled to soften her words. "I think I'll take a walk. See you at the orphanage tomorrow?"

Elaine nodded, and Anika took Main Street toward the center of town.

I have no feelings for Tucker. Maybe this time when we part ways, we'll at least be cordial. That's all there is—remnants of a shared past. This time Elaine is wrong. I do not still love him. I could not possibly be that stupid. What is that silly old saying? Once hurt, twice as smart. No, I'm much older and wiser now, not some silly schoolgirl with hopelessly romantic notions. Tucker Truesdale means nothing to me—nothing!

Chapter 3

When Anika stumbled out to join the other boarders at Mrs. Jenkins's breakfast table, there sat Tucker. "You live here?" she asked.

His nod confirmed her bleary-eyed suspicions. *Wonderful. Not only does he volunteer at the orphanage, but he also rooms at my boardinghouse.* This news was anything but good, especially after the restless night she'd spent. She didn't desire to spend days on end with him constantly underfoot, but so far that appeared inevitable.

"Mr. Truesdale, tell us about yourself," Mrs. Jenkins encouraged.

"Well, Mrs. Jenkins, I'm a lawyer, here on business, but I grew up the son of a poor Nebraska farmer. Studied hard and worked my way through law school."

"Did you know that Miss Windsor"—she smiled at Anika—"is a lawyer?"

Anika spoke up, "Yes, he does know that, Mrs. Jenkins. We

attended law school together."

"Really?" Amazement filled that single word. She shook her head. "Small world."

"That it is," Tucker agreed.

And feeling smaller all the time.

"So what brings you here?" Mrs. Jenkins sent a conspicuous smile in Anika's direction.

"You're correct, Mrs. Jenkins. I'm the reason Mr. Truesdale came to town. He's dragging me to court and filing an appeal against me and the women I represent." Anika's eyes dared him to deny it.

"Oh my." Mrs. Jenkins fanned her warm face. "Oh my, indeed."

The remainder of breakfast was a quiet and slightly uncomfortable meal.

An hour or so later, Anika walked toward the Stevens's place, which lay past the livery stable on the far end of town. At least she had succeeded in putting the barrier back into place between her and Tucker. *I can't afford to be his friend.*

"I thought we'd agreed upon a truce." Tucker called out from behind her.

She turned, and he lagged about twenty feet back.

"Only at the orphanage," she reminded him.

As he drew closer, her heartbeat quickened.

"So then the rest of the time I'm fair game?" His face was relaxed, his smile genuine, and her heart warmed up to him.

"Fair as any deer within the range of a hunter with a rifle."

She kept her voice modulated and her tone carefree. He needn't know the havoc he wreaked on her insides. *How can I keep myself safe from his charm? The truth—remember the truth.* She spoke her thoughts aloud: "You're here for one reason, Mr. Truesdale, and one reason only—to beat me in a court of law and to take from my clients what is rightfully theirs."

In his eyes she saw regret. "I wish it didn't have to be this way, Anika." He pronounced her name with tenderness, and the coolness of her attitude melted at the same pace as a block of ice in this Arizona heat. "I was hired to do a job."

"As was I," she reminded him. "Which makes our consorting impossible."

"Impossible, huh? Aren't you friends with other attorneys?"

"Tucker, we gave up our friendship a decade ago when we never spoke again after the suffrage rally. That last year of law school, you became an avid spokesman against suffrage, and we were at odds—you always fighting my attempts to promote women being given the ballot. No, we are not friends."

"I'm sorry. I was wrong—not about suffrage, but the way I handled the ending of our engagement."

She didn't desire this discussion. *And why is he on this road anyway?* "Are you following me? First you show up at the orphanage, then at *my* boardinghouse, and now on my way out of town."

He laughed—the warm, rich, inviting sound that was uniquely his. "No, I'm not, although circumstantial evidence would prove otherwise. I'm on my way to a barn raising."

Stopping, she shook her head. "Why?"

"I like getting involved in a community while I'm visiting. Our court date isn't for a couple of weeks, and I'm prepared, so I might as well do something useful until we go to Tucson for the big day. Don't tell me you're raising a barn today, too?" He cocked an eyebrow in that irresistible way of his.

"Yes, well, no, not exactly." She started walking again, south down Main Street past the residential section. "I promised to keep the children entertained while the men work and the women cook. How did you even know about this event?"

"Etta." He said her name as if he'd known her for years. "I was in the café yesterday, and she told me her son had recently married. Said his pa had given him some acreage to build on and invited me to the barn raising today. Promised me some good home-cooked food if I came."

"And here you are." She shook her head in disbelief.

"Yep."

They'd neared the edge of town and continued following the dusty road through the desert. A wagonload of people passed them, waving.

"How far do we have to go?" Tucker asked.

"It's a mile past the livery stable."

"I'm surprised you chose to walk in this heat."

"Me, too." *I needed to clear my head—clear you out of my thoughts, yet you're here.*

"Hard to believe it's September. Does it ever cool down?"

"This is cool—at least cooler than July and August."

"How long have you lived in Arizona Territory?" he asked after a few minutes of silence.

"Almost five years."

"And what brought you?"

"The plight of the women and children here in the West. Often they lose their husbands and fathers to Indians or in gunfights, and they have no way to survive. Many end up being forced into unsavory positions in order to put food on the table."

For the first time, Tucker caught a tiny glimpse of Anika's vision and her heart for the oppressed and exploited. No matter what her views, her heart was pure gold.

"Many of the women who filed land claims are widows who need a way to survive. Some are children who grew up in the orphanage and have nothing but the clothes on their backs. My friend India and her husband, Joshua, teach them about ranching. I've set up crews to build houses, barns, and fences."

"Sounds like you thought of everything." Suddenly, winning did not seem very important to him. "Anika, if they hadn't hired me, they'd have hired another attorney."

She sighed. "I know, but I hear you're the best."

He winked at her. "Don't believe everything you hear. Tell me about life here in the desert and the names of the different cacti."

"When I first moved here, I hated everything about Cactus

Corner except the people. I hated the long, hot summers, but then I realized the payoff was little to no snow in the winters. So for about six months a year the weather is truly wonderful. Then the rest of the time it feels like an oven, but even that is without humidity."

"Hot, but not a wet-hot?"

"Yes."

She pointed out various species of cacti and desert trees and bushes. "The tall ones with their arms reaching heavenward are saguaros. The ones that look like round mouse ears are prickly pear. And the cholla, or jumping cactus as it's better known, is the worst and most feared. If you get too close, it attaches itself and is quite difficult to dislodge.

"The trees with the green trunks are paloverde—or 'green tree' in English. Many of the names are Spanish, named by the early settlers to this area. Those bushes with the yellow blooms are greasewoods. Around June the cacti bloom, and it's truly beautiful."

He knew she saw a beauty he'd yet to find. To him it all looked brown and unbecoming, except the mountains off on the horizon. Now those were beautiful.

"We're here," she announced. Sure enough, a large crowd gathered about fifty feet from them.

His head and heart fought the ultimate fight, and while he called himself every kind of fool, he bowed from the waist and said, "Thank you, madam, for sharing the walk with me. Might I have the pleasure of accompanying you home this evening?"

Anika waged the same war within herself. He saw the struggle plastered across her face. "I don't think—"

He laid his fingers across her lips and whispered, "Shh. Don't think at all, Anika. Just say yes."

Her eyes were large, round, and filled with uncertainty. She closed them and sighed. Her breath caressed his fingertips where they still rested against her mouth. When she opened her eyes, he nearly drowned in a pool of hazel. *I'm still in love with her.* He lowered his hand, and her lips beckoned his. Moving his head toward hers, he anticipated the feel of her kiss. It had been much too long since their last one.

"I can't." She backed up a couple of steps. "Excuse me." She nearly ran toward the crowd, leaving him to recover alone.

"What am I doing?" He ran his hand through his hair, took a deep breath, and headed up the small knoll toward the crowd.

"That was quite the intimate scene a moment ago," Elaine said.

Anika's face heated up. "Did everyone notice?" She covered her hot cheeks with the palms of her hands.

"The three of us certainly did," Jody assured her.

"What's going on?" India questioned.

"I'm so confused." Anika shook her head, seating herself on a wooden bench. "The past and present are seeping together, and I no longer know if what I feel is current or just leftovers from an era long ago."

She stood with determination. "No matter, I can't give in. He is still the opposition. Let's focus on the task at hand." She smiled at her friends. "Are you three cooking or babysitting?"

Both Jody and India were cooking. Elaine followed Anika to the shade of a large paloverde. "Let's gather the children here, and we'll play games. I thought of several—Button Button, Fox and Geese, and Hunt the Thimble."

Elaine smiled. "Always favorites. I'll collect the children."

While waiting, Anika's gaze wandered to where the men worked. Tucker's long, lean form caught her attention immediately, and her heart responded with a tightening. *Why, why is this happening to me?* Try as she might to deny it, these feelings were real, persistent, and very much a part of the present.

The morning flew by in fun, games, and laughter. Several times Anika noticed Tucker watching her, and she quickly turned away. When dinnertime rolled around, the children dispersed into their parents' care. Elaine and Anika joined India and Jody on a blanket under the shade of a cottonwood near the bank of the Pantano Wash. Anika had thankfully lost track of Tucker's whereabouts and hoped not to see him again today.

But that wish wasn't to be. Joshua moved toward them, Tucker in tow. After kissing India's cheek, Joshua turned to Anika. "I met Mr. Truesdale this morning. We spent the hours discussing law versus ranching. I've yet to convince him ranching is much more satisfying than even practicing law can be. I understand he's been introduced to each of you."

The four of them nodded or answered, "Yes."

Joshua joined his wife on the blanket. "See, there is plenty of room for you. Sit there between Jody and Anika." He pointed to a wide space on the blanket.

Tucker settled next to her; his expression pleaded for forgiveness. "Do you mind? I can eat with someone else."

"You're fine." Her smile felt tight, forced.

"He did have several offers from the female persuasion," Joshua said, biting into a fried chicken leg. "Why he chose us, I'll never know." He chuckled.

That notion bothered her as much the thought of dining next to him.

"How's the judge?" Tucker asked, raising a buttermilk biscuit to his mouth.

"My father is well," Anika assured him. She hesitated to offer more information but decided every reminder of their differences was a necessary evil. "He has been largely involved in the Hull House in Chicago. Are you familiar with it?"

"Yes."

"What is the Hull House?" Elaine's lifted brows caused her forehead to wrinkle.

"It's a settlement house project founded by Jane Addams and Ellen Gates Starr," Tucker answered, taking a sip of lemonade. "Within a year of its opening, over one hundred settlement houses cropped up all across the United States." Tucker continued, "They are largely connected to the Progressive campaign, operated mostly by women, and have propelled thousands of college-educated women into careers in social work."

His astute knowledge of the subject surprised Anika, and she continued where he left off. "More importantly, in the last four years, this has given women a significant voice to be reckoned with in American politics. This is a huge stepping-stone, leading toward the ratification of enfranchising women. I believe very soon each of us will have the privilege and responsibility of voting." Anika's tone was passion-filled.

"A hard-fought battle," Elaine said.

"Yes, but we've made great strides in the last few years, thanks to men like my father who aren't afraid of women with rights." Anika couldn't help but glance at Tucker. "Did you know that last year Colorado became the first state to adopt an amendment giving women the right to vote?"

"Really? I didn't realize that," Jody said.

"We're close. I know it. We have to be." Anika laughed. "Sorry, this subject fills me with excitement."

They all laughed. Tucker smiled in her direction, but his stare was miles away. The subject switched to ranching, and nothing more was said about suffrage. Tucker finished his meal in silence, and Anika dealt with mixed emotions. It seemed she'd succeeded in distancing them, but was that what she truly wanted?

Anika rode home in the wagon with Joshua and the ladies. She didn't see Tucker again and told herself she was glad, but her gaze kept roaming over the horizon, looking for him anyway.

The next morning at Sunday service, she caught a glimpse

of Tucker at the back of the church. He disappeared, though, as soon as the last amen was said. She should be patting herself on the back for the success of her plan of avoidance, but instead she missed him.

Anika spent the following week feeling restless and downcast.

Chapter 4

Today, Tucker would face Anika for the first time in two weeks. He'd avoided her up until now, realizing that their deep-seeded beliefs didn't mix. She was still a suffragist, and he'd never agree with her on that point. How had he failed to remember? He'd promised himself there'd be no more attempted kisses. No more thinking about her—period. Yet here he was contemplating her again—probably for at least the hundredth time in the past fourteen days.

As he made his way down Main to catch the stage, the sun was just rising over the Rincon Mountains. Something about a new day usually gave a man a feeling of expectation, but today his only feeling was dread. Certain Anika would take the same coach, he anticipated an uncomfortable ride to Tucson. Four hours and twenty miles in a Concord with her could make a man forget why he was here and forget that she was the enemy.

He knew he went into this courtroom at a severe disadvantage because his mind was elsewhere. He'd mulled over every way possible they could make a life together, but there were no answers. He prayed God would change Anika's heart and she'd see the truth, but if it hadn't happened in the past ten years, chances were it wasn't going to happen now.

As he approached the stop for the stage line, he viewed Anika seated on the bench. A satchel rested next to her, and she read over some paperwork. Tucker claimed the other end of the bench and cleared his throat. "Good morning, Anika."

Glancing up, she nodded her head once. "Tucker." She returned her gaze to the paperwork in her hand.

The stage rolled to a stop in front of them. One of the lead mules pawed the ground. Both Tucker and Anika paid their fares and climbed inside. He took the seat across from her.

"Looks like we're the only two heading for Tucson this early," Tucker commented.

"Appears so." Anika kept her gaze focused out the window. "Us and a bag of mail."

The first hour of their trip was quiet, except for the creaking of the coach and the thudding of the team of mules' feet against the hard ground. The Concord provided a smoother ride than many of the older-model coaches, but there was still some jostling and jerking. Anika finally gave up trying to read, returned her stack of paper to the satchel, and rested her head against the tall, straight seat back, closing her eyes. Wordlessly, she clearly let him know she was uninterested in conversing.

Though he wished he could remain oblivious to her, his senses were keenly aware of her presence. With every breath, he drew in the rosewater scent of her. His gaze constantly returned to her face, admiring her pronounced cheekbones, the silky sheen of her hair, the curve of her brow above her closed eyes. But it was the fullness of her lips that made him remember the sweetness of touching them with his own.

Dear Lord, I love this woman. I guess I always have. Will You change her heart? Help her to see the truth. He wished for the freedom to glide the tips of his fingers across her cheek, to lightly kiss her rosy pink lips, and to wrap her in arms that longed to hold her forever. Shaking his head to dispel the feelings, he focused on the rugged terrain outside of the Concord. He, too, was beginning to appreciate the beauty God had sewn in this land—land that appeared harsh and relentless.

Upon arriving in Tucson, he was surprised by the size and sophistication of the town. He longed to ask Anika many questions but knew she'd not appreciate his inquisitiveness. Streets were lined with buildings—some made from adobe, others with clapboard siding, and even some with brick. The place wasn't nearly as rugged as he'd anticipated. He'd almost expected to see a gunfight in the middle of a street or a herd of cattle being driven to market through the center of town. It was no Chicago, but certainly more advanced than he'd imagined.

When they reached the stage stop, he climbed down first. Propriety insisted he assist Anika. He wrapped his long hands around her slender waist, lifting her to the ground. Spots of pink dotted her cheeks, and she kept her eyes averted from his gaze. His heart beat faster just being near her.

He hired a buggy to take them from the stage stop to the courthouse. Again he aided Anika and then climbed up himself. This time they were much closer in proximity than they'd been in the stage. The rear seat of the buggy allowed mere inches between them, and Anika leaned as far right as possible. The tension between them only grew, and Tucker decided he must say something, anything to break the strain.

"I'm surprised by the town's bustling activity and size. It certainly isn't the little frontier place I'd expected."

"No. Tucson hasn't been considered a frontier town for almost a decade now. During the mid- to late eighties, things began to change. She's no booming metropolis, but neither is she a hick town." Anika adjusted her coffee brown skirt, trying to keep it from encroaching onto his lap.

The buggy driver rolled to a stop at the corner of Pennington and Court, in front of the modern brick courthouse. Tucker paid the driver and followed Anika up the stairs and into the building. The sheriff's office was housed just inside.

Tucker trailed Anika down the hall to the correct door. Judge Joseph Daniel Bethune had just been appointed this year to the Supreme Court of Arizona Territory and would be presiding over their case. When they entered his courtroom, it was filled with women already seated and some standing in the back. This surprised Tucker. He'd apparently underestimated Anika. He may have been the expert on land issues, but she understood the human side of trying a case. She hoped to gain the judge's sympathy by filling his courtroom with the potential *victims*.

Anika seated herself on one side of the court, and Tucker took his place on the other. The space dividing them was a visual reminder of the chasm that lay between them and their fundamental beliefs.

Everyone in the courtroom rose when the judge entered; his black robe billowed behind him as he strolled toward the bench. Taking his seat, he banged the gavel, calling the court to order. Tucker noted the surprise in the judge's eyes when he observed his entire courtroom filled with women—all ages and sizes.

The judge explained that since Tucker filed the appeal, the court would hear his testimony first. Anika would have a chance for rebuttal when Tucker finished presenting his line of reasoning. Tucker spent the next two hours explaining why the documents filed by Miss Windsor on behalf of said women were being appealed. He supported his cause, citing facts from similar cases.

He'd done this long enough to know that when he finished stating his defense and offered his closing arguments, the judge was leaning heavily in his favor. Unless Anika presented strong support to sway the judge's opinion, Tucker was sure His Honor would rule in support of the men. Thank heaven this was a man who wasn't moved by the sight of a courtroom full of women hoping to win his sympathy.

Tucker felt good about the way the morning had gone— that is, until he glanced in Anika's direction. Their gazes met, and her hazel eyes reflected that she, too, recognized the judge's leanings. A deep sorrow settled over him as he realized the case would end this afternoon. He'd be around another few days to file paperwork, but then he'd move on to the next case, in the next town—without Anika.

"Court will recess until two o'clock this afternoon."

Upon the judge's announcement, Tucker made a beeline over to where Anika sat. Somehow he had to grab another few moments with her.

Tucker moved across the courtroom toward her, and she wanted to run out the door. Thoughts of facing his gloating only increased the desire, but instead she raised her chin and looked him straight in the eye. He'd not see her turn tail and run.

In his eyes resided sympathy, which she wanted no part of either. *I don't want your pity or your pride.* She willed her expression to remain cordial.

"I wondered if you'd join me for the noon meal?"

His request baffled her. "You want to eat together?"

He nodded.

"We're opposing counsel," she reminded him.

"Personal—not professional. A shared meal with an old friend." His lips turned up in a tiny smile, and his eyes pleaded with her to say yes. But it was the nostalgic tone in his voice that awoke a longing within her to agree and spend time with him. After all, by this time next week he'd be nothing more than a memory.

Against her own good judgment and common sense, she

nodded in concurrence. When he took her elbow and escorted her from the courtroom, she noted the shock in many of the people's eyes. They were no more surprised than she by her own foolish behavior, but knowing he'd leave soon caused her to throw caution away like a piece of rubbish.

They walked the two blocks to the café. Anika's heart pounded like a tom-tom in her chest. *What am I doing? Consorting with the enemy—that's what I'm doing.* But her heart argued she was grabbing one last memory of Tucker to file away—hopefully a sweeter memory than some previous ones they'd shared.

Tucker pulled her chair out and waited for her to settle in before seating himself. He smiled, and her stomach curled up inside of her.

"Thank you for joining me. I just wanted the chance to apologize for the many mistakes I made with you back in Chicago."

Her eyes misted up, and she lowered her gaze to her lap, swallowing hard.

"Will you forgive me, Anika?"

She returned her gaze to his and nodded, afraid to try to speak past the lump in her throat.

"Thank you." He covered her hand with his and gave a little squeeze. "Now let's share a pleasant meal so we can leave each other this time with a kinder memory."

After Tucker ordered their food, he asked her to tell him about Tucson.

Relieved, she grabbed hold of the safe topic of conversation like a drowning woman would a lifeline. "Until the Gadsden Purchase in 1853, Tucson belonged to Mexico. The Mexican people living here say they didn't cross the border; the border crossed them—which is true."

A woman delivered their pot roast to them. Anika tasted hers. "This is very good." She took another bite before resuming. "Many of the prominent people are considered Tucson's Mexican elite. For instance"—Anika cut her meat while she continued to talk—"the stage line we traveled on today is owned by Mariano Samaniego. At fifty, he is the single most powerful Mexican in Tucson. He's a college-educated man and formidable in business."

Pausing, she took another bite of her roast. Tucker appeared genuinely interested.

"This is nice." She smiled at him. "Thank you for suggesting it." She'd relaxed considerably, and getting her mind off the case was just what she needed.

She went on with more information about Tucson. "Don Mariano started with a freighting business, hauling supplies to military posts throughout Arizona, New Mexico, and Texas. Sadly, when the railroad made its debut in this area in 1881, the freighting companies could not compete. Luckily, Mariano Samaniego had diversified, also investing heavily in ranching, which boomed in the eighties."

Stopping to enjoy a few bites, Anika let her gaze roam over Tucker's face—his strong jawline, his straight nose—and it settled on his warm expression. His eyes sent secret messages that thrilled and confused her. Her imagination must be running wild, because she'd testify that his face held adoration, and that simply could not be. He'd quit adoring her the day he discovered her political stance.

She looked away, refocusing on her story. "He owns two ranches, the Canada del Oro Ranch near Oracle and the Rillito Ranch on the southern slopes of the Santa Catalina Mountains. Not only that, but he owns a saddle and harness shop, runs several stage lines, and is a politician, having served in city, county, and state government."

"Very impressive." Tucker took his last bite of potatoes.

"Tucson is filled with fascinating people, but now it's your turn to talk so I can eat. Where are you living now?"

While Anika finished her dinner, Tucker gave her an overview of his life for the past ten years. The loneliness woven into his tone and story made her sad for him. His fame and reputation had come at great cost. No real home and no one—anywhere.

Chapter 5

Lunch ended on a contemplative note for both of them. Neither said much on their walk back to the court-house. Tucker noticed that Anika refocused, probably on her upcoming presentation before the judge. By the time they reached their destination, Anika was all business.

This morning's scene repeated; the judge called the proceedings to order. "Miss Windsor, you may begin."

Anika stood. "Your Honor, may I present to you Miss Katie Wells. Katie grew up in the orphanage in Cactus Corner after her parents were killed in an Indian raid. Katie has worked for the past four years as a laundress for the hotel in order to save every penny possible to buy herself a plot of land—a dream passed down to her by her pa."

Tucker eyed the young girl who'd known much hardship in her young years. Her tattered dress and blistered hands witnessed to the truth of Anika's words. Next Anika introduced the judge to Mrs. Hector Gonzalez, a widow. She was a plump older woman with sad blue eyes.

"Judge, Mrs. Gonzales came to Arizona Territory as a mail-order bride from back east. Shortly after she arrived, her new husband took ill. He died three months ago. His kin no longer welcome her on the family homestead, so this is her chance to start again, on her own."

Anika didn't cite previous cases but presented real people and their very real needs. With each story, Tucker's heart softened a notch toward these women and their plight. Anika practiced law very differently than he did. She connected with the human side—he only presented the facts, the laws, and the statutes. His respect of her grew. She really did care about the people behind the case. He didn't actually know any of the men he represented or why they desired land.

As Anika introduced several more women, each with her own tale of woe, a glaring truth struck him: Anika Windsor filed no claim for herself or the friends he'd met, only for truly destitute people who needed a hand up.

Finally, the judge interrupted. "Miss Windsor, I have heard enough stories. Please state your case." His tone carried an edge.

"Yes, Judge. I'm sorry, sir. I only hoped to make known to the court the needs represented here today, needs which are real. Mr. Truesdale implied that I, on a whim, decided to organize a group of women in order to *steal* the land from any men who might apply. That simply is not the case."

At her words, the jagged edge of guilt cut deep into his heart. He watched her pace across the width of the courtroom as she continued reciting the facts.

"This was not some plot for women to overtake Arizona Territory, but a genuine concern by me on their behalf. I knew the Carey Land Act was expected to be signed into law sometime this year, so I informed women who would benefit from this opportunity. Women who have no husband or father to care for them, women who are poor and need a break in life, women who are entitled to the same opportunities as men."

"Women who have no husband or father to care for them." Her words replayed in Tucker's mind. Suddenly Anika's stand for suffrage became clearer to him. She fought for "the least of these," the ones Jesus spoke of in the Bible who had no one else to stand up for their rights. Maybe Anika wasn't an extremist for suffrage but a defender of social justice for those who had no one else. He'd have to ask her some pointed questions, but maybe, just maybe, their views weren't as far apart as he'd once thought.

As she summarized her closing statements, a heavy weight lifted from Tucker's heart. She'd given up a life of wealth and privilege as the judge's daughter to come west and fight for women, children—even Indians. Anika cared about the human condition. She was living out her faith. A thought flittered through his mind. *Maybe it's my heart that needs to change.* After he spoke to Anika, he'd meet with the minister. He'd hash this out until he understood her motives, her beliefs, and God's Word on the subject. He refocused on what she was saying.

"I don't believe you should punish any of these women

because they stayed informed and prepared. Ignorance of the law is no excuse. And these men simply chose to remain unaware." She nodded her head once with her final phrase.

Upon returning to her seat, she glanced in Tucker's direction. He sent her an encouraging smile. The most amazing thing was happening inside him. He honestly hoped she would win. He wanted the judge to rule in her favor, even though the loss would cost him his untarnished record. He was humbled, startled, and astonished by his own change of heart. Had to be God. Well, maybe God and love.

The judge called for a brief recess to review the facts. Anika closed her eyes and prayed. *Lord, not for my sake, but for the sake of these women, let justice reign.* In all honesty, unless God intervened, Anika knew the judge leaned in Tucker's favor. Her heart was heavy with grief. Anika kept her eyes forward, unable to glance back at the women whose futures rested in the judge's hands and unable to look at Tucker lest she see a smug expression plastered across his face. She couldn't bear that—not now.

The judge reentered, and Anika stood. As soon as he settled at the bench, his gaze rested on her, and she knew. Her heart felt as if it were bleeding into her chest, and tears formed at the back of her throat. Swallowing suddenly hurt, and her vision blurred. She blinked excessively to rid her eyes of the excess moisture.

"Miss Windsor, though you brought up some valid points, I must rule in favor of Mr. Truesdale and the men he represents."

She heard a unified gasp behind her. Closing her eyelids for the briefest of seconds, she reined her features and emotions in. She could not let them, or Tucker, see her devastation.

The judge continued, "You chose to only inform women about the land act; therefore, it is my belief the men were not provided equal consideration under the law. As a representative of justice and the court, I contend you had a responsibility to all, not just the ones you deemed worthy. I order that all land claims must be refiled in a more equitable manner for all involved."

Anika nodded her head, acknowledging the judge's decision. She planted a stoic expression across her features, but inside her heart cried out at the injustice.

"You and Mr. Truesdale may take turns filing the claims until the thirty parcels are gone, and you may claim the first one."

How kind of you, Judge.

"I trust you and he can work together in an equitable manner for all concerned?"

No! she wanted to scream, but instead she replied in a calm, steady voice, "Of course, Your Honor. We are both professionals."

"I'm pleased to hear that, Miss Windsor. I'll expect all land claims refiled in a timely manner." He banged his gavel once. "Court adjourned."

Anika ignored Tucker and tried to console the discouraged women surrounding her. A glance in his direction did reveal a quiet, contemplative man, not someone celebrating another victory under his belt.

"Please give me a few days to figure this out," Anika pleaded. "I know you all have so many questions and concerns, but I need time to find the answers."

She shook a few hands, hugged a few teary-eyed women, and then made her way out of the courtroom. *Lord, please show me the best answer for these women. Please help me find the best solution.*

Chapter 6

Tucker followed Anika from the courthouse and into the bright rays of sunshine, which seemed mocking. How could he tell her how sorry he was that he won? She'd surely not believe him. He ached for her and the loss all those women now faced. How could he tell her how wrong he'd been about so many things, but especially about her? How could he make this right? As a lawyer, he knew talk was cheap; he'd have to show her.

That's what he'd do. He'd show her—show her he loved her and help her find a solution to all of this. Anika hired a buggy, and Tucker decided to grant her some alone time to think. Knowing he'd be the last person she'd wish to have seated next to her, he stuck his hands in his pockets and strode toward the stage stop. Unfortunately, they'd have to ride the same coach back to Cactus Corner, unless he waited until tomorrow. He wasn't willing to do that. Hopefully, on the buggy ride, she could compose herself and face the ride home with him.

Anika was seated in the Concord when he arrived at the stop. He paid his fare and climbed aboard. Besides freight, they were again the only two heading southeast to Cactus Corner.

"Hello again," he greeted as he settled onto the bench seat across from her.

"Hello." Her tone dripped with frost.

He plunged ahead. "You presented your case well."

The frost in her voice was nothing compared to the coldness of her stare. "Don't patronize me, Mr. Truesdale."

"I assure you, I'm not. I don't offer praise lightly, nor do I speak it to merely flatter. I believe you should have won."

"Then why did you oppose me?" He spotted a glimmer of belief in her eyes.

He spoke with frankness. "I was hired to do a job, and I did it to the best of my ability."

"Is that all the law is to you—a mere job?"

The truth apparently astounded her, and he knew he'd offended her sensibilities. Anika held a deep love and respect for this land and the laws that governed it. She always had.

"How can you fight for causes you don't believe in and for people who shouldn't win?" The frost had been replaced with fire—fire and accusation.

"When they hired me, it appeared that some—pardon my misguided observation—suffrage-driven women wanted to dominate the land in this area. I had no idea that you were the brains behind the movement, nor did I know or understand the motive."

"And now?" She raised a brow in challenge.

He sighed. "Now I wish the women you represent had won."

"Why?" she demanded.

He smiled. She wasn't going to let him out of this conversation without extracting a pound of flesh. "Because I glimpsed your heart and understand why you stood in the gap for them." He paused and glanced out the window at the passing scene. He desired to word his next question very carefully—not as a challenge, but as an interest. "Was it because of your father that you became involved in suffrage?"

This time it was her turn to smile. "No, it was because of me that my father became involved." He noted the faraway look in her eyes. "Even as a very little girl, I wanted to help people, make things better for them. Have you heard of the *Chicago Legal News*?"

"Of course. What lawyer worth his salt hasn't?"

"My father subscribed from the onset, so when I learned to read, I'd read his copy. This of course pleased my father. He thought it was rather adorable. I actually became interested in what Myra Bradwell had to say, especially on her support of many reforms but particularly on women's suffrage. And she always had the blessing and support of her husband."

Anika tilted her head to the side. "I've never been radical like some of the leaders of the movement, but I do see the need." She smoothed the cotton of her skirt. "Did you know that twenty-five years ago, Mrs. Bradwell passed the bar with honors yet wasn't allowed admission into the Illinois bar until 1890, simply because she was a woman? She fought their refusal all the way to the Supreme Court but was told, 'Man is or should be a woman's protector and defender.' But I ask again, what about all the women who have no man to protect or defend them?"

Frustration changed the tone of her voice. "I do believe man as protector and defender to be the way God designed marriage to work, but not all women are married. Don't they deserve some say over who represents them in government? Whose rules and laws they must live under?"

Tucker had no opportunity to respond, except to nod his head in approval.

"Since my mother died when I was only a toddler, Myra Bradwell became the woman I admired most. She was a legal reformer who poured her life into this country. When one door closed, she just went on through another one. Do you realize the Chicago Legal News is the most circulated legal newspaper in the nation?"

Tucker laughed. "As a matter of fact, I do. I'm a lawyer, remember? Didn't Mrs. Bradwell die earlier this year?"

"Yes, sadly, in February. Her daughter has taken up where her mother left off. Do you know her most famous words?"

"No."

" 'It is not a crime to be born a woman.' "

"Just because people don't support suffrage doesn't mean they consider being a woman a crime." Tucker couldn't help but defend his position. "I hold my own dear mother in high esteem, I assure you."

"Why are you so opposed to suffrage?"

Tucker thought for a moment before answering. "I've always believed man was designed by God to be the head of the household. In the New Testament, God places man over his wife as He placed Christ over the church."

Anika nodded her agreement. "Why would the enfranchisement of women change that fact?"

"Maybe it wouldn't, but history shows it very well could."

"So you would deny progress because of what may or may not happen?" She sat up straighter and was clearly incensed by his answer. "That is truly ridiculous. If a woman goes against her husband and God's Word, that is between her and God. But it shouldn't be controlled by government!" She pointed her finger at him. "What about the growing number of women who have no husbands or fathers? Should their rights be denied only because their married counterparts might be less submissive?"

Anika didn't give him a chance to answer. "That is as absurd as believing our ancestors should have stayed in England because life here may have been worse, not better. Living is a risk, and most everything has both a negative and a positive side. Does that mean we should keep everything the same and never change?"

She was still passionate; that was for certain. Tucker saw a different point of view than he ever had before, but he still wasn't entirely convinced the movement as a whole was good or right. He was seeing suffrage in a more positive light, but he still wanted a minister to explain the biblical stance on the subject.

"Well?" she asked after a few moments.

"The jury is still out, but I am weighing your words. I want to ponder them in light of God's Word and in prayer."

She smiled, and delight trickled through him all the way to his toes. She leaned her head to the left ever so slightly. "Are you admitting, Mr. Truesdale, that I might be right and not a horrible, godless person for being a suffragist?"

"I am only admitting, Miss Windsor, that I will consider your theories."

"Well, that is certainly a better response than I received ten years ago."

"It is. And for that I am most sorry."

Anika rolled over for what she felt certain was at least the twentieth time. Sitting up, she straightened her covers and lay back down, staring at the ceiling. She had no idea how to handle this setback. *How do I decide who gets land and who doesn't?* She pictured each face and heard the hopes and dreams they'd shared echoing through her mind. *Lord, how can I ever figure this out? Give me Your wisdom.*

She rose and paced the length of her bed. The room was small and dark. She pushed aside the burlap covering the window and looked out at the night sky. The street was empty, and the moon illuminated the buildings.

Finally, the nights were cooling off some, and her room

wasn't as stifling as it had been the prior few months. Autumn in the desert was not even close to the season back home. How she missed the red and gold leaves falling to the ground in a mass of color. Here in Arizona, there were no distinct seasons, and though she'd grown to love the place and its people, she missed home every fall. She let the burlap drop back over the window and sighed.

She longed for sleep—a few hours' reprieve from the daunting task before her. And then there was Tucker weighing on her mind, as well—so charming and appealing yet so completely wrong. Wrong in the way he practiced law, wrong in his rigid religious beliefs, and wrong in the way he'd failed her at the first sign of trouble.

She pulled her cloak from the wardrobe, slipped it over her nightclothes, and buttoned it all the way to her chin. As quietly as possible, she opened her door and slipped from her room. Tiptoeing toward the kitchen, she thought she'd heat a cup of milk. That was her father's remedy for sleepless nights when she'd been a child.

Inching her way in the darkness, she kept her right hand on the wall. Choosing not to use the electric lights, lest she wake another boarder, Anika rounded the corner into the large kitchen. At the stove stood Tucker, his hair rumpled and his clothing wrinkled from the stage ride home.

She paused, debating whether to steal away sight unseen, but in her indecision, he must have sensed her presence. He turned, and the candle on the pie hutch outlined his face.

"Couldn't sleep either?" he asked in a low voice, almost a whisper.

She shook her head.

"I'm having a cup of warm milk. Would you like one?"

This time she nodded, and Tucker added to the pan more fresh milk from the pitcher next to the stove. He stirred the liquid, and Anika settled at a small worktable, perching atop a stool. Tucker's back was to her, and she contemplated the scene before her. This is how being married to him might have been—sharing a quiet kitchen in the middle of the night.

A wall of anger rose up inside her—anger at what they'd missed because of his inability to even discuss their differences and anger at the injustice that took place in the courtroom today.

Tucker placed a cup in front of Anika and one across from her. He pulled another stool up and joined her. She fought an urge to turn her back on him the way he had on her all those years ago.

"Is the case weighing on your mind?" Tucker asked.

Again she only gave him an acknowledging bob of her head and wrapped her hands around the warm cup. Something about warmth always exuded feelings of comfort, calmness, and peace.

"When would you want to start filing the claims?" Tucker broke the few moments of silence.

He didn't understand. She didn't want to talk to him about the case. "I will need a few days." Her tone rang with agitation.

"I'd like to have everything filed by the end of next week."

So you can move on and leave us here to live with the havoc you've caused? "Of course you would." The words were curt. "Your job is done, and all twelve of your clients win." Anika pushed her half-empty cup aside. "But I have to decide which dozen ladies now have to lose." She slid off her stool and reached for her mug, planning to finish her milk in the sanctity of her room at the opposite end of the boardinghouse from where the men lodged.

Tucker grabbed her arm. "Wait, Anika. Why are you so angry?"

She yanked free from his grip. "I'm angry because you come into people's lives, you turn them upside down, and then you leave. But after you're gone, those women have to live with the consequences." *And I have to spend years trying to forget you all over again.*

"How can I help?"

This was her chance to use her bargaining power. She spoke the thoughts that had plagued her all night. "Let my clients have all the parcels closest to the populated areas in the county."

Tucker pictured the map and knew Anika was asking him to file his claim for the least desirable pieces of property, leaving the prime real estate for her clients.

"You know I can't do that." He spoke softly, regretfully. "What you ask isn't in the best interest of my clients. I have to do right by them, Anika."

Her jaw tightened. "You've already admitted their winning the case was an injustice."

"They hired me to represent them to the best of my ability. I can't deny them that right. How can you even ask?'

"Two wrongs don't make a right. They don't deserve the best land." She placed her hands on her hips. "They don't deserve any of it and should be grateful for whatever they receive."

Tucker knew Anika was tired and overwrought, so he'd not take her request as unethical. He'd file it under the category of a desperate woman trying to claw her way out of a tough situation. "Anika, if I could, I'd give you the thirty parcels and forget this ever happened, but you know that's not possible. The judge made a ruling, and we must abide by it."

She hung her head just as a lone tear rolled down her cheek. Tucker groaned and pulled her into his arms. She didn't pull away, nor did she respond to him, but remained stiff in his hold. He lowered his head and kissed the tear off her check. Then he whispered near her ear. "I'm so sorry. I truly am."

She pulled back and searched his face with intense eyes.

His gaze fell on her lips. They were slightly parted and beckoned him. In her eyes resided confusion, fear, uncertainty, and yearning. The yearning reflected his own, and he lowered his head, his lips finding hers. The years disappeared, and every ounce of emotion he'd ever felt for her hit him with the force of a gunshot.

Chapter 7

This is where Anika belonged—in his arms. When their lips met, she relaxed in his embrace, and he savored the feel of his arms around her. Oh, how he'd missed holding her, loving her. And he did love her with his whole heart.

When his lips separated from hers, he longed for more of the sweetness they offered. The expression on her face was charming and slightly dazed, as if she, too, just discovered what had been missing from her life all these years.

If only we can reconcile our differences. As they gazed into each other's eyes, he felt hopeful. He'd meet with the minister tomorrow morning.

He watched the anger return to Anika, her face growing cold and her eyes hard. "How dare you?"

He dropped his arms from her waist and took a step backward, wondering where the tenderness had gone. He caught a glimpse of something out of the corner of his right eye, and her palm connected with his check. She appeared as startled as he, and he rubbed his face where the imprint of her hand left a sharp sting.

"Guess I should have stepped back a bit further." He continued rubbing his face. *So much for resolution.*

"You had no right to do that," Anika snapped. "No right whatsoever!" Fire burned from her eyes.

"I'm sorry. I thought—"

"No, Tucker. That's your problem. You don't think. You don't think about the cases you take or how they might affect people's lives. You don't think about breaking a girl's heart just because her views aren't identical to yours. And you certainly don't think about why kissing me is a bad idea, a very bad idea."

"Anika—"

"No!" She shook her head—the movement causing her hair to fly about. "Don't try to argue your way out of this. And don't ever try to kiss me again!" She spun around, leaving a stunned Tucker in her wake.

What in the world just happened? One moment she was soft and pliable in his arms, and the next she was "madder than an old wet hen," as his midwestern grandmother used to say.

Tucker cleaned up their mess and headed back to his rented room.

After an almost sleepless night, he decided to talk to the minister, even though no hope of he and Anika repairing their broken engagement remained. He still needed to understand the whole issue.

He slipped from the boardinghouse shortly after dawn, opting to eat at Etta's rather than chance another encounter with Anika. During breakfast, he wrote out the questions he had about how the Bible relates to suffrage. When he was done, he moseyed over to the church, hoping not to arrive too early. He found Gavin McCurdy sweeping the vestibule.

"Good morning." Tucker shook the reverend's hand. "Would you have a few moments to solve a mystery for me?"

"Certainly. Come have a seat. What's on your mind, lad?" the minister asked.

They stepped outside and sat on the steps leading up to the door of the church. "I need to know how God's Word speaks to the suffrage movement."

"Suffrage?" The reverend stared off into the distance. "Some woman giving you trouble?"

Tucker nodded. "I suppose you could say that."

"You got yourself a feisty one, do you?"

He didn't have himself anything, and that truth brought with it an ache to his heart. "Not exactly. We parted ways over this very subject, but I may have been too harsh, so I want to understand the Bible's stance. I've searched but found nothing that speaks directly to suffrage."

"Well, it's not addressed straight on. You have to dig deeper to find the answers."

"So what are they? Is God for or against suffrage?"

"Let's look for ourselves." The minister rose. "I'll get my Bible, and we'll search it together."

Tucker followed him through the foyer and into a small office. Gavin picked up his worn Bible. The pages were dog-eared and well read. "Let's look at Genesis chapter 2, verse 18." His pages crackled as he found the spot he wanted. "It says it wasn't good for man to be alone, so the Lord made a 'help meet for him.' The original language doesn't translate well into English."

Reverend McCurdy held up both his hands. "A helpmeet is someone who fits you like your right hand fits into your left." He joined his hands together, lacing his fingers between each other. Raising the joined hands, he said, "Before the fall, God designed the perfect partnership between a man and a woman. Now let's look at what happened after the fall."

He turned the page of his Bible. "Genesis 3:16 is the consequence of the sin in the garden or the result of the fall." He cleared his throat and read, " 'And thy desire shall be to thy husband, and he shall rule over thee.' " He looked at Tucker and shook his head. "Sad, isn't it? Sin took us from the perfect partnership to man ruling over woman. Is that how God intends it to stay?" He shook his head. "I think not."

He began turning the pages of his Bible again. "Let's look to Paul and the New Testament and see what he has to say on the subject. In Romans 16, Paul shares his appreciation of the women in the church, the work they do, and the leadership they provide. Many of the names listed in Romans 16, verse 9 to be exact, are women, and he's giving them commendations. So Paul understood the value of a woman and her abilities, gifts, and talents to be used for the kingdom."

As Tucker listened, he still wasn't clear on the real issue. "Reverend, I appreciate what you're saying, but what does this have to do with suffrage?"

Reverend McCurdy smiled. "Patience, patience." Once again he flipped the pages of his Bible. "This last passage should clear it up. I'm going to read from Galatians chapter 3, verse 28."

Tucker noted that whenever the reverend quoted the holy scriptures, his tone took on authority and his voice grew stronger and surer. " 'There is neither Jew nor Greek, there is neither bond nor free, there is neither male nor female: for ye are all one in Christ Jesus.' " He closed his Bible and looked directly into Tucker's eyes.

"All the same in Christ Jesus." He nodded his head as if satisfied. "For some answers, we must take the whole counsel of God's Word. I believe, in Christ, God's plan is for us to be restored to his original intention." He joined his hands together again. "Neither male nor female, and as Ephesians 5:21 says, 'Submitting yourselves one to another in the fear of God.' "

Tucker nodded and scratched his head. "So what you are saying is that in God's eyes we are all equal and should treat each other as such?"

"Yes. You're getting it now."

Tucker tried to bring together this new way of thinking. "But what about women submitting to their husbands?" He rubbed the side of his head, trying to make all the pieces of this puzzle fit together in uniformity.

"That is a whole new topic. You asked how I reconcile suffrage with the Bible. I believe women should be given the same rights as men within society. I believe that is what God intended all along, but yes, a wife is still called to submit to her husband."

Tucker finally understood. Suffrage and marriage were two different issues. Most people, as he had, tried to tie them together. He felt as though a bright light had been turned on, and for the first time, he could see—and see clearly. "You believe if Christ were still a man walking here on earth, He'd give women the vote?"

"I do. And if that creates problems within some marriages, that is for a husband and his wife to work out."

Tucker nodded. He and Anika had done a poor job of working out their differences. Perhaps it was best they'd never married.

"As for marriage, Tucker, the verse on a wife submitting follows directly after the verse that tells us to submit to one another. What I believe Paul meant is that we are called to mutual submission, but if an agreement cannot be reached, then God has put the ultimate responsibility on the husband."

"No lording over her, but treating her as an equal?" The pieces fit now for Tucker.

"Precisely."

Tucker rose and shook Reverend McCurdy's hand. "Thank you so much. It all finally makes sense."

The information might not lead him back to Anika, but he

was at last free to understand her point of view. And hopefully someday he'd be a better husband to someone. The thing was, there was only one someone for him.

The door squeaked, alerting Anika that someone had entered her office. She ran her hand over her hair and rose from her desk, blowing out a loud puff of air as she walked to the front counter.

India wore a wide smile. "Hello, friend. I came to remind you that we're going to Tucson this weekend to visit Carrillo Gardens." A frown creased the spot above her nose. "Are you well?"

Anika sighed, knowing the dark circles under her eyes told their own tale. "I didn't sleep well last night."

"The case?"

Anika bobbed her head in acknowledgment. "And Tucker."

India raised her brows. "Tucker?"

"He kissed me." Anika blurted out what was uppermost on her mind, knowing she needed a listening ear.

"Is he hoping to resume where you two left off ten years ago?"

Anika nodded. "But how can we? He'll be leaving town in a week."

"But you wish he wasn't?"

"No," Anika answered quickly and emphatically.

India made no comment but studied Anika with those intense eyes of hers.

"Oh, I don't know." Anika lowered her head. "Why do I keep reliving the kiss? I've thought of nothing else since it occurred approximately fourteen hours ago."

India grew serious. "Oh, but I think you do know why, Anika. You are still in love with Tucker."

"What is wrong with me? How can I be? Did I not learn a thing from the past? From our past together?" Anika paced to the window and back to the counter. "I'm so disappointed in myself. Not only did I allow him to kiss me, but I nearly swooned in his arms." Anika threw her hands up, feeling helpless.

India giggled. "Then you enjoyed the kiss?"

Anika leaned toward her. "Why would a woman enjoy kissing a man who broke her heart?" She shook her head. The mystery of it astounded her.

"Why, indeed?" India cocked her head to the right. "Unless of course she still cared deeply for him."

"The story only gets better," Anika assured India. "Reality squeezed through my momentary lapse of judgment, and anger hit me with the force of a dust devil. Without thinking but riding the high tide of my emotions, I slapped him."

India gasped. "You didn't?" Her eyes had grown wide as saucers.

"Oh, but I did." Anika rubbed her forehead.

"What did poor Tucker do?"

Anika laughed and shook her head. "His expression went from contentment to surprise to shock."

"Poor man."

"Poor man! What about me? How dare he think he can kiss me just because he once had that right."

"Maybe you should approach him and ask his intentions."

She'd not lower herself to approaching a man to inquire about his intentions. If Tucker had intentions, which he clearly didn't, he'd have to speak them without her probing. Anika decided there had been enough Tucker talk, so she introduced another topic. "I forgot about the trip to Tucson this weekend. I really don't have time—"

"You cannot change your mind at this juncture. Besides, you've been working much too hard. This break will do you good. Joshua thinks you, Jody, and Elaine should all stay at the ranch on Friday so we can leave at daybreak on Saturday. We'll spend the day and evening at Carrillo Gardens, then stay at the hotel, attend worship in Tucson, and return Sunday by suppertime."

Anika didn't wish to go, but she'd agreed earlier, back when her life was simpler. Besides, this would allow her to avoid Tucker and any accidental encounters they might stumble into at the boardinghouse.

"I'll make arrangements with Jody and Elaine to get out to the ranch tomorrow evening."

"No need. Joshua is sending a buggy for you. He'll have you picked up at six sharp in front of the boardinghouse."

Just as India left, several of the women began arriving for the afternoon meeting. Most of the thirty managed to be in attendance. Together they would find a way to divide the remaining claims among them. Anika wished this had turned out differently, but one must learn to adapt to the bumps in the road. Somehow they'd band together and solve this problem.

Chapter 8

Sure enough, early Saturday morning, Anika, Elaine, Jody, and India headed out the kitchen door at the ranch. Joshua had parked the carriage in front of the house, and sitting next to him on the bench was Tucker. Anika's steps faltered, and her heart fell at the sight of him. Her eyes darted to India, who shrugged and mouthed, *I'm sorry.*

"You're sorry? Why didn't you tell me?" Anika whispered through gritted teeth for only India's ears.

"I just found out myself, only ten minutes or so ago. Joshua invited him." India waved and smiled up at the two men who were talking to each other and oblivious to Anika's extreme discomfort.

She wished she'd followed her heart and stayed home. Now it would be a miserable time.

Upon spotting her, Tucker appeared as uncomfortable as she was. He apparently had no idea she'd be there either. His surprised expression spoke for itself, and then resignation

157

settled onto his face.

The girls chatted most of the way, but Anika found it difficult to concentrate on anything other than the man next to Joshua—the man with the broad shoulders who'd already broken her heart once and had a likely chance of doing it again. Anika finally focused on Joshua and Tucker's conversation, tuning out the discussion on the orphanage.

"No other businessman, Mexican or Anglo, has done as much for Tucson as Leopoldo Carrillo did in the seventies and eighties," Joshua informed Tucker. "He died near the end of 1890, but a few years before that, he took his love of gardening and his love to make a profit and opened a resort for the people of Tucson. It's quite a place and has been called Tucson's crowning glory."

When they finally arrived at the gardens, it was about ten in the morning. Joshua continued his narrative as they parked the buggy. Now everyone listened intently. "It's an oasis of natural beauty in the desert; it contains rose gardens, fruit trees, and man-made lakes. Not only does it have all of that, but it also has a luxurious saloon, private rooms, hot baths, and a dance pavilion."

Everyone climbed down from the buggy, and they walked toward the entrance together.

"Sounds pretty fancy for the desert," Tucker said.

"That it is," India agreed. "Tucson's most prominent citizens hold their formal parties here. And tonight, my husband and I will be dancing under the stars to Carrillo's orchestra."

India and Joshua shared a private look, and Anika suddenly longed to share personal moments with someone special.

"There is also picnicking and boating," Elaine said.

"And music on Saturday nights and Sunday afternoons." Jody finished the repertoire.

After paying and entering through the gate, the six of them found a grassy spot. Jody and Elaine spread the blankets, declaring this the perfect picnic place.

Anika glanced in Tucker's direction, and he, too, seemed to doubt that proclamation. She wondered if he remembered their picnic on Lake Michigan. Now that had been perfect. Maybe she could have one more perfect day with Tucker before he left for good. A longing settled deep inside for that one more day with the man she'd love forever.

India began unpacking the picnic basket, and Anika helped. Before long they were enjoying fried chicken and all the fixings. Everyone chatted, except Anika and Tucker—they both ate in silence. She wondered what he was thinking. Was he reminiscing, too?

As soon as the food was cleared away, Tucker rose. "Anika, would you take a walk with me in the rose garden?"

Her heart sped up at the thought of being so near him. All eyes were on her, and everyone waited for her answer. One more day. One more chance. His eyes were soft, inviting, and his expression hopeful. She nodded, all the while declaring herself crazy.

He reached out his hand to assist her up from the blanket.

As always when they touched, currents surged through her and her heart pounded with the same intensity as horse hooves racing across the desert floor.

Tucker looped her arm through his and steered her in the direction of the roses. "My mother grows roses," he informed her. "The scent always makes me homesick for my family and Nebraska."

"I understand. Picnics make me homesick for Chicago."

"And Lake Michigan," they said in unison.

Anika smiled up at him. The memories of her and Tucker before their fallout were tender. Somehow she'd shoved them all away and only remembered the pain of their last day together. Maybe one day she'd bring them out, dust off the cobwebs, and ponder the fine times they had shared, but for now, she couldn't bring herself to do that. It would need to be a time when she was alone and free to cry.

She finally asked, "How is your family? I always envied you having all those brothers and sisters."

"And I envied your status as an only child. You had your father's undivided attention."

They passed by some lavender roses. Anika stopped and ran her fingers across the velvet-soft petals. "Yes, but being an only child was often lonely. You, on the other hand, had nine playmates around at all times."

Tucker chuckled. "Perhaps that was the problem. They were around at all times." He grew serious. "No, I am grateful for my family. They are all I have that truly matters in this world."

Her heart felt heavy for him, maybe because her lot in life wasn't that different, but at least she had the children at the orphanage and some dear friends. "Did Katherine marry Ethan?" Anika plucked a petal and rubbed it under her nose. "He was trying to win her heart when we parted ways." They had begun a slow saunter through the variety of rosebushes.

"Married with five children, all boys—rough, rowdy boys."

"Poor Katherine." She laughed. "And your parents? How are they?"

"Growing older and more in love with each other every day."

Anika was feeling extra emotional today, and his words caused her eyes to tear up. That was the saddest part of her life—she had no one to grow old with.

He stopped, turning to face her. "Anika, there are so many things I want to say, but most of them are too late. But the one thing I will say is I'm very sorry—for many things, starting years ago. I'm sorry I kissed you yesterday, and I'm sorry I spoiled today for you by being here." His expression was pensive. "Joshua twisted my arm into coming, and it never occurred to me you'd be here, as well. Had I known, I would have declined immediately, no matter how much arm-twisting Joshua did."

Sincerity and humility filled his eyes and voice, and her heart was moved, but with Tucker, her heart was easily moved. "I, too, am so sorry. There is just so much emotion between us. I overreacted and I apologize. Let's have a nice day today and we'll part as friends." She grabbed his hand and led him on down the path to finish the rose garden tour.

Part as friends? He kept hoping they'd somehow not part at all, but she continued to give him the clear message that she was done and they were over long ago.

"A pleasant day together, before we part, sounds nice," he said, echoing her phrase. They stopped to inhale the fragrance of a red rosebush. "I didn't know roses would grow here in the desert."

"I think they take a lot of extra effort, but with patience and love, they do quite well, as you can see."

"Patience, love, and probably a lot of extra water," Tucker joked.

After they'd seen all the roses, they toured the fruit trees, took a boat ride on the man-made lake, and then rested in the afternoon shade of a heritage oak. He studied her while her eyes were closed. He'd forgotten how beautiful she was and had no idea how he'd leave her behind and go on with his life. But he must. And how he dreaded it.

Finally, the sun set and the orchestra began to play. Joshua and Tucker were kept busy between the four women. The group had a good time, and Tucker cherished the moments Anika was in his arms. He'd forgotten how much fun he and Anika always had when they were together.

By the end of the evening, Tucker decided he needed to leave town as soon as possible. Why torture himself with Anika's presence longer than necessary?

He spent all day Monday preparing the paperwork for the land claims and then purchased his train ticket to Nebraska. He telegraphed the judge and heard back from him. That night he tossed and turned but didn't dare go after warm milk for fear of running into Anika. The temptation to pull her into his arms would be too great. He'd go to her office in the morning and turn over the paperwork to her. Then he'd bid her a casual adieu, even though his heart would be breaking inside his chest. A fact she would never know.

Chapter 9

Anika had just arrived at her office and was removing her cloak when Tucker entered. She smiled at him. They'd had such a wonderful time the other night, and her heart danced at the sight of him. She moved toward the counter. "Hi, Tucker."

"Hello, Anika." His eyes were warm and inviting. He laid a stack of paperwork on the counter.

"You're here on business, I see." She'd hoped otherwise.

"Yes, business and good-bye."

That one word stole her breath, but she maintained her poise outwardly. On the inside, however, was a different story.

"When are you leaving?" She tried to sound casual but wasn't sure she'd managed.

"This afternoon."

She nodded and swallowed, finding the simple function difficult. "Where to now?" The cheeriness in her voice sounded false even to her ears.

"Home." He paused. "For the first time in six years, I don't have a 'next' case." His gaze never left her face. "It's time to re-build relationships with the people I love and figure out what to do with the rest of my life."

"Does that mean you're thinking about settling down?"

"Yes, I think it's time. Traveling has grown tiresome."

Stay here. Settle down with me. But suffrage still sat lodged between them like a giant chasm, making reaching out to each other impossible. The lump tightened in her throat, and she shifted her gaze to the pile of paperwork, lest he catch sight of the tumultuous feelings brewing within her.

"I wish you the best." She pointed to the pile. "What do you have here?"

"All my claims are ready to be recorded. The men filed for the outlying land, just as you requested."

She felt heat rising up her neck and flushing her face. "Tucker, I'm so sorry. I was feeling desperate that night, and when a person is unable to sleep, she might say most anything. I would never want you to do something unethical or compromise your integrity—"

"Shh." He placed his index finger against her lips. "It's truly all right. I showed them the county map and gave a list of pros and cons for each parcel. They made the final decision." He pulled the map off the top of his pile that showed where he had marked the twelve parcels that he'd filed claims on.

"Thank you, Tucker." She didn't even try to hide the emotion in her voice or the tears pooling in her eyes.

He reached across the counter and squeezed her hand. "It's the very least I could do." Clearing his throat, he said, "I also telegraphed the judge"—he pulled another piece of paper from his pile and laid it in front of her—"and he's granting permission for two women to co-own one piece of property. Should either someday marry, subdividing would be permitted. This way no one loses out—at least not completely."

Now a few of the tears that had been pooling spilled over, running freely down her cheeks. "You did this for me?"

He nodded. The expression on his face was so tender, Anika had to look away. It left her feeling too vulnerable. "I didn't just want to be part of your problem. I needed to help you find a solution. Granted, it's not perfect—"

"It is. It's great." She swiped at the tears. "Thank you." He'd provided the answer she couldn't figure out on her own.

"I could postpone my trip if you'd like me to stay another couple of days to help get your paperwork ready, as well." He sounded hopeful.

She shook her head, knowing another couple of days with him and she'd no longer care if women ever got the vote. She'd be willing to move to Nebraska and live on a farm if that was what he wanted. As painful as saying good-bye would be, delaying the inevitable would only increase the difficulty. "Though I deeply appreciate your offer, now that you've given me a plan, I'll be fine."

Disappointment settled over his features. He held out his hand. "Well, good-bye, then."

Instead of taking it, she walked around to his side of the counter. Maybe she'd fought long enough for other women. Maybe this time she needed to fight for herself, her future, her happiness. She took his hand in hers, stood on tiptoe, and kissed his cheek.

"I'll miss you." She forced the words past the lump in her throat, making them sound croaky.

He laid his hand on her cheek, and his eyes glistened brightly. "I love you, Anika."

Did she hear correctly? She searched his face, and his love was there in plain sight for all to see. "Did you say that you love me?"

A grin split his face. "I did."

She placed her hands on each side of his face and pulled his head toward her. Their lips met in a passionate explosion.

When they parted, she adopted a playful attitude, moving a couple of steps backward and then placing her hands on her hips. "The funny thing is, Counselor, I'm in love with you, too. So what do you *propose* we do about it?"

He pulled her back into his arms. His face had relaxed, and he looked at peace. "I propose that we get married and procreate little lawyers for the future generation."

"You do, do you?" She grew serious. "I do want to marry you, Tucker. And I do want to have children with you, but—"

Again he covered her lips with his index finger. "But you're concerned about suffrage—our original problem." He stole a quick kiss. "I resolved that issue a couple of days ago with

Reverend McCurdy." He briefly conveyed the gist of their conversation and the conclusions he'd drawn.

As he explained, her heart grew lighter and lighter. "Why didn't you tell me?"

"I was under the impression it wouldn't matter to you one way or the other."

She felt amazed. "Wouldn't matter! How could you think that?"

"Your reaction to my kiss, for one thing."

She smiled and shook her head. "I couldn't risk the damage your kisses might do to my heart. I already hurt so much at the prospect of your leaving." She grinned and cocked her head to one side. "But now you may kiss me as often as you like."

He accepted her invitation and gave her a quick peck on the lips.

"But my 'but' a few moments ago wasn't about suffrage." She backed out of his arms. "I do want to be your wife, more than anything—as you must realize since I declared my love before I knew anything about your views on suffrage changing."

He nodded and grinned. "I never thought you'd love me enough to walk away from your views, and now you don't have to." His look told her it meant everything to him that she'd put their love first. "What is your concern?"

"I don't care where we live, though I'd love to stay here, but I want to spend the rest of our lives together. Not me waiting at home for you to return from winning another case somewhere far away."

He grabbed her hand and pulled her back into his arms. "I've waited a long time for you, and I'm ready to plant some roots. I never want to be away from you again," he assured her. "Not ever. And I think living here is a really good idea."

"So what you're saying is this spinster"—she pointed to herself—"and this lawyer"—she pointed at him—"have resolved not only their legal issues but all their personal ones, as well?"

He raised his brow. "Except one. How soon can we make this official?"

She laughed. "Is this weekend soon enough?"

"No, but for you, Anika Windsor, I'll wait."

They sealed their future with a kiss.

JERI ODELL

For Jeri Odell, writing is a privilege and a passion. She loves sharing God and His truths through both the written and spoken word and is humbled and honored that He has allowed her childhood dreams to come to fruition. Her heart for every woman is spiritual growth and an intimate, vibrant relationship with Jesus Christ. Her goal and her constant prayer are that her words will bring God glory, challenge women to walk more closely with Him, and point the lost to the Savior. "I have nothing to offer anyone—in and of myself—but He offers more than we can imagine," Jeri says.

Her greatest pleasure, second only to God, is being a wife and mom. She and Dean have been married almost thirty-four years and have three adult children, two of whom are married. Family has filled their lives beyond measure.

She has also written four novels for Heartsong Presents and a nonfiction book titled *Spiritually Single*. She is the recipient of the Romance Writers of America's 2002 Faith, Hope & Love Inspirational Reader's Choice Award for the Short Historical category. Along with writing, Jeri has spoken at women's events and retreats. You may visit her Web site at www.jeriodell.com.

The Spinster and the Doctor

by Frances Devine

Dedication

For Mom—I wish you were here.
Special thanks to my friends:
Carol, Patty, Della, Evelyn, and Doris.
Your prayers help make this possible.

Marion and Megan,
I couldn't finish anything without your help.
Thanks to Vickie, Jeri, and Lena
for letting me be a part of this exciting book.
My kids and all my angel grandkids, you make me believe.
And to my heavenly Father, thank You for giving me this.
I love you all.

For God sent not his Son into the world to condemn the world;
but that the world through him might be saved.
JOHN 3:17

Chapter 1

Elaine Daly gathered a deep breath and filled her lungs with early morning air. After five years in Cactus Corner, she still hated the heat and dust, but she loved the calm and quiet of the desert morning. The half-mile trek from the orphanage to the church and back had offered a nice stretch of the limbs and allowed for contemplation and reflection.

She crossed the dusty street, clutching the tied-up bundle of donated clothing tightly as she almost tripped over a rut. All she needed was to drop them and have to wash them out in the hot sun today. She stepped up onto the board sidewalk and headed past the bank. As she neared the café, the familiar sound of laughter and banter broke the silence and the aroma of strong coffee wafted out through the open door. Elaine glanced in. Etta Stephens was said to make the best flapjacks and eggs in Arizona Territory, and the packed café testified to that.

Elaine walked on, slowing her steps as she approached the

vacant mercantile. The building had been empty since John and Rebecca Lane moved back east. Elaine's friend Jody McMillan had it in her head to buy the place, which was right next to the town orphanage. There was no denying they needed more space. The overcrowded children's home's large front parlor had recently been converted into a dormitory, relegating the visitors' area to a small room in the rear, formerly used for storage. But whether the church board would agree to expansion was anyone's guess.

A sudden scream pierced the morning air. Elaine froze in her tracks. Whirling, she turned and peered through the abandoned store's dingy window. Another scream rent the silence. She jerked back around as she realized the sound was not coming from the mercantile. Hitching up her skirts, she bounded up the wooden sidewalk toward the large adobe house that sat at the end of the dusty street. One more nerve-shattering shriek knifed through her as she reached the door of the orphanage. Her survival instinct kicked in and, dropping her bundle, she snatched a broom from the porch—it would have to serve as a weapon.

Elaine warily crept through the door, prepared to swing the broom with all her might if anything threatened. The hallway was clear. She tiptoed to the door on the left and peered into the room just as another scream issued forth. The daytime staff, mostly volunteers, stood in a circle in the middle of the new dormitory. Carla, the cook, glanced around, her brow furrowed.

"What in the world is going on?" Elaine flung the broom down and made her way over to the circle. She squeezed between Carla and the parlor maid.

Jody knelt on the hardwood floor, patting the golden curls of a tiny girl who sat holding a cornhusk doll. The child couldn't have been more than two. Suddenly the girl clutched her doll tightly, opened her rosebud mouth, and screamed.

Elaine's mouth dropped open. "Jody, who is this child, and why is she screeching like a banshee?"

Jody's blue-green eyes swam with unshed tears as she met Elaine's gaze.

"We're not sure. John Turner brought her in and just dropped her. We think she may belong to"—a crimson flush washed over her face, and she swallowed—"one of his saloon women."

Elaine's knee popped loudly as she knelt beside Jody. She sighed. At forty, she felt much younger, but her right knee apparently didn't agree.

"Does she have any injuries?"

"None that we could find. And no signs of illness either. She just screams." Jody inhaled deeply, then let the air out in a whoosh. "We've tried everything to reach her. She doesn't respond to anything."

"Did you send for Doc Howard?"

"Yes, but apparently he's gone to Tucson to pick up the new doctor."

Elaine let out a little breath of exasperation. "If only the

Jacobsons were here." The couple who served as house parents for the orphanage had gone to San Francisco to visit relatives. A much-needed vacation.

"I know. When will they be back?"

"Not until tomorrow. We'll have to deal with this ourselves."

Jody stood and smoothed down her skirt, throwing a glance of regret in Elaine's direction. "Elaine, I'm so sorry to leave you with this situation, but I can't stay. I promised to sit with Mrs. Wright today while Mr. Wright runs some errands. He's afraid to leave her alone."

"Then of course you must go. And don't worry. We'll just have to do the best we can until the doctor gets back." Elaine rose, then bent and picked up the child, watching closely to see if there was any reaction. When the little girl remained silent, Elaine glanced at Jody, who smiled and shrugged.

Elaine spent the morning in the parlor, rocking the child, who didn't utter a sound as long as the back-and-forth motion continued. But every time Elaine grew fatigued and stopped for a moment, a scream would issue forth from the little pink lips. No sign of agitation, just the ear-piercing scream.

The soft little body curled into Elaine's arms, and as she gazed at the child, an unfamiliar warmth spread through her chest. Of course, she had always loved children. Why else would she have spent fifteen years of her life raising her brother and sister after her parents died? And she certainly would not have left her comfortable home in Chicago five years ago to come out to this despised desert to help the Jacobsons if not for the love she had for children. No, right now she would be enjoying the fragrance and beauty of the May flowers that bloomed each spring on the green, green lawns of her friends and neighbors there. And soon she'd be enjoying summer picnics by the cool lake. The season she missed most was autumn. Nostalgia washed over Elaine as her mind conjured up pictures of red and gold leaves sparkling in the morning sun. She could almost feel the crisp, cold air coming off Lake Michigan. Elaine sighed. Even more important than these pleasures, she could be cradling her infant niece in her arms, or she might, perhaps, even have a family of her own.

An unaccustomed wash of hot tears filled her eyes. Shaking her head, she blinked them away and sat up straight. She had chosen this life and did not regret her decision. Not in the least.

The child screamed again, and Elaine, who had been wrapped in her thoughts, realized she had stopped rocking. She began to move vigorously back and forth. *Then who would have been here for this little one?*

At noontime, Elaine carried her charge to the dining room and coaxed some soup into the little mouth. When the toddler smacked her lips with obvious enjoyment, Elaine and Carla exchanged pleased grins. As long as a child could enjoy food, the situation wasn't hopeless.

"What shall we call her? Until we find out her name, I mean."

"Hmm, how about Sunny? To match that hair."

Elaine thought for a moment and smiled. "No, let's call her

Autumn." She reached over and turned the little face toward her. "You're my Autumn for now. Is that okay?"

For a moment, Elaine thought the deep blue eyes showed awareness, but then the soft lids came down and the child's lips opened wide. Elaine braced herself for the scream. When it didn't come, she cast a puzzled look toward Carla, who grinned widely.

"What?"

"She's waiting for another bite of that soup."

Dr. Dan Murphy jumped down from the buggy, hefted his trunk from the back, and followed the white-haired man into a small adobe house.

"You can just toss your things into the storage room off the side." Doctor Howard waved his hand toward a door. "I put a cot up in there. Guess you won't mind that until I get moved out of here." The aged doctor's mouth twisted up into a grin.

"Not at all. From what you've told me about that cabin in the mountains of Wyoming, I'm sure you can't wait to get out of here and take it easy."

"Well, I can and I can't." A pensive look crossed the doctor's face. "Hated it here when I first came, but I've gotten used to Cactus Corner. I'm probably going to miss it at first. I've patched up a lot of ranch hands. Doctored a bunch of kids. Most of them are grown up now." He chuckled. "It was wild country when I came out here in '52. Belonged to Mexico back then. I was a young pup like you and just about scared out of my britches at all the goings-on."

Cactus Corner's newest citizen smiled at being thought of as a young pup. He had just turned forty-five last month. "I'd like to hear all about it sometime, sir, if you don't mind."

"Oh, you will. If not from me, from someone else. Still a lot of old-timers around." He threw his hat on the table. "Well, I'm sort of tuckered out after that long buggy ride. Think I'll take a nap, and then you can go with me on my rounds. Meet some of the people you'll be caring for. They're good folks, albeit a little rough around the edges."

A loud pounding caused both men to turn. The door flew open and a young boy of about eight or nine crashed into the room. A large calico cat clutched beneath his arm wriggled furiously and made its escape, running out the open door.

"Doc! You must go to the orphans' home. I promise Miss Jody I tell you as soon as you got back."

Dr. Howard grabbed his medical bag and headed for the door, motioning for Dan to follow. "What's wrong, Pedro? One of the young'uns sick?"

"Don't know, Doc. Miss Jody, she say to tell you she needs you. I wait on your porch all morning." His dark eyes crinkled with laughter, and he flashed a dazzling grin. "But I get so very hungry, I run to my *casa* to get some grub."

Dan held on to the side of the buggy as Doc Howard raced through town. The doctor pulled the horse to a stop in front of a large adobe house. Dan looked on in amusement as the older doctor jumped down, waving his buggy whip at two boys playing beside the railroad tracks. "Hey, you young rascals! Ray and Charlie!"

Two guilt-filled faces turned their way.

"Get away from them tracks. You want to get yourselves killed?"

"No, sir!" the boys yelled in unison, then ran in through the side gate and took off around to the back of the house.

Dr. Howard shook his head. "I've been telling folks we need to move the children to another location ever since the railroad came through. I hope someone doesn't have to get killed before they'll listen to me."

Dan nodded. "It does seem hazardous." *Just another case of folks not caring.* He followed Doc Howard up the stone walk and stood to the side as the older man tapped on the door. A little girl with bronze-colored skin and long black braids opened it. She stared at the doctor with wide dark brown eyes, then scooted aside for them to enter, yelling loudly, "Miss Elaine, the doctor is here."

"All right, Rainsong. I'm coming."

Dan stared at the woman who came through the door. Her deep auburn hair had come loose on the sides and hung in bouncy curls on each side of her face. She appeared to be in her midthirties. Her dark blue eyes stared into his, and a delicate pink flush washed over her very attractive face. Lowering her gaze, she shifted the child she carried in her arms and turned quickly to the older man.

Elaine swallowed with difficulty. She couldn't believe she had been staring at the stranger. What must he think?

"Dr. Howard, thank the Lord you're here at last. We have a situation."

"A new child, right?"

"Yes, but more than that."

She led the men down the hall and into the parlor. Her glance shifted to the stranger, and she blushed as she caught Dr. Howard's amused smile.

"Elaine, let me introduce you to Cactus Corner's new physician, Dr. Dan Murphy. Dan, this is Miss Elaine Daly. She assists Mr. and Mrs. Jacobson in the care of the children."

Elaine offered her hand to the new doctor and instantly wished she hadn't. His strong hand enveloped hers, and heat rushed through her palm and up her arm. A little involuntary gasp escaped her throat, and she felt heat rise to her face.

A scream reverberated through the room. Elaine started, jerking her hand free as both men looked at the little girl with concern.

"And that," Elaine said, her voice shaking, "is one of the problems." She moved to the rocking chair and sat down with Autumn on her lap. She motioned for the doctors to take a seat on the sofa. Once they were seated, she quickly apprised them of the details.

"Hmm, well, let's get her onto a cot, and I'll take a look."

Doc Howard rose from the sofa and picked up his bag.

"Er—maybe I'd better hold her. She screams every time I put her down."

He blinked in surprise and peered at her through his spectacles. "Nevertheless, I think you'd better put her down so I can examine her. I've attended to screaming children before."

Elaine rose reluctantly and led the way to the toddlers' nursery.

Apparently one of the volunteers had taken the two- and three-year-olds outside to play, leaving the room vacant. Elaine laid Autumn down on a small cot and, after giving the child an encouraging pat, stepped back.

Elaine glanced at the stranger and felt a twinge of pleasure when he smiled at her sympathetically. She let her lips form just the tiniest smile, then looked away.

Dr. Howard gently examined Autumn, seemingly undeterred by her screaming. After a while, he stepped back, snapped his bag shut, and motioned for Elaine to pick the child up.

They went back into the parlor, and Autumn quieted as soon as Elaine sat down and began to rock her.

"Doctor, what's wrong with the poor little thing?" Elaine waited anxiously for his answer.

"Not exactly sure. No sign of injuries, anyway. And the child isn't ill." He twisted one side of his moustache. "She could be deaf. Or it could be some sort of shock. I'll know more about that after I talk to Turner." He shook his head and sighed. "To tell you the truth, Elaine, I think the child is just spoiled."

Elaine stared at Doc Howard, then down at the little girl who sat peacefully looking up at her. Laughter tickled her throat, and she chuckled. *Well, the little stinker.* "Spoiled? Do you really think that's all it is?"

"Mm-hm. Of course, I don't know for certain. But I'd just about be willing to bet on it." He stood up. "Send for me if you need me, and I'll let you know what I find out from Turner."

"I will, Dr. Howard. Thank you. At least she's not ill or injured."

Both men headed for the door, where Dr. Murphy turned and smiled.

For the first time, Elaine noticed the enticing gold flecks that sparkled in his dark brown eyes. *Stop it, Elaine. They're just brown eyes. Stop it before you make a fool of yourself!*

Tipping his hat, he said, "Good day, Miss Lainey. Don't let little Autumn wear you out."

She gasped as he turned and followed Dr. Howard down the path. He called her "Lainey." No one had called her that since she was eighteen. A smile tugged at her lips. *Lainey.* She liked it.

Chapter 2

Dust swirled around Dan's boots as he walked down the street. When he neared the saloon, a cacophony of noise assailed him. He paused and gazed at the swinging doors. Drawing in a deep breath, he took a determined step forward and pushed his way into the smoke-filled room.

Men in various stages of intoxication stood at the bar and sat at the tables. A garishly painted woman tripped across the outstretched boot of a customer at a gaming table. Ribald laughter reverberated against the walls. Loud angry voices floated down from the upper rooms, and something crashed to the floor. Dan blinked against the acrid smoke that burned his eyes. He clenched his teeth as memories assaulted him.

Five-year-old Dan squirmed and twisted, trying to see his mother's face, but her arms held him tight against her. She coughed, and a glob of blood hit Dan's hand. A jolt of fear pierced him as she fell to the floor, pulling him with her.

"Ma!"

She hit the floor with him still clutched tightly to her chest. Terror held him in its grip as her loud, rasping breaths suddenly stopped. Burly arms pulled him from his mother's grasp, and he struggled against them.

"No! Ma!"

He twisted and turned, striking out at the tall figure who held him captive. Bending forward, he bit down hard on the man's hand. The man cursed, and then a blow landed on Dan's head. . . .

A loud guffaw brought Dan back to the present. A shudder ran through his body. Maybe it hadn't been such a good idea to volunteer to do this for Doc Howard. Clenching his fist, he strode to the bar.

"What'll it be?" The surly bartender didn't bother to turn around as he continued wiping down bottles.

"I'm looking for a woman named Mary."

"Yeah? Well, we got three of 'em." The bartender faced Dan and gave him the once-over.

"The one I'm looking for was taking care of a baby until recently."

The man raised his eyebrows, and his lips turned downward. "What interest would you have in that baby?"

At the suspicious tone, Dan held up both hands. "Nothing except pure concern. I'm the new doctor in town. I need some information about her medical history."

"You mean if she's been sick or something?"

"That's right." Dan smiled.

"Ain't never been sick as far as I can remember. Mary took good care of the kid." The man narrowed his eyes and glared at Dan.

Dan nodded. "I'm sure she did. But most children have some sort of childhood disease at one time or another. I really need to speak to Mary, if you'd just tell me where she is."

"Charlie, quit bein' so contrary." A frowsy-looking redhead with kind eyes sauntered over and grinned at Dan.

"So you're the new doc, huh?"

"Yes, ma'am. Just arrived yesterday. Would you by any chance be Mary?"

The woman chuckled. "Nope, name's Lottie." She tilted her head toward the stairway and grinned. "Mary's busy right now. But I could probably tell you anything she could. We all took care of Baby."

"Well, Lottie, that's kind of you. Any information would be greatly appreciated by me as well as the good women at the orphanage."

Lottie frowned. "Humph. Good women, eh? And what does that make us girls in here? I can just imagine what they think and say about us." She slid onto the stool next to Dan. "You might want to buy me a drink. Turner don't take too kindly to idleness."

Dan smiled. "I'll tell you what, Lottie, how about if I just pay for your time and we forget the drink? Will that satisfy your boss?"

"Don't know why it wouldn't." She motioned the bartender

over. "Charlie, the doc wants to talk and is willin' to pay for it. So you just mark down two drinks every fifteen minutes or so."

"I dunno, Lottie." Charlie scratched his chin and frowned.

Lottie gave a huff and retorted, "Never mind what you dunno." She smiled and softened her voice. "It'll be okay, Charlie. Just do it."

"Well, okay. If you say so." He cast a sideways look at Dan. "But you call me if you need me."

"Come on, Doc. Let's sit over at that corner table. It's a little bit quieter there."

Lottie slid off the bar stool, her red and white satin skirts swinging around her legs, and motioned for Dan to follow.

A half hour later, satisfied that Autumn was a healthy little girl, Dan left the saloon. As he stepped outside the doors, his eyes met those of a woman just coming out of the general store across the street. He tipped his hat. She gave him a cold stare and turned away.

Uh-oh. I've only been in town one day and I've already given the good ladies of Cactus Corner ammunition against me.

"Miss Elaine, Miss Elaine. That baby won't hush up, and I'm tryin' to do my 'rithmetic."

"*A*-rithmetic, Charlene."

"Yes, ma'am, that's what I said—'rithmetic."

Elaine sighed and brushed the stringy blond locks from the girl's forehead.

"All right, Charlene, bring her to me. I'll take care of her." She looked into the girl's face. "Why are you doing your homework in the toddlers' room anyway? You're supposed to use the dining room table."

"Grace asked me to help watch them while she went to fix bottles. But those babies are makin' me crazy."

"Get your things and go into the dining room. I'll watch the toddlers until Grace gets back."

"Yes, ma'am." The girl made a beeline for the door.

"And go find your ribbon. It seems to have fallen out of your—" Elaine stopped talking, as the girl was already out of the room. She groaned. This was the most hectic day they'd had in a long time. There were usually at least two volunteers each day to help the Jacobsons and Elaine with the children as well as to oversee the younger volunteers who came in from time to time. But Mr. and Mrs. Jacobson's train would not arrive until late afternoon.

Anika was in the middle of a legal dispute of some sort, and India was busy at the ranch. Elaine was tempted to ask Jody to come in, but her friend's boss had been keeping her so busy lately that Elaine hated to disturb her on one of her few days off.

Elaine entered the toddlers' room and found not only Autumn screaming but seven more youngsters, as well. Grace's helper, Jane, sat in the rocker with two crying babes in her arms. She cast a frantic glance at Elaine. Several older toddlers sat on the floor in obvious distress.

Grace came through the door, huffing and puffing and carrying a basket full of milk bottles. "Sorry, Miss Elaine. Cook was busy and couldn't help." She set the basket down and handed bottles out to the little ones who were not yet weaned.

"I understand, Grace. It's been a difficult day for all of us. I really think we need to move the children who are off the bottle into the next dormitory. The others' screaming just gets them all going, and nap time is almost impossible."

Elaine went over to Autumn's crib. The little girl drank peacefully, with a tiny stream of milk running from the corner of her mouth. Elaine glanced around the room. It was finally quiet now that the babies were eating. Breathing a sigh of relief, she waved to Grace and Jane and headed for the kitchen to help Carla.

She passed through the hall just as someone knocked on the front door. *What now? It had better not be those rascal boys playing tricks again.* She opened it to find herself standing face-to-face with the new doctor. His eyes crinkled as he flashed a smile.

"Dr. Murphy—" Elaine cleared her throat and tried again. "May I help you with something?" She reached up and patted at her wayward curls. *Why can't they ever stay in the bun where they belong?*

He looked down at her from his considerable height. Again that smile about knocked her off her feet.

"As a matter of fact, I think perhaps I can help you. I have some information about your newest charge."

"Oh." Elaine stepped back. "Do come in, please. We're

rather at sixes and sevens around here today, but I'm sure I can find a few moments."

He followed her to the small parlor, and they sat on the sofa. A lock of sandy hair had fallen across his forehead, and Elaine could almost feel her fingers brushing it back. She forced the thought out of her mind, wishing she had sat on the chair across the room so she wasn't so close to this man who left her flustered.

"It seems Miss Autumn's mother was one of the. . .er. . . entertainers at the saloon. She died shortly after the baby arrived. Since the mother had never mentioned family, there was nowhere for the child to go."

"Well, for goodness' sake! Why didn't they bring her here instead of waiting nearly two years?" Elaine felt the creases between her eyes and consciously composed her face.

He raised one eyebrow and said, "It seems some of the ladies in the establishment thought she would be better off with them than here."

She gasped. *They thought the child would be better off in a saloon than with godly Christian people?* "How could they possibly believe a child should be raised in a saloon?"

A painful look clouded his eyes, but the next moment his mouth twisted in a sardonic smile. "Ah. . .well. . .Lainey, there are worse places than saloons."

Heat warmed her cheeks. *Lainey.* That name again. She glared at him. "What exactly do you mean by that?"

"Nothing personal, my dear. I was merely stating a fact."

He rose and picked up his hat.

"Wait. What caused them to change their minds?"

"They didn't. Turner didn't want the child around anymore, so he took matters into his own hands."

"Did you ask about the screaming?"

"As a matter of fact, that was the clincher. Turner told them they'd spoiled her so much he couldn't stand to have her around anymore. Apparently her tantrums and screaming were hurting the business. There's not a thing wrong except she's been spoiled rotten." He gave a nod in her direction. "Well, Miss Lainey, I'll get out of your way. Don't work yourself to death."

"Thank you, Dr. Murphy. I do appreciate the information." She reached out her hand, which he took and held for a moment.

"You're more than welcome. I'll do anything I can for these orphans. And I'll do anything I can for you, as well." Turning, he left her standing in stunned silence.

Now what did he mean by that?

Dan ran his hand over the mare's glistening chestnut flank and gave her a final pat. He had run her harder than he liked to, but he'd wanted to see how she would do in an emergency.

"She's a beauty, Mrs. Dillinger. I'm surprised you can part with her, but I'm glad you are." He tied the reins to the back of the buggy. His newly purchased horse had rested enough for the slow trot back to town.

The young woman smiled and tucked a loose strand of blond hair behind her ear. "Just take good care of her. And please call me India. After all, we are neighbors now."

"I'm sorry I missed your husband. Maybe next time."

"I'm sure we'll see you in church. You can meet Joshua then."

The lovely young woman smiled broadly and waved to him as he pulled away in Doc Howard's buggy.

Dan whistled as he rode through the saguaro and other cacti, which grew profusely in the area. Mrs. Dillinger was a beautiful woman. She'd grace any big-city drawing room. He couldn't help but wonder why she chose to live in this hot and dusty country. Of course, Arizona Territory had its beauty. Like now with the sun setting behind the mountains. If a man didn't know better, he'd think the mountain itself was on fire. He had to admit he'd never seen a sunset like this in San Francisco. Still, life wasn't easy here. Especially for the women and children.

He had wondered about Miss Elaine Daly. It was obvious she came from back east somewhere. He grinned. The prim and proper Miss Daly hadn't said a word about his familiarity with her name. He had no idea why he was deviling her the way he was—trying to get under her skin. He couldn't deny the attraction he felt for her. A grin quirked his mouth. He had to admit he enjoyed the reaction he got when he called her Lainey.

Amazing, the difference in women. These ladies, although obviously used to hard work and no-nonsense lifestyles, were nevertheless genteel and gracious.

Then there was Lottie and her kind. Dan frowned, and his body tensed into the familiar fighting mode. Most likely Lottie's life had been a lot different from Miss Daly's or Mrs. Dillinger's. It wasn't her fault she hadn't had the same advantages as the other ladies. No doubt they snubbed her and made her feel like dirt under their dainty little shoes when they saw her on the street.

Dan took a deep, cleansing breath and relaxed. He wouldn't let the past mess up the chance of a fresh start here in Arizona Territory. He was going to stay on the straight and respectable path here. The "Lotties" would have to fight their own battles this time.

Chapter 3

The small visitors' room was stuffy—too stuffy. Elaine pulled at her collar, then grabbed her fan and waved it furiously.

Anika Truesdale shook her head and narrowed her hazel eyes. "Really, Elaine, I'd think after nearly ten years you'd be used to the weather here."

"Well, I'm not. It's not natural for it to be so hot in May." She gave another sharp pass with her fan to make her point.

"Well, it's natural for Arizona, honey," Anika drawled.

The four friends tried to meet at least once a week, although it wasn't always possible now that India and Anika were married. Today's meeting had begun with a lot of friendly banter and catching up on each other's events of the week. Elaine didn't know why she'd gotten so tense all of a sudden. But the weather wasn't helping.

"Are you sure it's the heat, sweetie?" India grinned, then ducked as Elaine's fan flew through the air, bounced against the wall, and almost landed on her head. A startled look crossed her face, and she stared at Elaine.

Elaine gasped in horror. What in the world had she done? "I'm so sorry, India. I don't know what came over me."

India nodded her forgiveness. "I think I know. Why don't you admit you're smitten with the good-looking new doctor?"

"Oh no! You can't be!" Jody lifted her hands to her cheeks, her eyes wide.

"Why, Jody, what do you mean?" Elaine asked. "Not that I care a whit about Dan Murphy, of course." Her heart fluttered, and she felt warmth creeping up her face.

Jody bit her lip. "Oh dear. I hate passing on gossip, but. . ."

"But what?" Anika leaned forward. "Just get to the point, Jody."

Elaine couldn't help but smile. Anika and her lawyer mind could never abide beating around the bush.

"Well—" Jody hesitated, then rushed on. "Mrs. Sanders thinks Dr. Murphy might not be quite nice."

Elaine's heart pounded. Why would Mrs. Sanders say such a thing?

India looked at Jody, a surprised expression on her face. "What's that supposed to mean? I've met him and I think he's very nice." She grinned. "My horses even like him."

"I hate to spread gossip, but for Elaine's sake, I think I must. Mrs. Sanders saw him coming out of the saloon week before last, and a few days ago, Mr. Sanders spotted him standing outside the saloon doors, talking to one of those. . .women."

Jody blushed and bent her head over the small garment she was sewing.

"Well, maybe someone was sick," India said.

Jody glanced up. "That's what I said, but Mrs. Sanders said no respectable doctor would treat those women and take a chance on spreading their disgusting diseases to the decent folk in Cactus Corner."

"Hmm." Anika tapped her fingers against the wooden arm of her chair. "She may be right. The bartender usually does their doctoring."

"How in the world would you know that?" India jerked her head up and stared at Anika, wide-eyed.

Anika grinned. "I am a lawyer, you know. We have ways of finding out things."

Elaine felt numb. She couldn't speak because of the lump in her throat.

"Elaine, you don't really care about that man, do you?" Jody asked.

"No." The word came out with a croak, and Elaine ducked her head and concentrated intently on the small shirt she was mending. "Of course not. I barely know him."

Mercifully, at that moment, India took pity on her and turned to Jody. "By the way, Jody, has Elmer proposed yet today?"

Anika and India exploded with laughter as Jody rolled her eyes and didn't bother to answer. Her employer made no secret of the fact he intended to make Jody his bride. Not that

Jody thought him repulsive, but she simply wasn't interested, and Elaine knew his constant wooing was about to drive Jody insane.

Just then, Grace peeked her head through the door.

"Everyone's tucked in. Do you mind if I join you?" A few months ago, Anika had recruited the girl to women's suffrage, and since then, Grace had almost become Anika's shadow.

"Grace, what in the world are you wearing?" Elaine stared at the pant-covered legs.

"It's a bloomer outfit, ma'am. I waited until I went off duty to put it on."

Elaine heard a muffled snort coming from India's direction and had to press her own lips together to keep from laughing. Jody had turned her head and coughed into a hanky.

Anika stood and took the girl's hand, leading her over to a chair beside them. "Pay no attention to them, my dear. You look absolutely delightful. I've been thinking of making a bloomer outfit for myself. I hear they're all the rage among the suffragettes in England and even New York."

Elaine was thankful for the laughter and the change of subject.

A short while later, when everyone had left, she stepped outside and watched the moon rise above the mountains. She shivered as cool air tickled her skin. She should have remembered to wear her shawl. That was one good thing about the desert. Although she was burning up a short time earlier, nighttime always brought a cool breeze.

She went back inside and said good night to Mrs. Jacobson, who was just coming out of the kitchen. Once in her room, she fidgeted as she tried unsuccessfully to keep her mind on her devotions. Finally, she gave up and went to bed.

Thoughts of Dan Murphy's kind eyes pressed into her mind, and she tried fruitlessly to block them out. He seemed so nice, and she had to admit her pulse raced whenever he was near.

"Oh Lord, I almost fell in love with a scalawag."

Through her open window, the cicadas seemed to mock her. She could almost hear them chiding, "You did, you did."

Slinging her coverlet back, she strode to the window and slammed it shut. "There," she muttered, brushing her hands together.

But as she lay back on her soft pillows, a sob caught in her throat as her own thoughts echoed the words. *I did. I did fall in love with him.*

Dan patted little Sam Carter on the shoulder and handed him a piece of licorice. "You're a trouper, Sam. I think you may be the best patient I've had all day." He didn't mention that the little boy was the only patient he'd had all day.

Mrs. Carter's tired eyes rested kindly on Dan as she clutched the bottle of cough syrup he had given her for her son. "I wish I had the money to pay you, Dr. Murphy." She bit her lip, and Dan could see embarrassment written all over her lined face.

"Don't worry about it, Mrs. Carter. I can't wait to sink my

teeth into this wild plum cobbler. It's payment enough."

A hint of a smile touched the woman's lips as she lifted her toddler from the cot. She headed for the door, then stopped and turned. "I don't believe them rumors about you, Dr. Murphy. And my man don't, either."

Dan stared after her as the door swung shut behind her. Rumors? What rumors? He'd wondered why he'd had only a handful of patients all week. The first few days after Doc Howard left, the office had been full almost continuously. He'd thought maybe no one was sick, but it was highly unusual not to at least have headaches or rashes to treat. Come to think of it, the few folks who had come in had been from the Indian camp a few miles away or miners' families. Not one of the upstanding citizens of Cactus Corner had darkened his doorway this week.

Now that he recalled, he'd received some cool nods from the ladies of the town, and not a few skirts were swept aside as he walked down the street.

What were the rumors? And who started them? He inhaled deeply, then let the air out with a *whoosh*. So it had begun again. Only this time, he was innocent of any wrongdoing.

He washed up and changed his shirt, then grabbed his bag and headed out the door. He hadn't checked on the children at the orphanage in a few days. Besides, a visit with Miss Elaine was just what he needed to lift his spirits.

Grace answered his knock.

"How are you today, Miss Grace? Lovely as ever, I see."

The girl blushed and stammered, "I'm fine, Doc. Brother and Sister Jacobson are at a church board meeting. I'll tell Miss Elaine you're here." She scurried from the room, leaving Dan standing in the hall with his hat in his hand.

A few minutes later, Elaine walked in. How she managed to look so cool and crisp in this heat was a mystery to Dan. Unfortunately, the expression on her face was even cooler.

"Yes, Dr. Murphy? How may I assist you?" Not a trace of friendship or congeniality appeared on her face. In fact, she seemed to struggle with some emotion he couldn't identify.

"I thought I'd check in on the children," he said, attempting a smile.

"The children are all fine, Doctor. So if you'll excuse me. . ." The words trailed off, and she glanced toward the door.

He nodded and turned away, then with resolution wheeled back around to face her.

"What's going on, Miss Elaine?" He took just a tiny bit of satisfaction at the shocked look on her face. Apparently she hadn't expected to be confronted.

"I don't know what you mean."

Dan quirked an eyebrow. "Well now, let's see. I have very few patients, none of whom happen to be the so-called respectable citizens of the town; I'm getting the cold shoulder from said citizens; and now you're treating me as you would a rattlesnake getting ready to strike."

He watched with interest as Elaine's face flamed. She opened her mouth, shut it, and then opened it again.

"Miss Elaine, one of my patients tells me rumors are going around town about me. I think I have a right to know what they are so I can either admit them or defend myself."

Elaine felt tension clamp down on her from her head to her toes. She realized she was twisting a section of her skirt and forced herself to open her hand. Uncertainty gripped her. It had never occurred to her that the stories were untrue. After all, why would anyone make up such atrocities? But he looked so confused and even a little hurt as he stood facing her. What if he truly was innocent? It was easy to jump to conclusions. Elaine had been guilty of that herself at times.

She swallowed and took a long, shuddering breath. "Dr. Murphy, would you like to come in for a moment? Perhaps we should talk."

A look of surprised relief passed over his face, and he followed her to the small receiving room in back.

Elaine sat down next to a small table, motioning him to the chair on the other side. Could she really do this? Maybe one of the men should be talking to him. But then, most of them believed he was guilty. Still, such a delicate subject. She could feel warmth on her face just thinking about it, but having admitted to herself that she was in love with him, she felt she owed it to him to push through her embarrassment.

She glanced at him and was surprised to see sympathy on his face.

"Miss Lainey, if this is too difficult for you, don't feel that you have to tell me anything."

She straightened her back and looked him in the eye. "I'm fine, Dr. Murphy."

She began with the incidents at the saloon. "I realize the first time was probably when you went to find out about Autumn."

"Yes, you're right. It was."

"Well, what about standing in the doorway with one of those. . ." She stopped and blushed again, then, frustrated at her own emotions, she took a deep breath and exhaled loudly. They wouldn't get anywhere if she couldn't stop blushing.

"Her name is Lottie," Dan said, coming to her rescue. "I was giving her instructions on how to care for one of the girls who'd come down with a very bad case of tonsillitis."

"Oh." Elaine paused. "But. . .should you be treating those women? I mean, after all, you could pass something on to other people."

"What exactly could I pass on to these 'other people'?" Dan scowled. This was the first time she'd seen him with anything less than a pleasant expression on his face.

"Well, I don't know." She frowned and blew a strand of hair from her eyes. "Mrs. Sanders said some kind of disease could be passed on."

"My dear, the type of disease the good Mrs. Sanders was referring to can't be passed from patient to patient by a doctor."

"Oh." She wasn't sure what to reply, since she had no idea what sort of disease he was referring to.

"Didn't Dr. Howard give medical treatment to the folks at the saloon?"

Elaine shook her head. "My friend Anika said the bartender took care of them."

Anger washed over his face. "Well, just so you know, physicians take an oath to give medical care to all who need it. And I intend to do just that. If anyone, including you, has a problem with that, I'm sorry, but that's the way it is." He stood, gave her a short bow, and then strode from the room.

Elaine listened to his boots as he walked up the hallway. Suddenly she jumped up and ran out into the hall just as he reached the front door. "Doctor, wait."

He stopped and turned, his brow raised, a question in his eyes.

"Don't you want to hear about the other things being said?"

His lips turned up slightly at one corner. "Not particularly. I think I have a pretty good idea of what's being said. I hope in the future you'll give me the benefit of the doubt before you believe the rumors, Miss Elaine. I may be rough around the edges, but I'm not immoral."

Elaine's heart fluttered. She could feel the throb of her pulse in her neck as relief washed over her. She held her hand out to him. "I believe you, Dr. Murphy."

With two strides, he was standing in front of her, her hand in both of his. Warmth filled his eyes as he gazed into hers. "Thank you, Lainey. But are you sure you want to be my defender? It may cost you in terms of friendship."

Elaine jerked her chin and gave a tight little smile. "My friends won't turn against me." Gently she slipped her hand from his warm grasp. "Good day, Doctor. I'll be praying for you."

Chapter 4

Elaine stopped and stood gaping at the crowd gathered around the door of the general store. What in the world was going on? And how would she ever get through the shoulder-to-shoulder throng? Well, the flour bin was almost empty, so she really had no choice.

"Excuse me." She squeezed between two strange men at the edge of the crowd. Twisting and elbowing her way, she managed to get to the door, where she slipped inside. The crowd there wasn't as large. Mrs. Granger locked the door and motioned for her to follow her into their private quarters in back of the store.

"Elaine, you shouldn't have come out. It's getting pretty bad on the street."

"But what's going on?" Elaine followed the storekeeper's wife to the corner, where they sat in high-backed rockers.

"You didn't hear about the copper strike last week?" Mrs. Granger fanned herself and gazed at Elaine through wide blue eyes.

"Well, yes, I did hear that someone had found copper up in the mountains. What does that have to do with this?"

Mrs. Granger sighed. "Unfortunately, it seems everyone from a hundred miles around has heard about it, too. They've been pouring into town like ants since yesterday. Many of them came without any mining gear at all, expecting to buy it here. And expecting credit. We sold what we had on a cash basis, but we've run out. We simply weren't prepared for the rush. Some of them are getting downright ugly."

Elaine gasped. "Isn't the sheriff doing anything to control them?"

The woman gave a short laugh. "He's trying. But the jail won't hold them all."

"Can't you get more supplies?"

"Fred's heading to Tucson today. He's tried to reason with the miners, but some of them can't be reasoned with. Like that crowd outside." She brushed hair from her forehead and breathed deeply. "I was just getting ready to lock up and put the closed sign on the door when I saw you coming. I suppose you need something for the orphanage."

"Yes, tomorrow is baking day, and we're about out of flour." She looked questioningly at the older woman.

"Sorry, dear. That's gone, too. I'll have someone bring some over from my own supply—enough to make a few loaves." She peered at Elaine. "But you really shouldn't go back through that crowd. And it wouldn't be safe to go out the back way either. No telling who'd be out there."

"Well, no one bothered me on my way in. I'm sure I'll be fine, and I really have to get back." Elaine rose. "Anything you can send will be fine. We'll get by."

They walked to the front of the store. Mrs. Granger put the CLOSED sign on the door, and the crowd began to thin out just a little.

Mrs. Granger unlocked the door, and Elaine slipped through. Seeing the angry faces of the men in the throng, she almost turned around and knocked on the door. But no, she had to get back to the orphanage. Taking a deep breath, she stepped forward and began to make her way back through the jumble of sweating, mumbling bodies.

"Hey there, pretty little lady." A hand grabbed Elaine's arm and yanked her around. She found herself nose to nose with a grinning, bearded round face. She almost retched from the foul smell emanating from between the man's broken, rotted teeth.

"Let go of me." She jerked her arm, then yelped as he squeezed it tighter, pulling her close to him. Laughter met her on all sides, and she felt herself getting dizzy.

"Let her go. Now!" She heard Dan Murphy's voice and felt strong arms catch her just as darkness overcame her.

"Elaine, dear, wake up."

Elaine's eyes fluttered open as gentle hands patted her cheeks. Martha Jacobson's worried face looked down at her. As she raised herself onto one elbow, she saw that she was lying on her bed at the orphanage.

"What? How did I get here?"

"Dr. Murphy carried you here after he rescued you from that mob of ruffians."

Elaine's heart raced as the memory of her assailant flashed through her mind. "Oh, I need to thank the doctor. Is he still here?" Her hero. Her knight in shining armor. Warmth rose from her chest to her face, and she felt the corners of her lips tilt upward.

Martha smiled and cast a knowing glance toward her. "I guess you're feeling better. But you'll have to wait to thank the young doctor. As soon as he knew you were all right, he slammed out of here. He was quite angry."

Elaine stood and smoothed her skirt, then went to the small mirror over her washstand and arranged the hair that had come loose.

"You lie back down, now. The girls and I can manage."

"Nonsense. I'm fine. I was just overcome from nerves and the lack of air. Oh, Mrs. Granger will send some flour over later. They're out of everything in the store."

"Yes, I heard. I'm afraid our sweet little town won't stay the same now that the miners are here. A few of them will bring families, of course, but most of the miners are a rough bunch."

They left the room, and Martha headed for her desk in the kitchen while Elaine went to check on the children. Grace was rocking Autumn, and the little girl seemed contented as she lay with her head against Grace's chest, her thumb in her own little rosebud mouth.

Elaine smiled and ran her hand over the soft curls. "We really need to make her stop sucking her thumb."

"Yes, ma'am. That we do." Grace looked at Elaine, and they exchanged knowing smiles. Little Autumn had almost stopped the screaming. They weren't about to upset her just yet.

Jane rushed in carrying a stack of diapers. When her eyes rested on Elaine, they lit up with mischief. "Miss Elaine, you are so lucky."

"What do you mean, Jane?"

"What do I mean? Well, I would give just about anything to be carried in the strong arms of a handsome man like Doc Murphy."

"Jane Andrews, that's not very nice. I was unconscious."

"Yes, ma'am." The girl giggled and put the stack of diapers away.

Elaine let out a huff and walked out of the room. There were several volunteers helping out today, so she mostly went from one group to the other making sure all was well and giving occasional instructions. This, of course, left too much time for free thinking, and Elaine found her mind wandering to Dan Murphy. Her cheeks flushed as she thought of Jane's words. She couldn't help but wonder how those arms would have felt if she'd been awake. *Stop it, Elaine.* All she needed was to get people gossiping about her, too.

The rumors about Dan seemed to be getting worse instead of dying down. Elaine knew most of the *respectable* folks were going to a doctor in another town and continued to snub Dan every chance they had. She'd made several of the ladies angry when she defended him at the last sewing circle. Since then, she'd gotten the cold shoulder from a few people herself, although most folks stood by her even though they thought she was deceived.

She was happy the Jacobsons hadn't been swayed by the gossip. They liked the new doctor and didn't care who knew it, although they thought he was unwise to continue to give medical treatment to the saloon girls. Elaine had to admit to herself that she agreed. Those creatures had done fine with the bartender to take care of their medical needs, and she simply couldn't understand why Dan couldn't see it, as well. After all, they'd chosen the sort of life they lived, hadn't they?

If he aimed a little to the left, he'd make it this time. Dan leaned back in his chair with his boots propped up on the desk, then aimed the wadded-up paper and sent it sailing, giving a satisfied grunt when it landed in the can on top of the bookcase.

Pushing his boots against the desk, he slid his chair back and got up. How pathetic was he anyway to be so easily entertained?

He grabbed his hat and slung it on his head as he went out and locked the door. If anyone needed his services after hours, they could come looking for him. He intended to go to the hotel and check on the miner who'd come down with a fever earlier in the week. It probably wasn't anything serious, but with so many strangers crowding into town, he didn't want to risk an epidemic.

The town was quiet today. Since getting their supplies a couple of days ago, all the miners were up in the mountains searching for copper. He passed the dress shop, which was closed for the day, and sauntered through the door of the hotel.

"Howdy, Doc. What can I do for you?" The desk clerk ran a feather duster over the long counter.

"Hello, Bob. I just came to check on the miner who was ill."

Bob stopped dusting and scratched his ear. "He hightailed it out of here with the rest of them."

"Hmm. Did he appear to be all right?"

"As far as I could tell. Didn't seem sick to me. He probably just had a touch of the sun or something."

Dan frowned. "Maybe." Shrugging, he said good-bye and left. He stood outside the hotel with his hat in his hands, running his fingers around the brim. He wondered if he could get by with going to the orphanage to see Elaine. Probably not. Since she'd agreed to let him call on her last week, he'd already been over there three times. He grinned. No sense in pushing his luck. He'd never imagined he'd feel this way about any woman.

He crossed the street and headed down the sidewalk to the café. *Might as well eat supper,* he supposed. Etta usually closed up by seven on weekdays. She had a huge crowd for breakfast and lunch, but it was pretty slow at supper, except for Friday night. Today was no exception. There was only one other customer in the place.

Dan sat at a table near the door and looked over at the menu on the chalkboard.

"What'll it be, Doc?" Etta's cheerful voice rang out through the room.

"I'll have the meatloaf dinner, Miss Etta. It's been awhile since I had it, and I think I hear it calling me. A cup of that great coffee, too."

Etta laughed and went to get his coffee. She placed it on the table and headed back to the kitchen to get his food. He knew she did all the cooking and serving. The girl who'd worked for her had quit, and now she was stuck with it all.

"When are you going to get some help, Etta?" He took a sip from the steaming mug. "You can't run this place by yourself forever."

"Matter of fact, I just hired someone. She came in looking for work this afternoon. Starts in the morning."

"Well, that's good. Who is it?"

"She's not from around here. Came in on the train this morning, looking like a little lost kitten. Had a tiny baby in her arms. She didn't say why she landed here in Cactus Corner, but I guess that's her business. I put her up in my spare room."

"Are you sure that's wise, Etta? Moving a stranger into your place?" Dan shook salt on his potatoes, then put the shaker down. No insult to Etta's great cooking. He just liked a lot of salt.

Etta wiped the dusting of white granules off the red-and-white-checkered tablecloth. "Maybe. But she and that baby looked as though they needed help even more than me. And sometimes you just have to trust people." She grinned. "Besides, she's not big enough to do me any damage even if she tried."

Dan shook his head as she walked away. He ate his meal, then sat back with a slice of apple pie and another cup of coffee.

A murmur of voices drifted in from the kitchen, then footsteps. Dan inhaled sharply as an all-too-familiar scent pervaded his nostrils. "Dan, I'd like for you to meet Lila, my new waitress."

"Well, small world, isn't it, Dan?"

Dread surged through him, and he knew the women he'd see before he even raised his head. His heart thumped loudly, and he felt sick as he glanced up at the familiar blond hair and curvaceous figure of the woman who stood over his table, smirking at him.

Would it never end? Would trouble follow him wherever he went?

Chapter 5

What was the use of even trying? Just when he'd begun to think maybe there really was a loving God up there somewhere, the same old garbage came raining down on his head. Dan let the door of the orphanage slam shut behind him and mounted his horse, slinging his medical bag over the saddle horn.

Sure, she'd allowed him to give medical treatment to the children, but he could tell she'd rather have had a witch doctor had one been available. She at least could have listened when he tried to tell her about Lila. But no, she stood there with that frozen look on her face and handed him his hat.

Pain shot through him. Pain he thought he had gotten rid of years ago. And all because Lila had decided to get her revenge. Apparently it was time to move on again. He had hoped it would be different this time. *Thanks a lot, God. If You're really up there, You're not doing much of a job taking care of my life.*

Elaine choked back tears as she peered through the lace curtains and watched Dan ride away. Uncertainty nibbled at her mind.

"Do you think you might have been a little bit too hard on him?"

Elaine turned and stared at Anika. "Too hard?"

"You might have listened to his side of it." Sympathy was written all over Anika's face.

Oh no, she'd heard it all.

"Sorry. I didn't mean to eavesdrop. The walls are thin."

"But, Anika, that woman came right out and told Etta he'd run out on her. After getting her. . .well, you know."

Her friend pursed her lips and looked thoughtful. "I know. I heard all about it. But who's to say she's telling the truth?"

"Oh, I don't know." Elaine dropped onto a settee. "But why would anyone lie about something like that? And besides, what about all the other rumors?"

"I thought you didn't believe the other rumors."

"Well, I didn't, but. . ."

Anika sat next to her and patted her hand. "Honey, it's not my place to give you advice. Especially when you didn't ask for it. But even criminals get a chance to defend themselves."

Elaine sat frozen as she watched Anika get up and leave the room. Was she really being unfair to Dan? Respectability was as much a part of Elaine as the color of her hair. So much so, that the very hint of a lack of virtue was enough to fill her with horror. Her decision to believe Dan when the rumors had first started had surprised her as much as anyone else. She'd had little experience with men and, even when she was a young girl, had never fancied herself in love. And now, the possibility that she'd been foolish in her defense of him, especially since the whole town knew she'd agreed to let him call on her, sent waves of embarrassment through her veins.

But what if he *was* innocent?

The banging noise wouldn't go away. Dan threw the pillow off his face and sat up, groaning. The pounding continued, but now he was awake enough to realize it came from the front door.

"Coming!" He pulled his pants on and limped into the front office, carrying his boots. As he yanked the front door open, Joshua Dillinger dropped his fist, which had obviously been ready to pound on the door again.

"I've got a miner in the wagon. He's unconscious and burning up with fever."

"Let's get him into the examining room." Dan followed the rancher to the wagon and looked at the man lying there. Immediately he recognized the sick miner from the hotel. They carried the limp figure inside and laid him on an examining table.

"How long has he been like this?" Dan ran a practiced eye

over the unconscious miner and stuck a thermometer into his mouth.

Dillinger swiped a hand through his hair. "I've no idea. I found him like this on my property early this morning. A pack-laden mule was grazing nearby. The miners have been filing across our land headed for the mountains all week. This one, obviously, didn't make it."

"His temperature's raging." Dan laid the thermometer down and opened the man's mouth with his fingers. He gazed at the white-coated tongue and red throat, then probed the man's neck. "I remember seeing him in the crowd around the general store one day. And he was staying at the hotel—which means others have been exposed." Dan spoke quietly, reflectively, to himself and was surprised when he heard Dillinger's voice.

"Exposed to what?" The man stood in the doorway to the outer office, frowning.

"I can't say for sure until I examine him more thoroughly, but I'm afraid it may be influenza." He dipped some water into a glass and managed to get a trickle down the man's throat.

"That's serious, isn't it?"

"It can be if left untreated. Hopefully we've caught it in time."

"But if it should become an epidemic?"

Dan's lips tightened, and as he spoke, he could hear the grimness in his own voice. "Let's hope it doesn't come to that."

"What are you going to do?"

Dan sat silently for a moment. What should he do first? He

made a sudden decision. "I'm going to get someone to stay with the patient while I go up in the hills and check for signs of the sickness among other miners."

"I wish I could stay, Doc, but I have pressing matters at the ranch."

"One of the women from the Indian camp helps me out occasionally. If you could stop by there on your way home, I'd appreciate it."

"Consider it done." The two men shook hands, and the rancher left.

Dan lifted the miner and placed him on a cot against the wall. He took a bottle from a cabinet in the corner and managed to get a spoonful of medicine down the man's throat, then dipped a cool cloth in water and washed the hot, red face.

Sighing, he spread a blanket over the man's body and stood. He washed his hands, then went into the main office. His packed suitcase, in the middle of the floor, caught his attention. He'd forgotten he planned to leave this morning. It seemed the right thing to do yesterday, but now, with a patient in the other room, his plans would have to wait. He carried the bag to his quarters and stowed it, then made a pot of strong coffee. It seemed as though he wouldn't get to run from his troubles this time. At least not yet.

When he rode into one of the miners' camps a couple of hours later, he found no sign of sickness. As he went from site to site, he breathed a sigh of relief as no more cases of influenza appeared. Perhaps it was just an isolated case.

He went back to town to discover the miner awake. His fever had broken and he appeared to be recovering. Perhaps he'd get to remove himself from his place of torment after all.

Elaine's face crossed his mind, and he hesitated. Maybe he wouldn't leave just yet. This time he had something to stay and fight for.

"Miss Elaine, wake up." The insistent voice penetrated Elaine's sleep-fogged brain, and she opened her eyes to see Jane bending over her bed.

"What is it, Jane? Have I overslept?" She yawned and looked at the girl, who still wore her nightdress with a shawl thrown over her shoulders.

"No, ma'am. It's only three o'clock. Two of the children are sick, miss. Mrs. Jacobson says you need to come now."

Wide-awake, Elaine got up and dressed quickly. When she got downstairs, she could hear coughing coming from the small infirmary. Martha Jacobson was bending over Rainsong, wiping her face with a wet cloth.

Elaine hurried to her side, glancing at the next cot where Grace was holding Pedro's hand as he moaned in his sleep. "What seems to be wrong with them?" She reached over and brushed the little girl's damp hair back from her forehead.

"I'm not sure," Martha answered. "They are running fevers and coughing. Maybe it's merely a summer cold. But I really think we need to send for the doctor and have him check them over." She glanced at Elaine with an apologetic little smile. "With George in Tucson picking up the new wagon, I'm afraid you'll have to go, dear."

A knot formed in Elaine's throat, and she forced herself to relax and swallow. Her heart sped up. *Stop it, Elaine. He is the only doctor in town. You can do this. For the children.*

Hastily twisting her hair up, she grabbed a shawl and headed down the dark street. As she neared the doctor's office, she heard voices raised in what sounded like an argument. Peering ahead in the darkness, she gasped. The young woman, Lila, stood with her arms tightly around Dan's neck.

His eyes met Elaine's, and he jerked away. "Elaine, this isn't what it looks like. I promise you."

The Lila creature cast an amused glance at Elaine. "Don't believe a word he says, honey. Trust me." With a laugh, she sauntered off down the dusty street toward the café.

Dan took Elaine's hand. "Please let me explain." The pleading in his voice made Elaine's heart race, and a sick feeling clutched at her stomach.

She jerked her hand away and stood stiffly, speaking through tightened teeth. "Dr. Murphy, what you do is of no concern to me. We have sick children in the infirmary who need your assistance." She turned and hurried toward the orphanage. As she neared the sheriff's office, she crossed the street and broke into a near run.

Before entering the orphanage, she brushed away the tears that flooded her eyes and spilled down her cheeks. This time

she had seen the truth with her own eyes. There was no denying now that the only man she'd ever fallen in love with was
a scoundrel.

Chapter 6

Dan sat by Pedro's bed and felt his pulse again. It was too fast—much too fast. He looked up at Mrs. Jacobson, who stood with a pan of water and some clean cloths. The worry on her face matched the concern on his.

"I think I've done all I can for now, Mrs. Jacobson. Keep the children cool and give them the medicine every four hours. Try to get clear liquid down them." He paused. "Pedro came and got me when the miner accosted Miss Elaine. Was Rainsong, by any chance, with him that day?"

"Yes, as a matter of fact, she was. I sent them to tell Elaine to add white thread to her list. Why?"

"One of the miners was ill. It's obvious they were exposed at that time." A sick feeling washed over him. "Has Elaine shown any symptoms?"

She shook her head slowly, frowning. "No, none that I'm aware of."

"Do you know where she is?" He intended to find out for

sure. Whether she wanted to see him or not.

"Probably in the kitchen. Or perhaps in the toddlers' room. She spends what time she can with Autumn."

He closed his bag and stood. "Thank you, ma'am. I'd better talk to her."

Elaine wasn't in the toddlers' room or the kitchen. He found her in the backyard hanging sheets out to dry. She looked both directions when she saw him as if searching for a way to escape.

"How are the children?" She averted her eyes and gazed at the railroad tracks as though watching an invisible train go by.

"About the same. I'm afraid it's influenza. One of the miners came down with it. He's doing better, but it's much more dangerous for children. You'll need to watch them carefully."

She nodded and bit her lip, then bent down and pulled another sheet from the basket at her feet.

"I believe they were exposed the day the mob was outside the general store."

"Oh no. They'd been sent with a message for me, but I didn't see them in the crowd." She concentrated on the sheet, two little furrows between her eyes.

"Have you had any symptoms? Sore throat, headache?"

"No."

"Elaine, please look at me."

She lifted her face and looked straight into his eyes. The pain and accusation he saw there overwhelmed him. She cared about him. But she didn't trust him. Well, why should she? The evidence against him was pretty strong.

"Listen. I couldn't sleep last night. I went outside to get some air. Lila was there before I knew it. She'd been drinking. She tried to talk me into. . .well, never mind. The next thing I knew, she had thrown her arms around my neck. That's when I saw you. I know it looked bad, but I had nothing to do with it."

A shadow of doubt crossed her face, then straightening her shoulders, she glared at him. "Well, perhaps she loves you. Perhaps she's desperate for her child's father to marry her. Although I don't know why any woman would want a scalawag who walked out on her when she was—" She stopped and blushed.

"I'm not her baby's father, Elaine."

"Oh, then why would she say it's you?" She placed her tiny hands on her hips and tapped her foot on the ground.

"Because she hates me and wants revenge."

A startled look crossed her face. "Revenge for what? Walking out on her?"

Dan sighed. "No. We never were together. She wanted a relationship. I didn't. So she drifted on to someone else. She hates me because I killed her lover in a gunfight." There. He'd said it. She'd turn and run now. But at least it would be for the truth.

Her mouth opened slightly, and his eyes were drawn to her soft lips. Oh, how tempting to take her in his arms and claim those lips as his own.

Gasping, she drew back. Apparently she'd read his expression too well.

"So you're a cold-blooded killer? You killed the man out of jealousy?" Incredulity was written on her face.

Okay, so maybe it wasn't the passion in his eyes that had caused her to gasp.

"No, Elaine. It wasn't like that. It's a long story. But I was protecting someone when I shot the man."

"Mm-hm. Well, Dr. Murphy, I'd say that's a pretty wild story, and it's your word against hers. Since she has a little baby as evidence, and I can't imagine anyone claiming a killer as her child's father, I'd say her story rings a lot truer than yours." She picked up the empty basket and headed for the house.

"Elaine, please send for me if you have any sign of illness."

Tossing her head, she went in and shut the door firmly behind her.

Dan inhaled and blew out a loud breath. He didn't know what it would take to convince her of his innocence, but he'd be blamed if he'd give up trying.

Elaine straightened and wiped her sleeve across her perspiring face. She'd been bending over the ironing board longer than she wanted to think about, and the muscles in her back and shoulders were screaming at her. With sick children in the house, everyone had a little more work to do. She put the iron away and took the stack of shirts and dresses to the dormitories.

Three days after the children became ill, they still weren't over the sickness. Elaine had managed to avoid Dan each time he'd come to check on them. He had stressed extreme cleanliness, and they had complied, boiling everything they used and scrubbing their hands with strong lye soap dozens of times a day. Thankfully none of the other children were showing symptoms, but several miners and a few of the townspeople were ill. Dan had told India and Joshua that the sickness was definitely some strain of influenza and was reaching epidemic proportions.

That wasn't the only thing India had told her. In no uncertain terms, she'd informed Elaine that her husband believed totally in the doctor's innocence, and many of the townspeople were also rethinking their original position on the subject. Even Etta, who had championed the young woman in the beginning, was starting to be disenchanted with her. In fact, she had told Jody that if it weren't for the baby, she'd send the girl packing.

Elaine sighed. She dared not get her hopes up again. And besides, if he was innocent, he'd probably never forgive her. She'd been pretty hard on him.

Deep in her thoughts, she headed down the hall toward the kitchen. Just as she reached the kitchen door, Dan walked out, almost running into her.

She drew in a sharp breath and stammered, "I d—didn't see you c—come in."

"Apparently not, or you'd have hidden again." A sad smile appeared on his lips.

"Excuse me? I most certainly have not been hiding from you." She could feel her cheeks flaming. A dead giveaway.

He leaned against the door frame, and the gold in his eyes flickered as he looked at her. "You don't need to hide from me, Elaine. I won't force my attentions on you."

Elaine's heart raced as she watched him walk away and out the front door. She went into the kitchen and sank into a chair at the table.

Carla looked up from the dishpan. Removing her dripping hands, she dried them on a white cloth. "Miss Elaine, I think you need a cup of strong coffee. You've been going like a wildfire all day."

"Thanks, that sounds wonderful." She leaned against the tall ladder back of the chair and watched the wiry cook as she poured strong, black coffee and set the steaming mug on the table in front of her. Elaine added sugar and cream, then inhaled gratefully as she lifted the mug to her lips and let the sweet, milky liquid trickle down her throat.

"Oh, that's heavenly. Who would think coffee could be so refreshing on a hot day like this?"

"Hmm, you need to get off those feet more often. I see you scurrying all around the place day and night."

"Well, we all have to do our part. The volunteers are working hard, too." In fact, India and several of the ladies from the church had helped nearly every day. They couldn't always stay long because of other responsibilities, but they did what they could. Anika and Jody had come at night a couple of times and promised to help out on the weekend if the children were still ill. Elaine breathed a prayer of thanks for her friends.

She stood and stretched. "I'll send Mary and Charlene in to help with supper. They should be finished with their studies by now."

After locating the girls and sending them to the kitchen, she headed to the toddlers' room.

Children in varying stages of walking and running tripped around the room. One little boy stood firmly and let out a yell as another child attempted to take a wooden horse from his hands. Ellen, one of the volunteers, settled the argument by distracting both children with other toys. Autumn lay in her crib with her arm around a stuffed bear and her thumb in her mouth.

"How in the world does she sleep with all this noise going on?"

Ellen shook her head. "I was wondering the same thing. She must have been tired. She's been asleep since right after lunch. She's usually the first one up after nap time."

Elaine walked over to Autumn's crib and placed her hand on the soft curls. She didn't feel hot. Ellen was probably right. The child was merely tired. Still, Elaine determined to check on her later to make sure. As tiny as she was, influenza could be especially dangerous.

Dan opened a can of beans and poured them into a bowl. He wasn't too excited about eating cold beans, but he didn't want to build a fire on a hot day like this. He thought longingly of Etta's hot bread and beef stew. She always had stew on Tuesdays. He crumbled a piece of two-day-old corn bread into the beans and tossed in some stewed tomatoes a patient had given him for payment. Cutting some onion into the mix, he sat at the table and tried to enjoy his meal. Actually, it wasn't bad.

I'll bet Elaine's a good cook. Dan threw his spoon down. Couldn't he do anything without thinking about Elaine? Her blue eyes appeared in his dreams. The sound of her laughter would ring out across the street when he went outside. He'd turn only to find some other woman laughing outside the dress shop or walking a child. Often he'd feel a wave of anger that anyone should dare to have Elaine's laugh. Then he'd direct the anger at himself for being such a fool.

He scraped his bowl, then washed and dried it and the spoon and put them away. He went outside and stood on the weathered board sidewalk. The air was beginning to cool. Maybe he'd take a walk.

"Doc! Doc!" Startled, Dan looked down the street. Charlie and Ray came up the street in a dead run. This didn't look good. He met them halfway down the block.

"What's wrong?" He grabbed each boy by an arm as they skidded to a stop.

"Miss Elaine says come fast." Ray gasped and choked out the words. "That baby, Autumn. . .she's been taken with the sickness."

Chapter 7

B ut why can't we help? We ain't tainted, you know." The plump redhead stood outside the door wringing her hands, frustration and indignation written all over her face. Her companion stood quietly, with her head down.

Elaine had never experienced embarrassment the way she did at this moment. She knew the women were from the saloon. What in the world should she do? With eight sick children and several of the staff down sick, she desperately needed the help. But these creatures? Surely not. On the other hand, to send them away would be depriving the exhausted staff and volunteers of extra helping hands.

"Look, lady, I know you think we're trash. But we heard Baby was sick, and we're the ones raised her, you know. Mary here was the closest thing to a mama the little one had. Please, if you'd at least let us see her for a minute."

Elaine glanced at Mary, who lifted soft brown eyes filled with pleading. She couldn't have been more than eighteen or nineteen, and beneath the paint, Elaine could detect a vulnerability she wouldn't have expected to see in a saloon girl.

Surprising herself, she pulled the door open wider and motioned them in. She hardly knew why and knew even less what to say to the two. Should she offer them chairs?

She ran the back of her hand across her forehead and felt herself sway. A pair of firm hands grasped her arms and lowered her to the settee.

"Mary, find someone and fetch some water. Honey, stay with me, now. Don't faint."

Elaine could hear the words but couldn't find the voice to answer. The room was spinning wildly, and she closed her eyes and gave in to the darkness.

"Elaine, wake up."

Someone was shaking her. She wanted to tell the person to stop but didn't have the strength to form the words.

"Elaine, can you speak?" She recognized Jody's voice, filled with worry.

She opened her lips and breathed. "Jody? What happened?"

"You fainted. That's what." Relief filled her friend's voice. "Nearly scared me to death. I thought it was influenza."

Fear clutched her. She couldn't be sick. The children needed her.

"It's not, is it?"

"I don't think so. You don't have any of the symptoms.

Seems like plain old exhaustion to me." Jody stooped beside her and patted her hand. "But just to be sure, we sent for Dr. Murphy."

Elaine tried to sit up, but Jody pushed her back down. "Don't even think about it until the doctor gets here."

"But, Jody, I don't want to see him."

"Well, that's too bad, because you're going to." She stood and looked down at Elaine. "You know, you're just about the only one in town who still believes the rumors about Dan Murphy. Don't you think it's about time to consider the possibility that he may be innocent?"

Elaine pushed herself up and glared at her friend. "I have work to do. Let me up."

"Sorry," Jody said with a triumphant grin. "Martha says you're not to do anything till the doctor looks you over."

Elaine jerked her head around, and her gaze fell on the two women from the saloon. They were standing in the corner of the hallway self-consciously but looked at her with sympathy. Whatever was she going to do about them?

The door opened and Dan burst in. His eyes widened at the sight of the saloon women, but when he saw Elaine, he hurried over to her. Before she had a chance to protest, he lifted her into his arms and started up the stairs.

Unfamiliar feelings coursed through Elaine. Her skin felt hot where his hands gripped her arm, and the scent of his cologne made her head reel. She snapped to herself. "What are you doing? Put me down."

"You need to lie down while I make sure you're not ill. Miss McMillan, will you come with us and help her get into bed?"

"I'd be more than happy to, Doctor." Was that a tinge of glee in Jody's voice? Oh, would she get an earful when Elaine was strong enough to deliver it.

An hour later, Elaine lay propped up on soft pillows while her friend fed her sips of soup. "For heaven's sake, Jody, I can feed myself."

"Dr. Murphy said you're not to do anything until morning." Jody held the spoon up to Elaine's lips.

"Well, he didn't mean I have to be fed like a baby. Give me that spoon."

Jody laughed and relinquished the utensil. "Okay, I'll let up. But promise me you'll stay in bed until morning. I'm going to stay overnight so you can rest."

"What about church? Who's going to teach your Sunday school class?"

"They've canceled church tomorrow due to so much sickness. Dr. Murphy said there shouldn't be any more public gatherings than are absolutely necessary."

"But, Jody, I'm needed to help."

"Well, we have two new volunteers."

"Really? Who?" At the look on Jody's face, she knew. "Not those—"

Jody interrupted her friend. "Mr. Jacobson says we need everyone who is willing to help. After the initial shock, Martha agreed." A peculiar expression crossed Jody's face. "Dr. Murphy said not to worry. They don't bite."

Elaine pressed her lips together. "He would."

Jody sighed and shook her head. "You're making a mistake, Elaine. Dr. Murphy is an honorable man."

Pain jabbed at Elaine's stomach. She pushed the tray away and turned over onto her side. Jody's footsteps whispered across the floor, and Elaine heard the door shut softly as her friend left the room.

Thoughts whirled around in her mind like fireflies, darting here then there. So the whole town was coming around to Dan's side? But they'd all been just as adamant before that he was guilty, so who was to say they were right about his innocence? Did she dare believe in him?

She tossed her head back and forth in an attempt to clear the thoughts away. A pair of gold-flecked eyes made their way into her mind. "Oh, go away and leave me alone." She crammed a pillow down over her head, but somehow she knew those eyes would find her there, too.

Dan chuckled to himself as he rode up the rocky mountain path. What a sight it had been to see Lottie and Mary working side by side with the upstanding ladies of the town. He cut the laughter short and frowned. He wondered how often those upstanding ladies stopped to scrub their hands to make sure something didn't rub off on them. Well, he hoped something would rub off. Maybe something like Lottie's full-hearted kindness or Mary's sweet compassion. Dan sighed. It wasn't that he thought their lifestyle was right. The Lord knew he didn't think that. But he knew that most of them had become trapped by one thing or another and would give anything to be able to settle down and live decently and respectably.

He didn't know Mary's story, but Lottie had told him her father had sold her when she was thirteen. She'd been beaten and almost killed before she lost her will to fight. It didn't take long after that for her to completely give up any thought of things changing for the better.

It was another "Lottie" he'd been protecting when he killed Lila's lover. Dan had been walking by a saloon on the outskirts of San Francisco when a scream pierced the air. He took the outside stairs two at a time and crashed through the door just in time to see Tom Furley's fist land on Annie Carter's face, causing blood to gush from a two-inch gash. The ensuing fight had ended in Furley pulling his gun. Dan drew his own and fired before Furley had a chance to shoot.

He'd lived with the guilt ever since. Maybe he could have talked the drunken man into putting the gun away. Dan sighed. He'd never know. All he knew was he hadn't worn a holster since. Like Lottie, he just wanted to settle down and live a decent, God-fearing life. But trouble seemed to find him wherever he went. People judged harshly. Even then, when he'd saved the woman's life, folks pointed fingers and raised their eyebrows. And Lila had vowed to get revenge. Dan supposed it was easier to turn her rage on him than on the lover who'd betrayed her.

After searching for an hour, Dan found another miner down with the sickness and managed to get him into town with the help of the man's friend.

They'd turned the hotel into a makeshift hospital for the miners and others who had no one to care for them in their sickness.

Finally, when he'd treated the last sick miner and everyone was as comfortable as possible, he headed home to get a couple of hours of sleep. If he didn't get some rest, he wouldn't be any good to anyone.

Sun was streaming through his window when he awoke. He jumped up and quickly washed up, not bothering to heat the water. After he was dressed, he headed out the door. His stomach felt hollow, and after a moment's hesitation, he turned and walked to the café. Lila or no Lila, he was stopping for a hot breakfast.

The café was locked, and a CLOSED sign hung on the door. Puzzled, Dan went around to the back entrance and knocked. After a moment, he heard footsteps and muted coughing. The door opened. Etta stood holding Lila's baby. Lines of tiredness crossed her face.

"Dan, I'm so glad you're here. I couldn't leave the baby and didn't want to take him out with all the sickness. But I don't know how much worse it would be. His mama's down with something. I think it's this influenza that's going around. I've been taking care of her the best I can, but. . ."

Another fit of coughing erupted from the cot across the room, where Lila lay writhing and moaning. When Dan touched her face, the heat was almost enough to burn his hand.

He looked at Etta. "Are you or the child sick?"

"No, thank the good Lord." She shook her head. "What can we do, Doc? Can you move her to the hotel?"

Dan frowned. The hotel was full of sick miners. He hated to take a woman there. Even Lila.

"Are you willing to take care of the infant until Lila's well?"

"Sure. Got nothing else to do. No sense in opening up. People are scared to leave their houses anyway."

"Give me a few minutes to check with the Jacobsons. Since the sickness is already there anyway, maybe they'll agree to care for one more. I don't know where they'll put her, but a pallet on the floor would be better than the hotel right now."

Elaine watched as Dan carried Lila into the house. She'd only seen the woman once, and it had been dark, but she tried to restrain her curiosity. What did she care what the woman looked like?

She led the way to the small visitors' room where three cots had been set up. One of the staff members lay on one of them, her small form still as death.

Elaine pulled down the blanket on one of the cots and watched as Dan placed the woman gently between clean white sheets. He checked her pulse, then straightened up and turned to the woman on the other cot. After checking her vital signs, he looked at Elaine.

"Thank you for taking Lila in. I wouldn't have liked to leave her around the baby any longer. He's already been exposed to the influenza, and at his young age, he'll have little chance to survive if he catches it. We can only pray he hasn't already."

Elaine stood frozen, unable to speak. Between the extreme tiredness and the emotional stress of being in Dan's presence, she was feeling dizzy again.

"Elaine, are you all right?"

Her heart leapt at the concern in his voice. "I'm fine. I'm just tired." She pulled at the button on her throat. "Of course, it was the Jacobsons' decision to allow her to stay here. But I'd like to think I wouldn't turn a sick woman away from the door."

A tender look crossed Dan's face, and he placed his thumb on her chin, turning her face up so that she had to look at him. "Of course you wouldn't, Lainey. I know that."

Tears filled her eyes and threatened to overflow. Blinking, she cleared her throat and clasped her hands behind her back before she could make a fool of herself by flinging herself into his arms. The thought warmed her cheeks, and she cleared her throat again. "Would you like to check on the other patients while you're here?"

He looked at her silently for a moment, tenderness and yearning in his gaze, then a veil seemed to cover his expression. "Yes. Have you seen any improvement in anyone?"

A twinge of disappointment gripped her. Then she firmed

her chin. "Rainsong doesn't seem as feverish today. But she still can't keep any nourishment down."

Side by side they walked to the infirmary, where three people kept around-the-clock vigil with at least one staff person in the room at all times. In addition to Rainsong and Pedro, nine more patients tossed restlessly in the infirmary, including three toddlers and one infant.

Elaine and Dan walked over to the crib near the window. Little Autumn lay still and silent.

Mary sat by her side, constantly dipping cloths into cool water and sponging the child's hands, arms, and legs. She looked up at Dan as he and Elaine stopped by the crib. Her eyes were brimming over. "Please, Doc, don't let Baby die."

Chapter 8

The night breeze fluttered the lace shawl that lay across Elaine's shoulders and caressed the skin at her neck. She shivered, and a sigh of pleasure escaped her lips. Fifteen minutes had passed, and she knew she had to get back inside, but the thought of facing the stifling heat and the smells of sickness inside the orphanage was almost more than she could bear.

At least the epidemic seemed to be dissipating. There had been no new cases for the past few days, and some of the earlier victims were showing signs of improvement. Thankfully they hadn't lost anyone. Dan had said Rainsong and Pedro should be well enough to leave the infirmary in another day or so. Autumn was also getting better, much to Mary's delight—although she still had to be practically hauled away from the child's bedside to get a few hours' sleep each day.

Elaine inhaled deeply and attempted to rein in her thoughts. Her intention had been to spend a few moments mentally preparing for the chores that must be done before she could retire for the night. Her thoughts, however, had taken on a mind of their own, and no matter where she tried to guide them, they skipped and danced right back to Dan Murphy. She had stopped denying, at least to herself, her feelings for the handsome doctor. But she was so ashamed of herself for believing all the rumors that she couldn't bring herself to spend any more time than necessary in his presence.

How could I have thought he was capable of such deeds? He's proven his character over and over again.

"Elaine! Come quickly!"

At the sound of Martha's frantic cry, Elaine rushed into the house and down the hall to the infirmary. *Lord, please don't let it be a new case of sickness.*

The fear on Martha's face caused Elaine's heart to race.

"What is it? What's wrong?" The sound of her own voice matched the expression on Martha's face.

"Lila's taken a turn for the worse. I've sent for Dr. Murphy, but I need you to sit with her until he arrives." She paused and inhaled deeply. "It's really bad. I don't know if she'll make it."

As Elaine's hand rested on Lila's face a few minutes later, she wasn't sure either. The young woman's skin was hot and as dry as parchment. She moaned and thrashed from side to side. Suddenly the thrashing stopped, and she grew still.

"Please, Lord, no. Don't let her die without knowing You." Elaine hardly knew she was praying aloud. She leaned her head down to Lila's chest and breathed a sigh of relief when she detected a heartbeat. "Heavenly Father, forgive me. I've been so bitter toward this woman, I haven't even prayed for her. I don't know her heart, but You do." She sobbed the last few words. "If you'll give me another chance, I'll tell her about You."

A gentle hand touched Elaine's shoulder, and she glanced up to find Dan gazing tenderly at her. She stood and moved aside so that he could attend to Lila.

"Elaine, will you hold the lamp close so I can get a better look at her throat and eyes?"

She complied, all the while watching Dan's hands as he examined his patient. Such strong hands, and yet so gentle.

Finally, Dan stood and washed his hands in the clean water one of the staff had brought, then turned to Elaine and motioned her out into the hall. "Continue with the medicine and keep her as comfortable as possible. Try to get water down her. At this point, that's about all we can do."

"Do you think—" Elaine stopped, unable to voice her fear.

Dan rubbed his eyes and took a deep breath.

He's exhausted. He needs to get some rest.

"I really don't know. Her condition is poor, but she has a couple of things going for her. She's a strong woman. And she has you to pray for her." He looked at Elaine intently, searching her face. "Take care of yourself. Get plenty of nourishing food and make sure you don't overtire yourself." He reached down and brushed back a strand of hair that had fallen across her cheek.

Elaine closed her eyes and sighed. If only she could stand

here like this forever. Suddenly she felt his lips brush against her forehead. Startled, she opened her eyes. The love in his eyes almost took her breath away. With sudden resolve, she decided it was time to let him know she trusted him.

"Dan, I'm so sorry for my attitude lately. I was terribly confused. I shouldn't have condemned you the way I did."

A look of tenderness crossed his face. "Shh. It's okay. I know things looked bad. I don't blame you."

She bit her lip, and her eyes filled with tears. "I want you to know I believe in you. You're a good man, and I know you're innocent."

The gold in his eyes flickered, and his smile was warm. "Thank you. You don't know how happy it makes me to hear you say that. I could handle everyone's doubts but yours."

Elaine sat and stitched as she watched over Lila. She laid the small shirt she was mending aside and reached over to feel the young woman's forehead. The skin was cool and moist to Elaine's touch. *Thank You, Lord.*

"Could I have some w—water, please?" Lila's cracked voice wasn't much more than a whisper, but Elaine's heart jumped with excitement.

"Of course you can." Elaine poured a little bit of water from the pitcher on the bedside table. "Here, let me lift your head a little."

Lila took a few sips, then lay back on the pillow. Her eyes

still appeared tired as she looked up at Elaine. "I could hear you praying for me." Her words held a measure of wonder. "Why would you care if I died?"

Elaine struggled to find the right words. "I just couldn't bear the thought of you dying. Especially when I wasn't sure if you even knew about Jesus."

"I do." Her voice seemed stronger now. "My mother took me to church when I was little. I accepted Jesus when I was thirteen." She stopped speaking and took several breaths before continuing. "Mama died of the typhus a few months later. I guess I blamed God. My granny tried to keep me straight, but I was so bitter. By the time I was sixteen, I'd just gone wild, I guess."

"You know God will forgive you, Lila. You can start over."

"I know. I'm a little scared at the thought of what I'll do with my life, but I'm going to give it back to God right now and ask Him to help me."

Lila closed her eyes, and after a few moments, Elaine thought she'd gone to sleep. But she stirred and her eyes opened slightly. "All that stuff about Dan wasn't true. We never were together."

"I know." Elaine smiled. "But thank you for telling me."

It was over. Finally. Dan yanked off his boots and fell across the bed, not even feeling the wrinkles in the rumpled sheets. He was going to sleep the rest of the day and all night. Then he'd get cleaned up and go have a long talk with a certain auburn-haired woman.

Dan and Elaine stood side by side and watched as the train pulled out of the station. They stood silently until the last car was out of sight.

"Do you think they'll be okay?" Elaine squinted, trying to see the caboose in the distance.

"I think they'll do marvelously."

"Lila showed me her grandmother's letter. She sounded so happy and excited to see her first great-grandchild." Elaine frowned. "Of course, Lila did lie to her and tell her she was a widow."

Dan laughed. "Well, she hasn't been back with God for long. Give her time."

The real surprise was Mary. During Lila's convalescence, the two young women had become friends, and Lila had led Mary to the Lord. Then, to be sure her friend didn't go back into a life of sin, she'd insisted on taking Mary home with her.

"I wonder how Lila's grandmother will react to Mary."

"Well, my dear, that's where you come in. Pray. A lot." He took her hand and placed it in the crook of his arm, gently leading her away from the empty platform.

"I will, Dan. I promise I will. And for Lottie, too. She has such a big heart and worked so hard to help the children." She felt tears rise to the back of her throat. "Now she's right back at the saloon. I had so hoped. . ."

A shadow crossed his face. "I know. I did, too. But remember, as they say, Rome wasn't built in a day. And now, Miss Lainey, what's this I hear about a Fourth of July picnic?"

She started at his sudden change of subject. "Oh yes, we have one every year. It's so much fun, Dan. You'll have to be sure and attend."

He chuckled, and she looked up into his eyes. Oh, those gold-flecked eyes.

"Yes, of course I intend to go. But I meant would you do me the honor of attending the event with me?"

Elaine's breath caught in her throat. She had begun to think she'd imagined his interest in her. In the weeks since the end of the epidemic, he'd not spoken of anything personal. In fact, he'd only come to the orphanage a couple of times a week to check on the children. But now his eyes seemed to burn into hers.

Oh, stop it, Elaine. There you go again, imagining things. He's just being friendly.

Realizing he was waiting for an answer, she swallowed. Well, she had planned to go to the picnic anyway. But she couldn't let him think she was expecting anything but friendship.

"That would be nice, Dr. Murphy. Thank you for asking me."

He threw back his head and laughed.

Now why is he laughing?

Chapter 9

Dan knew he needed to tell Elaine about his past. He'd imagined it dozens of times, each time changing the words and location. In one scenario, she looked at him tenderly with tear-filled eyes and assured him it didn't matter a bit. She was only sorry he'd had to endure so much. Then, in another, a look of disgust crossed her face and she turned and ran away from him.

Night after night he'd tossed and turned, weighing the cost of telling her. And tonight was no different. He knew, before their relationship could go any further, he had to be honest with her. If he asked her to marry him, and that was his intention, she had the right to make a decision based on the full knowledge of who he was.

Groaning, Dan turned over and sat up on the side of his bed. He lit the lamp on his bedside table and picked up his watch. He groaned again and flung himself back onto the bed. Four in the morning—another sleepless night.

"So, Elaine, dear, who will be escorting you to the picnic?" Mrs. Granger's lips tilted in a teasing smile as she added a spool of white thread to Elaine's sack.

Elaine blushed and tried to concentrate on the money she was counting out. "Why would you think anyone is escorting me? I usually walk over with the children and staff." There. She hadn't actually lied.

"Mm-hm. A number of things don't seem to be as 'usual' lately, do they, now?"

"Mrs. Granger, really. . ."

"Oh, all right, then. I'll stop teasing. But everyone knows you and the doc are sparking."

"Wh–what?" Elaine almost dropped her reticule. Grasping it, she yanked the strings tightly.

"Well, there's no shame in being courted, you know. And personally, I think it's about time you two continued what you started a couple of months ago."

Elaine mumbled good-bye and left with her purchases. How mortifying. Was the whole town talking about her and the doctor? Because other than being kind and attentive, he certainly hadn't made any declarations of affection toward her. True, he'd asked to court her at one time, but that was before Lila came to town and the rumors got so bad. Then the epidemic hit right afterward.

Early this morning he'd dropped some medicine off at the

orphanage for one of the children, and he'd asked if he could come over tonight to talk to her. Maybe he wanted to tell her he'd made a mistake when he'd asked to court her. At the thought, a knot formed in Elaine's stomach.

"Elaine! What's wrong with you? I've called your name twice."

Startled, Elaine looked up to see Anika standing in the doorway of the office she shared with her husband.

"Sorry, I didn't realize I was here. I guess I was daydreaming."

"Hmm. Do you have time to walk over to the café with me? I was just about to take a break."

"I'm afraid not. I told Martha I'd start the ironing this morning. We did laundry yesterday, so there's a lot." Elaine puckered her forehead and bit her bottom lip. "Oh, fiddlesticks. Maybe I will go with you. A few minutes won't hurt."

The two walked in perfect step, their heels clacking against the boards. As they turned into Etta's place, the smell of coffee and fresh-baked pastries assailed Elaine's senses.

They found a table near a window and sat facing each other.

Anika groaned. "Etta's baking is wonderful for the palate but murder for the waistline."

"Like you have anything to worry about." Elaine grinned at her friend, whose statuesque form was the envy of just about every woman in Cactus Corner.

"Well, I have to be careful not to get too sure of myself. You know how trim May Johnson was, and she's big as a cow since she had her baby."

"Anika! You don't mean you're—"

Anika glanced at her and laughed. "No, silly. But we do plan to have a family someday."

Elaine felt her face go hot. "Oh. Well, we shouldn't talk about such things."

"Excuse me if I offended your maidenly ears," Anika teased.

Elaine stood, her hand knocking over the saltcellar. Fumbling, she brushed the spilled granules off the cloth.

"Anika, I really should go on home. I'd forgotten I have to help Rainsong with her arithmetic before I can do the ironing." Elaine rushed out, feeling a twinge of remorse at the hurt and bewildered look on her friend's face. But she couldn't take the teasing and banter today. Not until she knew what was going on with Dan.

Dan and Elaine stood in the moonlight and listened to the night sounds. He reached over and took her hand. From their position on the stone patio behind the orphanage, they gazed out across the desert.

An ache began in the depths of Elaine's being at the sweetness of the moment. *Father, whatever happens next, no matter what Dan says, let me remember this sweetness.*

When she knew she couldn't bear another moment, she glanced up at him. "Whatever it is, Dan, you can tell me."

A sound between a sob and a groan escaped from his throat.

He raised her hand to his lips, then with a sigh released it and let it fall to her side.

"I know you've questioned my championing of the women who work at the saloon. I don't blame you. Maybe it's not the wisest course to take. It surely hasn't done my social life much good in the past."

He looked down into her eyes, and she could see the pain in his.

"Until I was five, I lived with my mother in a room above a saloon. She worked there, you see."

Elaine blinked, trying to absorb his meaning. "She was a cleaning lady?"

"No, a saloon girl."

A shock passed through her body, but Elaine took a deep breath and steeled herself against whatever might be coming next.

"I grew up being bounced on the knees of gamblers, drunks, and women of questionable morals and had no idea it was not an ordinary life for a child." Dan ran a hand over his face. "To this day, I don't know why my mother was reduced to such a state. I only know she was an angel to one small boy. She cared for me, protected me, and loved me. When I was five years old, she was killed. She'd picked me up to get me out of harm's way but never made it to the stairs. When the bullet hit her, she fell with me in her arms."

He stopped, and Elaine knew from the horror on his face he was reliving the moment from the eyes of that small child.

The blood rushed from her face, and she fought the dizziness that tried to overcome her. She couldn't faint. Not now. Dan was hurting. She could see the pain written all over his face, feel it in the trembling of his body.

She reached up and touched his cheek. "How horrible for you. I'm so sorry, Dan. What happened to you after that?"

"I was placed in an orphanage in a nearby city. Years later, when I was eighteen, I went back to try to find out more about my mother and why she was killed, but no one remembered her. Or if people did, they wouldn't admit it. I couldn't even find her grave."

He took her hand, which still rested on his cheek. "I'm not telling you these things to get your sympathy, Elaine. I want you to know why I am who I am."

He led her to a small bench at the back of the house, and they sat down.

"A benefactor, knowing my desire to study medicine, paid my way to medical college. I threw myself into my studies, and my benefactor, an established physician, took me in. Over the next eight years, I became quite successful. Then a typhoid fever epidemic hit the city. We eventually got it under control, but there were many deaths. Most of them on the docks and in the saloons. You see, the upstanding folks had to be taken care of first. When I realized what was happening, I headed down there, but it was too late. I did what I could but saved very few. One girl, not more than sixteen, died in my arms. I'll never forget the look of fear on her face."

He leaned back and closed his eyes, and Elaine thought her heart would break for him. She wanted to take him in her arms and comfort him, but somehow she knew his story wasn't over.

He opened his eyes and sat up straight. "After that, I left the city and opened up a practice in a small town. But before long, some of the good ladies there decided I was worthless and had no morals because I tried to help the unfortunates in the saloons. I realized some of them were there by choice, but most weren't. Besides, I had taken an oath. Of course, my practice dropped off, and I couldn't make a living, so I headed out to another town. And then another. But trouble followed me everywhere I went. I'm so tired of it all. I want respectability so badly. But I just can't seem to stay out of trouble."

"But, Dan, you haven't done anything wrong." Surprise filled Elaine as the words left her mouth. She really meant them.

"Do you mean that, Elaine? You're not shocked?"

"I probably would have been two months ago. God has changed me, Dan. I thought I had compassion before, but I know now the compassion I had was conditional. It took working with Mary and Lottie and being around Lila to show me the truth about myself."

Dan reached over and traced his thumb along her jawline and looked into her eyes, searching. Elaine looked back without trying to hide her feelings from him.

"Lainey." The word was only a whisper. He touched her face, caressing her cheek, and raised her hand to his lips.

When he lifted his head, Elaine realized that she was trembling from head to toe.

"Lainey, my Lainey. This isn't the moment for the question I want to ask you. You have the right to think over the things I've told you. And maybe you'll decide I'm not the man you want to give your heart to—the man you'd want to be a father to your children."

He bent down and kissed the top of her head. "I love you. Whatever you decide, I'll accept and understand."

Dan brought the buggy to a stop in front of the orphanage and turned to Elaine.

"It's been a wonderful day, hasn't it?"

"Yes, but I'm afraid you and I were perhaps the main attraction. I hope you weren't bothered by all the stares and knowing grins." Elaine shook her head at the memory. India and Anika had been the worst, but even Jody had done her share—the traitor.

He threw back his head and laughed. "Not at all. I rather enjoyed it."

She gave him a sidewise glance. "You would, you rogue." She smiled to soften the words. "It seems you've been accepted as a full-fledged upstanding member of the town."

He laughed again. "Yes, well, now if it only stays that way. I hope you didn't mind leaving while the fireworks were still going on."

"No, I was getting a little tired. And anyway, we can still see and hear them from here." She smiled secretly. She was pretty sure she knew why he'd suggested they leave early.

He jumped down and came around to help her out, and they walked hand in hand around the building and sat on the bench on the stone patio.

He turned to face her and looked intently into her eyes.

This is it. Oh God, please let this be it.

Before she knew what was happening, he'd slipped off the bench and knelt in front of her. Her heart fluttered wildly. *Yes, this is it. It has to be.*

"Elaine, will you do me the honor of becoming my wife?"

She gazed into his gold-flecked eyes, her mind racing as wildly as her heart. Could this really be happening to her? Surely she must be dreaming. But the hand that held hers was warm and strong. Yes, it was a dream. A wonderful dream come true.

"Yes, Dan. With all my heart, I will." Her words were strong, true, and sure.

Joy washed over his face. He examined her face as though wanting to make sure she'd really said yes. Then with a cry of jubilation, he jumped up and pulled her to her feet.

"My darling." His voice shook with emotion as he drew her closely to him. "I'll spend the rest of my life making you happy."

He lowered his head, and she lifted her face to his, eager, with joy in her heart. And as his lips claimed hers, she could hear the fireworks in the distance.

Or maybe it wasn't the fireworks at all.

FRANCES DEVINE

Frances grew up in the great state of Texas, where she wrote her first story at the age of nine. She moved to Southwest Missouri more than twenty years ago and fell in love with the hills, the fall colors, and Silver Dollar City. Frances has always loved to read and considers herself blessed to have the opportunity to write in one of her favorite genres, historical romance. She is the mother of seven adult children and has fourteen wonderful grandchildren.

Frances is happy to hear from her fans. Email her at fd1440writes@aol.com.

The Spinster and the Tycoon

by Vickie McDonough

Defend the poor and fatherless:
do justice to the afflicted and needy.

PSALM 82:3

Chapter 1

Autumn 1895

P lease, Lord, let someone other than Elmer buy my box dinner this year." Jody McMillan sighed and set the ACME Paperworks box that held her fried chicken meal on the table in her boardinghouse room and adjusted the frilly bow. She'd picked the blue gingham ribbon on purpose, hoping to entice someone other than her boss, Elmer Brody, to bid on her meal. Everyone in Cactus Corner knew by his trademark plaid flannel shirts that Elmer loved red.

She smiled to herself. In a moment of unabashed orneri-ness, she had even affixed a little bird that had fallen off her favorite hat to the bow, because her boss had hated birds ever since he was seven, when he'd been pecked by a crow. Every box social, her boss had purchased her dinner, and this year she was determined to dine with someone else.

She peeked out the window, delighted to see that a large

crowd had gathered in the churchyard. A flash of red snagged her attention, and she dropped the curtain as if she'd been burned by a hot coal.

Elmer owned Brody Freight Line, and his marriage proposals were as regular as his freight deliveries. She had no intention of ever saying yes to him. If he continued asking her to marry him, she just might have to seek other employment. Even though the town was growing because of a recent copper strike, few people in Cactus Corner had need for a female bookkeeper.

Jody sighed, picked up her decorated container, and covered it with a towel. If she could keep Elmer from seeing it, just perhaps she could dine with some other lonely bachelor.

She closed the door to her room at the boardinghouse and hurried down the hall, her shoes clicking on the shiny oak floor. If she was the last to arrive, Elmer would for sure notice which box was hers.

Couples moseyed arm in arm toward the church. Adolescent girls giggled, excited about a chance to spend some time with a young man, and blatantly displayed their boxes for all to see.

She drifted along with the noisy crowd. When had she lost the desire to be wooed by a handsome man?

At twenty-six, she'd long ago come to grips with her spinsterhood and had given up on marrying, even though her three closest friends had found love and married in the past year and a half. India, Anika, and Elaine, though spinsters for years, all now sparkled with a newlywed glow.

Jody was sincerely happy for each of them, although she felt left out and missed their weekly get-togethers. And now India was expecting a baby.

Jody attempted to swallow as her throat tightened. Would she never know what it was like to be a mother?

At least she had the children at the orphanage to cuddle, and they all needed cuddling. She would soon be able to lavish India's baby with kisses and hugs. Shouldn't that be enough?

She shook her head in an effort to shake off her melancholy. This was an exciting day—she felt it in her heart. Something good was going to happen, and she wasn't about to let self-pity ruin it.

As she neared the crowded area outside the church, her gaze landed on India waddling toward her. Most women who were in the seventh month of their pregnancy wouldn't dare be seen in public, but India didn't mind. In fact, if Joshua hadn't put a temporary halt to it, her friend would probably still be riding horses and herding cattle on their ranch.

Jody sighed, knowing that deep inside, she wanted the happiness her friends had found. But she wouldn't settle for marrying someone who didn't make her insides tingle.

"There you are." India smiled and rubbed her back with her fist. "I had just about decided you'd chickened out on attending today."

"Well. . .I can't deny I considered it."

India looped her arm around Jody's and tugged her toward the front of the crowd. She flashed a mischievous grin. "Elmer has been asking about you."

Jody emitted a very unladylike grunt. She spied Anika and Elaine chatting near the table holding a whole slew of colorful boxes with lavish decorations. It had been a good year since the last box social, and it looked as if the ladies in town had gone all out in their decorating.

This gathering had been her idea, and she fervently hoped they would earn enough money today to finally be able to buy the mercantile property next door to the orphanage so the children's home could be expanded. She and her friends had been saving money and organizing fund-raising events for two years now.

As she glanced at each container, Jody added up the amount she thought it would sell for. Like a dust devil spinning up a cloud on a hot day, a giddy excitement swirled in her stomach. They would make their goal today; she was certain of it.

Keeping her back to the crowd, she looked both ways, relieved not to see Elmer. She lifted off the towel, set the box on the table, and then put two others in front of it. If Elmer was watching, he'd think that one of those was hers.

Lucinda, a little girl from the orphanage, squealed and darted past her, dark pigtails flying. Pedro, another orphan, dashed by close on her heels.

Jody snagged Pedro's collar as he tried to slip past her. She gave him a stern glare. "Take that lizard to the other side of the church and let it go. You need to be on your best behavior today."

"*Sí*, Señorita McMillan."

She watched him head toward the church building and bit back a smile at the boy's attempted regret, knowing this wasn't the last time today she'd probably have to warn him about his behavior.

"Pedro at it again?" Elaine smiled as Jody approached her. "What kind of varmint was it this time?"

"A lizard."

Anika shook her head and chuckled. "That boy does love his critters."

"But Lucinda hates them—and he knows it." Jody moved into the shade of one of the huge saguaro cacti, for which the town was named, and her friends followed. Anika's and Elaine's husbands stood a short distance away, chuckling about something. Jody turned so she couldn't see them. Watching her friends' spouses only made her loneliness greater. Each of her three best friends had found her soul mate and true love, leaving her the only unmarried woman left in the town of Cactus Corner, except for the Widow Classen, who was in town visiting her sister.

The church bell clanged, and everyone quieted, turning in unison to face the front. Elaine leaned toward Jody. "Elmer's been looking for you. He asked me what your box looked like."

The eager anticipation making Jody nearly bounce on her toes slammed to a stop like a locomotive squealing to a halt at a washed-out bridge. She spun around to face her friend. "You didn't tell him, did you?"

Elaine's eyes twinkled as she shrugged. "Perhaps."

"Oh, Elaine. . ." She bit back her comment, knowing her friend was teasing.

As the pastor stood and began auctioning the boxes, Jody kept a running tally. After the tenth sale, she glanced around the crowd, wondering who might buy her container. Her gaze collided with Elmer's, and he lifted his straw hat. Jody quickly turned to face the front as the pastor lifted up a box decorated in red fabric. Perhaps Elmer would bid on this one. She considered turning and giving him a coy look so he'd think it was hers, but she shrugged aside the thought—tempting as it was. She wasn't one to play games with another person's emotions.

It wasn't that she didn't like Elmer—he just didn't make her heart sing. Only an inch taller than she, he was more than three times wider. His straw blond hair stuck out from under his hat in straight spikes that reminded her of a scarecrow's. He was a kind, albeit persistent, man, but she simply didn't love him. She wanted to like him, but the pressure of his constant marriage proposals had driven a wedge in their one-time friendship.

She shivered at the thought of them marrying. Her new name would be Jody Brody.

No, she'd rather spend the rest of her days as a spinster than marry Elmer.

Aaron Garrett surveyed the deed in his hand again. There had to be a mistake.

He had bought the old mercantile, sight unseen, on the recommendation of a business associate. The property wasn't nearly as large as he had been led to believe, and the man had stated explicitly that the mercantile bordered the railroad.

But that wasn't the case.

A run-down children's orphanage sat between his newly acquired land and the railroad tracks.

His father's investment company had devoted a fair amount of money to buy the old mercantile, which Aaron planned to tear down so he could build a hotel. The recent copper strike in the mountains north of town had brought an influx of miners, investors, and businessmen into the small town. If his instincts proved right, Cactus Corner would soon be on the map.

Aaron rubbed the back of his neck as he walked along the property line. Things were worse than he'd first thought. The property was almost too narrow for a hotel, and behind it, the land dipped swiftly down to form a gulley.

He longed to prove that he was just as sharp a businessman as his father, but what would he do now? Phineas Garrett had told him many times location was everything in real estate, but Aaron had messed up in a big way.

That was the last time he'd allow an agent to buy property for him. If a man wanted something done right, he had to do it himself.

He rolled up the deed, tapped it against his leg, and glanced around the town. The few people left on the street all seemed headed in the same direction. He'd noticed a huge crowd at the churchyard as the train rolled into town. Some kind of shindig was going on there. He hoped whoever worked at the land office hadn't left yet.

Smacking the deed against his thigh, he strode south past the closed café. The only building after that was the bank, so he crossed the street to check the buildings on the east side of Main Street. He passed a dress shop, a doctor's office, and the general store—all closed. Evidently when Cactus Corner held a gathering, the whole town showed up.

He stopped at the train depot, grateful to see the clerk still there. The man was removing his black cap as Aaron approached the counter. "Excuse me. Could you please tell me where the land office is?"

The clerk tapped on his straw hat. "Ain't got one. Tucker Truesdale, the town attorney, handles most all land deeds around here. 'Course there was the time when him and his wife—"

"Where can I find this Truesdale fellow?" Aaron wasn't in the mood for a rambling story. His reputation was on the line.

"Why, most everyone's at the box social over at the church. I'm headed there myself."

"Excellent. I'll walk with you, and perhaps you can point out Mr. Truesdale."

The skinny clerk nodded, put a board behind the grill in his window, then closed and locked up the depot office. They walked the short four blocks with the clerk talking the whole time.

Aaron just wanted to finish his business so he could find

something to eat and get a room at the boardinghouse. He'd traveled from Phoenix and was tired and dirty from the train soot. He knew the previous hotel had burned down a few months ago, and he hoped building a new one in Cactus Corner would earn his father's stingy praise, but so far, things didn't look good.

"That there's Truesdale."

Aaron watched a tall man stride to the front, drop some coins in the preacher's hand, then pick up a box covered in yellow ribbon and fripperies. The man's smile came easily as he held up the box and the crowd cheered. Mr. Truesdale sidled through the horde and stopped beside a pretty dark-haired woman. She looped her arm through his and gave a smile that sent a surge of longing through Aaron.

He'd love to settle down and get married, but he'd never met a woman who intrigued him enough to make him cease his endless work. Building hotels took up most of his time, and no woman wanted to come in second to a man's occupation.

As he made his way toward the lawyer, the man noticed his approach and handed the fancy box to the woman. She glanced curiously at Aaron, smiled, and then headed toward an empty quilt spread in the shade of the church building.

The lawyer held out his hand as Aaron stopped in front of him. "Tucker Truesdale."

Aaron shook hands and introduced himself. "I'm terribly sorry to bother you at a time like this, but I have a huge problem."

Mr. Truesdale's brows lifted. "What kind of a problem?"

Aaron held out the deed. "I bought the mercantile property through an agent but was under the impression that it bordered the railroad."

"No, it doesn't." The lawyer took the deed and looked at it.

"I know that now, but that doesn't help me." Aaron heaved a frustrated sigh.

Mr. Truesdale glanced over toward the woman and then back at Aaron. "I fail to see how I can assist you."

"I need to acquire the land by the railroad. I'm planning to build a hotel there."

"The orphanage is located next to the railroad."

Aaron restrained himself from sighing out loud. "I know that now. I don't suppose the land the orphanage is on is for sale."

Truesdale shrugged. "I doubt it. You're fortunate you bought the mercantile when you did. Some women—my wife included—have been raising money to buy that property so the orphanage could expand. They'll be sorely disappointed to find out it's been sold." He pressed his lips together and glanced toward his wife again.

Aaron wasn't sure if he'd been deliberately misled or if it was an honest accident, but either way, he'd lost money and his father would be furious.

Truesdale started toward his wife, but Aaron stepped in front of him. "I was deceived about that property. There's not enough room to build a decent-sized hotel, and there's a gulch in back." He waved his rolled-up deed in the air, more annoyed than he could ever remember. He knew his behavior wasn't Christian-like and lowered his arm.

Could things get any worse?

The animated pastor pointed his direction and held up a box dinner with a frilly blue ribbon tied around it. "Sold to the gentleman in the back for four dollars."

Chapter 2

Tucker Truesdale crossed his arms and stared at Aaron with upraised brows and an amused smirk. "Looks like you just bought yourself a dinner, Mr. Garrett."

"What? No, I didn't." Aaron darted a glance at the minister, who was looking across the crowd straight at him, motioning him forward with his finger.

The man hoisted the frilly box in the air. "Come on up and claim your dinner, stranger. Your generous donation will help our orphans."

Aaron groaned under his breath. He was starved, but a picnic with some farmer's wife or an old spinster wasn't what he had in mind.

Truesdale patted him on the shoulder. "Aw, don't look so troubled. It's for a good cause."

Mrs. Truesdale's shoes scuffed against the dry ground as she hurried to her husband's side, hazel eyes alight with excitement. "That's Jody's box."

Truesdale lifted his brows again and looked Aaron up and down. "Is it, now? Elmer will sure be disappointed."

With the whole town turned in his direction and suddenly silent, except for a squalling baby, Aaron had no choice but to accept his fate like a man. He plodded forward, hoping this Elmer fellow wasn't the beefy husband of the woman whose box he'd accidentally purchased.

He shelled out the money and claimed the container, surprised at how heavy it felt and at the delicious fragrance of chicken emanating from it. His stomach gurgled. For a moment, he considered letting the pastor keep his money and offering the box to be auctioned off again, but he didn't want to hurt some old woman's feelings or embarrass her in front of the townsfolk.

Sighing, he glanced around, and the crowd seemed to be waiting as a whole to see the box's owner. A loud murmuring erupted in the crowd as a woman of average height and slender build stepped forward, looking both curious and hesitant. Her honey blond hair glistened in the sunlight like a shiny gold coin. Her long blue dress swished around her legs, and as she drew closer, he saw that her eyes were a pretty blue-green. Surely she wasn't a farmer's wife.

Apprehension surged through him, and he glanced around the crowd to see if he'd upset some hulking husband. People visited in small groups, no longer paying them any attention now, except perhaps the lawyer's wife and two other ladies chattering beside her.

The pretty woman gave him a hesitant smile. "Um. . .that's my box."

Aaron grinned. Perhaps his luck had just changed.

Jody's heart still pounded a frenzied beat. Watching several men bid on her box had been nerve-wracking, but when the handsome stranger topped all offers, she'd been both relieved and thunderstruck.

How could she be expected to dine with a stranger?

She glanced at her three friends. Anika, Elaine, and India had their heads together, ignoring their own dinners, most likely scheming and matchmaking.

The gentleman cleared his throat and held out his hand. "I'm Aaron Garrett from Phoenix."

Jody shook his hand, trying to ignore its warmth. "Jody McMillan."

"Uh. . .would that be *Miss* or *Mrs.* McMillan?"

"Oh, it's *Miss*." She pulled her hand free and glanced past Mr. Garrett to see Anika motioning them to join her and Tucker. The last thing she wanted was to have her friends questioning this stranger and making him uncomfortable with their pointed questions. When she saw that Dan and Joshua had moved their quilts next to the Truesdales, Jody knew she had to get Mr. Garrett away from them.

He stood with her box under one arm, jingling some coins in his pocket with his other hand. He seemed as uncomfortable as she felt. Was he disappointed in her?

Jody swallowed the lump in her throat. "Um. . .why don't we see if we can find some shade?"

He nodded and looked around, then pointed to a place near several saguaro cacti a little ways past the adobe church. Jody took his offered arm and allowed him to lead her.

Behind her she heard Elaine call out in a singsong trill, "Jo—dy, come and eat with us."

With her free hand, she waved off her friends and could hear their not-so-subtle laugher as she and Mr. Garrett walked away. Tension tightened Jody's neck. Her irritation with her friends surged. Why couldn't they leave well enough alone instead of embarrassing her?

Mr. Garrett stopped in front of a tall cactus and stared at the ground. "Will this do?" He kicked away several small rocks, then glanced up.

Her gaze collided with his, and she thought she'd never seen brown eyes as intriguing as his. He wasn't especially tall, probably just under six feet, but his curly dark brown hair and hat made him seem taller. Dressed in his stylish business suit, he stood out in the casually dressed crowd. Jody realized she was staring and forced her gaze away. *What's wrong with me?*

Perhaps she *would* have been better off dining with Elmer. At least she knew what to expect with him.

Mr. Garrett set her box down and peeled off his suit coat. She shifted her gaze away, knowing she was blushing.

He spread the jacket on the ground with the lining side

against the dirt, then offered his hand. "Allow me."

Jody realized he meant for her to sit on his coat, and her insides turned to mush at the thought of such an intimate action. "Oh, that's not necessary. I'm used to sitting on the ground."

One of his dark brows lifted; then he pressed his lips together as if holding back his amusement. "I'm afraid that comment intrigues me so that I can't allow it to pass without further elaboration."

"Uh. . .well, I mean, I sometimes sit on the ground when playing with the orphans."

"Ah. . .sounds delightful." He chuckled, then held out his palm. "Please have a seat, Miss McMillan. I insist."

"All right, then." She took his hand, sat down, and re-arranged her skirt, just wanting this afternoon to end. When she got back to her room, she'd kick herself for organizing this event. What had she been thinking?

"So how does this work? I've never eaten at a box social before."

Jody tilted her head up, holding her hand over her eyes to block the sun. "Well, first you have to sit on the ground."

"Ah. . .point taken." Mr. Garrett tugged at his pant legs and eased down. He smiled, and Jody tried not to notice how white and straight his teeth were.

Focusing on their dinner, she dragged the heavy box toward her, untied the bow, pulled off the lid, and spread open two cloth napkins. Then she laid a plate on each one. "I hope you like chicken."

"Love it." The gleam in his eye told her he was telling the truth.

She loaded his plate with three pieces of chicken, green beans still slightly warm in their canning jar, and buttery new potatoes.

"Mmm. . .it looks wonderful. I haven't eaten since this morning before I left Phoenix."

Jody handed him his plate and silverware, wondering what business he had in Cactus Corner. She'd never seen him here before—she was sure she'd remember him.

He took a bite of chicken and closed his eyes. "This is positively delicious. I'm going out on a limb here, but this might even be better than my mother's. Please don't ever tell her I said that, though." One corner of his mouth quirked up, and he winked.

She couldn't help the delight that coursed through her. Elmer never seemed to notice her food that much, because he was always gawking at her. A shaft of concern for her boss speared her, and she glanced around to see where he was. She didn't want to marry Elmer but hated the thought of his being left to himself without dinner. When she noticed him eating with the Widow Classen and her sister's family, she blew out a sigh. Thankfully, he didn't look as if he missed her at all.

"Have you lived here long?"

She turned back to Mr. Garrett and nodded. "Most of my life. I was raised in the local orphanage after my parents died."

"Oh, I'm sorry." His dark gaze softened.

"It was a long time ago."

He pressed his lips together in a sympathetic smile.

Who was this man? And why were her insides in such turmoil at his nearness?

She picked a piece of the chicken's crisp buttermilk coating off her skirt and flicked it away. "So. . .are you in town on business or pleasure?"

Aaron couldn't help feeling sorry that Miss McMillan had lost her parents at such a young age. His father might be tough and expect a lot out of him, but his mother was the heart of his world. He couldn't imagine growing up without her encouragement and support.

He realized Miss McMillan was waiting for his response to her query.

"I'm here on business. Looking to purchase some land."

The pretty woman across from him brightened. "Oh, then we have something in common. I—well, I mean, the orphanage committee—will be buying land soon so the dormitory can be expanded. That's the whole reason for this gathering, and if my calculations are correct, we've finally reached our financial goal."

Two youngsters ran past them, squealing and laughing. He watched them, wondering if perhaps they were orphans. They looked happy enough, but what was it like for them to grow up without parents to love and guide them? He pulled his attention back to the comely woman across from him. "So you're looking to buy real estate?"

"Yes. We've been raising funds for two years to buy the old mercantile property."

He could tell by the way her lovely blue-green eyes glimmered that she was ardent about her cause. A shaft of guilt surged through him as he realized she'd be terribly disappointed.

As much as he didn't want to admit it, he liked her. But that was dangerous with both of them wanting the same property—property he'd already bought. He shook his head. What did it matter if this woman piqued his interest more than any other had lately? If he couldn't buy the land the orphanage now occupied, he wouldn't be in town long.

She chattered on and on about her cause, making him feel even guiltier. He'd purchased the land in good faith, not knowing she also wanted it. He decided to try a different approach.

"Have you ever considered relocating the facility? I mean, it can't be safe for the children with it being in such close proximity to the railroad tracks."

Miss McMillan blinked. "Why. . .no. They know not to play around the tracks, and the location is a perfect one, being so close to everything."

"But children need a place to run and play. Surely being located in town is a hardship for the youngsters. Wouldn't they be better off on an acreage where they could stretch their legs without fear of the railroad or town riffraff?"

"Just what is your interest in the orphanage? Are you some kind of inspector?" Miss McMillan hiked her cute chin and glared at him. "Because if you are, I can assure you the children are well cared for and loved."

He lifted his hands in surrender. "Now don't get your feathers ruffled, Miss McMillan. I'm just curious. I noticed the orphanage when I came into town and thought to myself that a railroad and children were a dangerous mix."

"Well, it's never been a problem. The orphanage was there before the railroad, and it will remain in the same location for many years."

Aaron sighed, even though he couldn't help admiring her spunk and determination. He glanced at the sky as his hostess scraped the remains of his meal off his plate. *What do I do now, Lord? Just give up? Or see if I can't help Miss McMillan understand that moving would be a wise decision?*

His concentration was pulled away from his prayers as she laid a huge slice of apple pie on his plate. With his mouth watering at the sight of the fat, juicy apples, he reached out, taking hold of the dish and a clean fork. For the next few minutes, he savored each delectable bite, wondering why such a good cook hadn't been snatched up by some local bachelor.

Miss McMillan ate her pie, taking dainty bites and occasionally wiping her appealing mouth with the corner of her napkin. For a moment, he could only watch her, fascinated with her mannerisms and capriciousness. She was all lady, but underneath her frilly layers, a passionate fire burned.

If he could spend time with her, he was sure he could change her view about moving the orphanage. It was in the children's best interest every way he looked at it.

"Will you be in town long, Mr. Garrett?"

"Well. . .that all depends." He pinned her with a smile. "Will you have dinner with me tomorrow night?"

Chapter 3

J ody's shoes tapped against the polished wood floor, then quieted as she stepped onto the braided rug. She paced to the window and back to the door of her small room in the boardinghouse. Mr. Garrett was probably waiting downstairs. She should have told him she lived at the boardinghouse, but it hadn't seemed a proper thing to be discussing with a stranger.

What was she thinking, agreeing to dine with him again?

She wasn't thinking. She'd been lost in those expressive brown eyes of his and listening to his wonderful voice. That and trying to avoid glancing at her friends, who'd stared at her and Mr. Garrett the whole time they ate.

She heaved a sigh, thinking about how withdrawn Elmer had been at work today. He'd looked wounded and asked her who that man was she'd eaten with. At least he hadn't pestered her and Mr. Garrett at the box social. She was thankful he hadn't even seemed to miss her with the Widow Classen stuffing him full of her homemade sausages and sauerkraut. Jody had been relieved to have Elmer's attention focused on someone else for a change.

She'd cringed this morning when Elmer had said, "Just remember, I staked a claim on you first. You tell that city feller I intend to marry you."

She'd tried to set him straight by informing him that she belonged to no man, but he'd simply glared at her and stomped off.

Oh. . .I have to find another job.

Jody rolled her head to one side and then the other, working the tension out of her neck as she pulled her thoughts back to the man she was to meet. Part of her desperately wanted to get to know Aaron Garrett better, and another part wanted to run the other way. Surely she was mature enough to have dinner with a man without making a big to-do about it.

There was no point in prolonging the inevitable. She stepped into the hall and closed her door, unable to deny even to herself that she was attracted to the suave, handsome stranger. But what could come of such an attraction? He lived in Phoenix and she in Cactus Corner.

Holding on to the railing with one hand and lifting her skirt with the other, she made her way downstairs. At least being seen around town on Mr. Garrett's arm would help refute Elmer's claim on her.

Jody's breath caught in her throat at the view of Mr. Garrett standing in front of the window with his back to her. He was a sight to behold all decked out in his fancy suit, his dark hair curling along his collar. Broad shoulders narrowed to a slim waist, and one hand in his pocket jingled his impatience.

Had her three close friends felt such a strong attraction to the men they'd married when they first met them?

Jody twisted her lips and forced that thought out of her mind. She would enjoy spending the evening with this handsome man, but that was all. She'd most likely never see him again once he concluded his business in town.

Aaron paced the foyer of the boardinghouse where he was staying. He stopped at the open front door and stared out, hoping to see Miss McMillan coming his way. She'd been hesitant to agree to dine with him, but when she learned he was staying at the boardinghouse, she'd finally relented and told him she'd meet him there.

But she was five minutes late, and he couldn't help wondering if she'd changed her mind. Perhaps he'd come on too strong the previous evening at the box social. He should have just told her he'd bought the mercantile, but he hadn't wanted to see the disappointment in her eyes.

A woman behind him cleared her throat. He spun around and stood face-to-face with the very female who'd occupied his mind all day. A faint rose color stained her lightly tanned cheeks as he stared at her.

"Good evening, Mr. Garrett. I trust you had a productive day."

Aaron gave a curt bow and smiled. "Let's say it was an

interesting day. Cactus Corner may seem like a sleepy little town, but there's a lot going on here."

She smiled, making Aaron's stomach quiver. He'd found a rose blooming in the desert. He offered her his arm and rejoiced silently when she looped her hand around it. "I explored the town earlier and found a quaint café that serves some delicious food."

"Oh yes. Etta Stephens is a wonderful cook. I occasionally eat lunch there. Gives me a break from the boardinghouse fare."

"Obviously you live here." Ah, that explained how she managed to slip up behind him.

Her cheeks turned pink again. "Yes. I suppose I should have told you, but it didn't seem a proper topic of conversation."

"Think nothing of it." Aaron escorted Miss McMillan out into the warm sunshine, ignoring the sweat trickling between his shoulder blades. One would think that this close to sunset the temperature would drop.

"That's my place of employment."

Aaron looked across the street to where Miss McMillan was pointing. "You work for the freight lines?" He chuckled. "Don't tell me, you're a driver?"

Mirth danced in her eyes as she shook her head. A faint scent of something floral drifted past on the hot breeze. "No, although there are days I wish I were. I'm the bookkeeper and process most of the paperwork."

"Ah, I see."

They passed the attorney's office, and Aaron helped her cross over the railroad tracks. Children ran around yelling and playing outside the orphanage as they approached the building.

"Miss Jody!" Several youngsters squealed her name and charged toward them. Dirt flew behind their little feet. Three Mexican girls and two boys of Indian heritage, who all looked to be about seven or eight, huddled around Miss McMillan.

She released her hold on him, opening her arms to envelop the whole group in a big hug. Aaron stood back and watched, mesmerized. The children were dirty and sweaty, while Miss McMillan was spotlessly dressed. She didn't even grimace at handling the grubby kids. Most women would have been put off, but not her.

And he admired her for it.

After she touched each child and greeted all of them, she sweetly sent them on their way, then glanced at him apologetically. "I'm sorry about the disruption. I volunteer at the orphanage, and they all know me."

"And love you, I'd say." Aaron tucked her hand back around his arm and proceeded toward the café.

She peeked at him out of the corner of her eye. "I suppose it's only natural for them to care for me since I love each of them. I, better than most people, can empathize with them, since I, too, grew up in the orphanage."

As they passed in front of the mercantile, an arrow of guilt drove its way into Aaron's conscience. He needed to tell her that he'd purchased the old store, but if he did, would she still dine with him? Perhaps he'd tell her afterwards.

"Oh!" Miss McMillan suddenly stopped and let go of his arm. She glided over to the filthy mercantile window, cupped her hands beside her eyes, and peered in. "This is the property we're going to buy."

Stepping back, she waved her arm to the right. "This purchase will enable us to greatly expand the orphanage. It will take awhile, though, because we'll need to raise money for the building." She turned back to face him, excitement glowing in her eyes. An enchanting smudge of dirt covered the tip of her nose.

Pushing his guilt aside, knowing he would be the source of her disappointment, he pulled out his handkerchief. When he held it out to her, she gazed at him questioningly with those beautiful aquatic eyes. He tapped his finger on his nose, and her brows lifted.

"You—uh—have dirt on your nose."

"Oh my!" She grabbed the clean handkerchief and rubbed her whole face.

He couldn't help smiling, as all she'd done was smear the dirt. "Please, allow me." He retrieved his kerchief and grasped her shoulder, ignoring her trembling, then gently wiped the end of her nose. He hoped she wasn't afraid of him, but it wasn't fear in her gaze, more like. . .wonder.

Aaron swallowed and stepped back, needing to put some distance between them. He wasn't sure, but he thought he might be shaking a bit himself. How was it this particular woman had such an effect on him?

"Is it gone?" She looked in the window and tilted her chin up as if trying to see her reflection.

He nodded and returned his handkerchief to his pocket, then started jiggling his coins. It was a bad nervous habit that he was trying to break. Closing his hand around the coins, he held it still.

"How mortifying!" She pressed her lips together and looked at two cowboys riding their horses down Main Street.

Aaron chuckled. "Think nothing of it, Miss McMillan."

She swirled around, cupping her fingertips together. "We don't hold much to formality here in Cactus Corner, and I realize we've just met, but would it be too forward of me to ask you to call me Jody?"

"Not at all. And you must call me Aaron." He bit back a smile when her cheeks turned pink again.

"All right, then, Aaron. Shall we continue on? I had an early lunch, and the fragrant aromas coming from the café are just about to do me in."

He bowed and held out his hand. "After you."

They placed orders for Etta's special pot roast and mashed potatoes, then Aaron studied his dinner partner. She waved at a couple sitting at the corner table, and he didn't miss their curious stares as they waved back. Jody's honey blond hair was braided and twisted into a becoming bun. Soft wisps fluttered around her face. She had an appealing habit of tucking the rebellious strands behind her ear, even though they refused to stay.

Glancing down at the table, he forced his thoughts back to business. He'd asked around town and learned that Jody held some position of respect with the board that managed the children's home. Winning her over to the idea of moving the facility could help his cause tremendously.

"So how long did you live at the orphanage, if I might be so bold as to ask?"

She glanced at him with those beautiful eyes that he could easily lose himself in. He straightened and leaned back in his chair, arms crossed over his chest.

"Oh, it was about twelve years. First I lived there as a child until I turned sixteen; then I lived and worked there until I got the job at the freight office when I was nineteen."

Aaron pressed his lips together. "That's quite a long time."

She nodded and smiled at someone he hadn't met across the café. He wished he could just enjoy this time with the lovely Miss McMillan, but he was a businessman and had decisions that needed to be made concerning the hotel.

"Miss—uh, Jody, have you thought any more about moving the orphanage?"

She glanced at him, confused. "Why, no, I haven't. I see no reason at all to relocate. I believe I clearly stated my opinion yesterday."

Aaron sighed. She was as stubborn as she was beautiful. His gaze landed on a plate piled high with roast beef, potatoes, and carrots the waitress was carrying to another table, and his stomach grumbled. One thing he agreed with Jody on—the fragrant odors of the café were tantalizing him.

He regrouped his thoughts and tried a different approach. This morning he'd poked around town and learned that there had been several close calls with the train and the orphans. One time, two brothers had even stowed away and weren't found until the train reached the next town. Aaron imagined Jody and the orphanage staff must have been frantic to find the boys. Perhaps if he hinted at those incidents. . . "Surely there have been events with the train and the children."

Jody grimaced and avoided his gaze. She toyed with the corner of her cloth napkin. "Well, of course there have. You know how children are fascinated with anything that is forbidden."

"Then I rest my case. It would be in their best interest if the orphanage was moved."

She stared at him wide-eyed. "Uh. . .no, that's not what I meant. You can't remove all temptations from young ones but rather must teach them how to handle such circumstances. Surely if you had children of your own, you would teach them to stay away from the railroad tracks, wouldn't you?"

He nodded. "Of course—if I had any. But I also wouldn't build my home next to the tracks where they would be tempted daily to rebel against my authority. It's the nature of youngsters to test rules. I fear one of these days, one of them could meet disaster by tempting fate. Besides, they would have fresher air away from the train, and you wouldn't have to worry about the noise waking the little ones from their naps. They'd have land to raise animals and grow a bigger garden. As far as I can tell, there are only positive reasons for moving."

Jody pressed her lips together and eyed him with a narrowed gaze. "Just what's your interest in all this? Why are you so concerned about the orphans?"

His heart lurched. He hadn't been prepared for her pointed question. Silverware clinked and the soft hum of voices distracted him. He knew he should just tell her the truth.

"Mr. Garrett, I asked you a question."

Aaron sighed. Just like that they were back to using surnames. He turned to face her. "My job is to scout out towns and find property to build on. I'm sure you're aware that the only hotel in town burned down."

Jody nodded. "Of course."

"With the recent copper strike and the influx of people, Cactus Corner is a good investment, and the town needs a new hotel. I wouldn't have even been able to get a room in the boardinghouse if it wasn't for the fact that someone else was checking out the same day I arrived."

"But I still don't see what this has to do with the orphanage."

Aaron leaned back in his seat as the waitress placed two steaming plates of aromatic food in front of them. His mouth watered, but he needed to finish explaining.

"I believe that the orphanage land is the best place to locate a hotel."

Jody gasped. "You can't be serious."

"Yes, I am. But I wouldn't even consider such a thing if I didn't feel it was also in the children's best interest to relocate."

Jody pushed her food around on her plate, having suddenly lost her appetite. So Mr. Garrett was merely a fortune hunter. A scalawag who didn't mind putting orphans out on the street to accomplish his goal. Disappointment coursed through her like a raging creek after a heavy rain. She had hoped something might develop between her and Aaron, but now that would never happen. She should have known better than to be swayed by a charming gentleman. He was merely a wolf in sheep's clothing.

Like a mother bear, she would defend the orphans and their home. "The current location has sentimental value since it was the only real home I can remember having. It may be in need of repairs, but that doesn't mean it should be torn down." She wanted to add, "just so you can build your swanky hotel," but didn't.

He lifted one hand in surrender. "I understand that, but surely the children's welfare is more important than sentiment."

Jody was too upset to reply. He made it sound as if she were thinking only of herself. She pushed her plate back, ready to get away from the infuriating Mr. Garrett.

Chapter 4

Aaron stood back, watching the three-man crew he'd hired dismantle the old mercantile. Their fervent pounding made the ache in his head worse. He needed to succeed at this job to earn his father's respect. Phineas Garrett was as stingy with his admiration and praise as he was with his money, and if it hadn't been for the inheritance left Aaron by his grandmother on his mother's side, he would most likely be working as a clerk for his father instead of building the hotels that made him and his father wealthy men.

He sighed, again regretting buying the mercantile land without first looking it over himself. He wouldn't make that mistake again. Once he got the crumbling building out of the way, he could more accurately measure the land and determine if there was room for a small hotel. He may have to build out over the gulch in the back, but that might not be a bad thing. The area underneath the hotel there would allow a place where guests could tether their horses out of the sun. It might work, if the slope wasn't too steep.

What he really wanted to do was make Jody happy and let the orphanage have the property, even though he still felt the children would be better off in a different location. But if he failed to accomplish his goal, his father would only chastise him further and deepen the chasm between them that Aaron had prayed God would close. He only wanted his father's love and respect, but so far he'd been unable to earn it.

Aaron rubbed the back of his neck and looked at the orphanage property. He hated going behind Jody's back, but it was time to approach the Jacobsons to see if they felt the same way about moving the orphanage as Jody did. He wouldn't have waited this long, but he had hoped to sway Jody to his way of thinking. The woman was as stubborn as his father.

He sighed and turned his gaze next door. If only he could purchase that land, too, then he'd have the perfect hotel location and plenty of room.

But that was a big *if only*.

Jody stomped toward the old mercantile, her footsteps pounding on the boardwalk like Indian war drums. She was certainly angry enough to start a war.

Here she'd let herself become enamored with Aaron Garrett, even though she tried to resist his polished charm, but now she was sure she was just another victim in a long line, probably all the way from Cactus Corner to Phoenix. She clenched her fist as she caught a glimpse of him standing in the middle of the street, surveying the building that was being torn down.

She clenched her teeth together and furrowed her brow. Of all the nerve!

Jody stepped off the boardwalk onto the hard-packed dirt street and bypassed a rancher on horseback. So far, caught up in his work, Mr. Garrett had failed to see her approach.

She marched up behind him and stopped, trying hard to ignore the delicious scent of expensive cologne wafting from him. She shook her head. It didn't matter if he smelled better than anything she could think of. Of course, as upset as she was, she couldn't think clearly anyway. "How could you?"

Mr. Garrett jumped and spun around. "Miss McMillan, you gave me a start. I was rather engrossed in this project and didn't hear your approach."

"Well. . .you know I'm here now, so you might as well answer my question." She crossed her arms over her chest, waiting.

His dark brows darted upward. "Sorry, but I didn't hear your question. What was it again?"

He tipped his hat to her and gave a smile that made her heart quiver. She and that heart would just have to have a talk later. Aaron Garrett was too nice-looking for his own good—but she wouldn't fall for his charm again.

"I said. . .how could you?" She welcomed his confused stare, which allowed her a moment to catch her breath and push aside her attraction to him.

"How could I what?"

The obvious fact that he had no idea what she was talking about irritated her even more. She flung her arm out and pointed toward the mercantile. "That! How could you not tell me that you'd bought the property after you learned how hard I'd worked to raise money to buy it?"

"Ah, that's what's gotten your feathers so ruffled."

Jody looked sideways at the sounds of a harness jingling and a wagon creaking. A mule brayed as if telling her to get out of its way.

Aaron took hold of her arm. "Let's clear the road before we get run down."

Jody allowed him to help her up the boardwalk steps, then jerked her arm free of his. Each pound of the hammer knocking boards loose only reemphasized her failure. A plank squealed as a worker pulled it free, and then it tumbled down with a loud clatter, sending up a puff of dirt when it hit the ground. This should have been a day for rejoicing; instead, it nearly broke her heart. The town might have a nice, new hotel—and she wouldn't argue that it was needed—but the orphans would lose out.

"Miss McMillan, I know this causes you distress, and that's the very reason I was hesitant to tell you about my purchase."

Jody narrowed her eyes and glared at him. "It would have been the courteous thing to do, especially once you knew *I* planned to buy it."

"I was going to tell you the night I took you to dinner, but then we argued, and the time never seemed right. I do apologize. I probably should have told you the day of the box social when I accidentally bought your dinner, but—"

Jody held up her hand. "Wait! You mean you never planned to buy my box?"

"Uh. . .no. It was an accident. I was waving a paper in the air, and the parson mistook it for a bid. That said, I'm most delighted I did purchase your dinner. I enjoyed the meal and my time with you very much."

She didn't want Aaron being nice to her or his voice softening when he talked about their time together. Jody stared into the eyes that reminded her of coffee and could read his sincerity. For a fraction of a second, she was tempted to forgive him. She knew for sure that was what the Lord wanted her to do.

Perhaps this *was* just an honest mistake, but now Aaron knew how much she wanted that land, and he was still going ahead with his plans.

Well. . .she had other plans. And she was sure Aaron Garrett wouldn't like them.

Jody smiled and looked around the partially dismantled mercantile where she and her friends were staging a protest. She could only imagine Aaron's expression of surprise and frustration when he and the crew returned from their dinner break and found the women camped out in the middle of their work area. She chuckled to herself at her ingenuity. Surely Aaron would see how determined she was and would sell the land to the board.

"Jody, I have to tell you this is the most outlandish idea you've ever come up with." Elaine settled into the rocking chair that she'd borrowed from her husband's office. "If I hadn't planned to work on these squares for a quilt for Autumn, I'm afraid I wouldn't have been able to join you." Her gaze landed on the doctor's office across the street. "I just don't know what Dan will say about this when he returns from the Johnson ranch."

"I agree. This *is* a crazy idea, but you inspired me, Jody, when you came out to the ranch yesterday, begging for my help." India lowered her cumbersome body into the chair Jody had scrounged from the orphanage. "I left Joshua a note, but when he gets back to the house, he'll be livid. Ever since I started showing, he's been so bossy, wanting to keep me close to home. I'm about to go stir crazy. I needed a good mission to concentrate on." She flashed an ornery grin.

Elaine shook her head and focused on stitching two fabric squares together. "He's only trying to watch out for you, India."

"I know, and I love him for it, in spite of the fact that it sometimes frustrates me." She fanned herself with a cardboard advertisement for the funeral home in neighboring Baxter Bluff.

Jody glanced across the street at the café, feeling both guilty for coercing her friends to stage this protest and glad that they'd so willingly come to her side to help the orphans. Delicious odors emanated from the café, reminding her that she'd skipped breakfast, and now the dinner hour was quickly passing. Perhaps once the ladies were settled, she'd ask Etta to fix a tray for them.

India squinted and pointed down the road. "Here comes Anika."

Anika was struggling to carry a side chair Jody recognized as coming from Mr. Jacobson's office. Jody stepped out from under the shade of the mercantile and hurried to help her. Anika handed the heavy chair to Jody. "I have a surprise. Be right back."

Her friend's skirts swished as she hurried away. Jody hoisted the chair over a small stack of boards pulled from the building and set it next to India's.

"Where's she off to in such a hurry?" India asked.

Jody shrugged. "Said she had a surprise."

Simon Fitzgerald, the banker, slowed his steps as he passed in front of the old store and gawked at them. "Just what are you ladies doing?"

Jody stared back. "We're declaring a protest to stop Mr. Garrett from building a hotel here. Everyone knows this is our land, and we're not giving it up without a fight."

Mr. Fitzgerald chuckled and shook his head. "Miss McMillan, I fear you're starting something here you won't be able to finish. Mr. Garrett is one determined man."

Jody crossed her arms and hiked her chin, ready for battle. "Well, he doesn't know what he's up against."

He laughed out loud as he crossed the street and entered the café at the same time the three men Aaron had hired moseyed out. They crossed the street, their voices getting louder the nearer they came. Suddenly, one glanced at Jody and grabbed one of his cohorts by the arm. Jody braced herself for another skirmish.

"Hey! What do you think you're doing?" John Simmons, a local carpenter and the tallest of the three, stepped forward, hands on his hips. "Get out of there before you get hurt."

"We're not leaving. And that's that."

John glanced at his coworkers, then back at her. "We don't get paid if we don't work."

Jody shrugged and stood her ground. "I'm sorry, but we're staying put."

John motioned to Clay Stuart. "You and Sam go work out back for a while. I'll go tell Mr. Garrett we got us a problem."

The two workers disappeared behind the back of the mercantile, while John spun around and headed back to the café. A moment later, Jody could hear pounding coming from behind the building. She heaved a sigh and readied herself to face Aaron.

"Whatever you have there, Anika, sure smells good." Elaine stood to help Anika with the crate she carried.

"Oh, what is it?" India asked.

Anika smiled and lifted her head as regally as a queen. "I thought since we were going to sit out here, we might as well try to raise some additional funds for the orphanage while winning people over to our way of thinking." She lifted a towel and revealed a platter of sugar cookies and a dozen muffins. "We'll have a bake sale."

India clapped her hands together. "What a wonderful idea. I'm famished. I need to sample some of those cookies."

They all laughed in unison.

"You're always hungry," Jody said, smiling at her friend.

"Well, I am eating for two."

"True." Anika placed the basket on what used to be the store's counter. "Now all we need is a table of some kind."

"Here." Jody crossed the room and picked up the end of a board. "We can use these."

"Good idea." Anika hoisted up the other end, and they placed the board on two crates, blocking the open doorway. They added another plank, then set out the items for sale.

Anika straightened and looked at Jody. "You do realize we're trespassing on private property. We could get in a lot of trouble."

"I don't believe Mr. Garrett is the type of man to press charges. I just hope he'll see reason."

Anika looked Jody squarely in the eyes. "You don't know what type of man he is. You've only just met him a few days ago. Or is there something you're not telling us?"

Jody glanced away. How could she explain her feelings? She was more attracted to Aaron than she'd been to any man she could ever recall meeting, but they were practically enemies now. Or would be soon. A measure of doubt niggled at her. This morning she'd been so certain of her plan, but now. . .perhaps they should just call off the protest.

"Oh, I see." Anika's lips twisted up in a wry grin.

"See what?" Elaine looked around as if she'd missed something.

Anika sashayed over to where India and Elaine were sitting. "She likes him."

"Who?" India furrowed her brows.

"Jody likes Mr. Garrett."

"I do not." Jody stomped to the middle of the room. "Don't go telling tales, Anika."

"But you see, it's not a tale. The truth is written all over your face and in your fervent denial."

Jody turned away and stared at the café door, her friends' soft chuckles echoing behind her. It wasn't true. It couldn't be. Perhaps she admired Aaron's fine looks and citified bearing and manners, but that was all. Wasn't it? She couldn't afford to like him.

Jody leaned against a pillar and sighed, wondering again if she was making a mistake. Had she once more plowed ahead without seeking God's guidance?

Yesterday she'd been so sure of her plans. So sure the protest would stop the work on the mercantile. But it hadn't.

She heard a loud crash out back, and the whole building shimmied. Jody swallowed and peeked at her friends to see if they'd felt it, too. None of them seemed concerned, and their happy chatter continued. They were probably planning how to matchmake her and Aaron.

Jody sighed. She'd prayed about what to do and thought of the protest, but had that been only her idea and not the Lord's?

Peering over her shoulder again, she saw Stanley Becket

looking over the baked goods. He selected several items, then handed Anika some coins. She turned and smiled, lifting her hand in the air. The coins in her fist jingled.

More money for the orphanage, but what did it matter now?

The banker pulled out a chair at Aaron's table and sat down without even asking permission. The little hairs on the back of Aaron's neck stood up. Trouble was brewing; he could feel it.

Had there been a problem getting his money from the bank in Phoenix? He had some working capital on hand but not a lot.

"There's a hen party going on at your mercantile." Mr. Fitzgerald motioned to Etta, who came and took his order.

Aaron waited until she left, then leaned forward. "Hen party?"

The banker rumbled a deep belly laugh and nodded. "There's a quartet of pretty women staking their claim on your property."

Aaron looked over his shoulder and out the window and saw the flash of a green skirt inside his building, just as John Simmons stomped into the café. Aaron's heart ricocheted as he recognized Jody's slim form inside the mercantile. What was that gal up to now?

His scowling crew foreman stopped beside the table, his hands on his hips. "We've got trouble, boss."

Chapter 5

Aaron stood on the boardwalk outside the old store with his hands on his hips, staring at the ground. Just how was he supposed to deal with this situation? He couldn't exactly stomp in and throw out the four ladies, especially with one being in a delicate way.

He glanced up at the sky. *I could use some help here, Lord.*

A tiny part of him wanted to laugh at the ridiculous situation. Jody had to know her little hen party wouldn't get her what she wanted, but in spite of the irritation and inconvenience it caused him, he couldn't help admiring her gumption.

She saw him staring and crossed her arms, glaring at him as if daring him to confront her. He thought of the scripture in Proverbs: *"A soft answer turneth away wrath: but grievous words stir up anger."* He'd try reasoning with her first.

With the doorway blocked with an array of baked goods on wooden planks, Aaron climbed in a window that had already had the glass removed, then dusted off his hands as he looked around. The women had quite a setup, with chairs, food, and things to occupy them.

"We're not leaving." Jody uncrossed her arms and sashayed toward him. "So don't bother to try making us."

Aaron sighed. "You do know what you're doing is against the law?"

When he got no response from Jody, he glanced at the lawyer's wife. She fidgeted and looked away. She knew he was right.

"Some things are higher than the law." Jody stared straight at him.

"That's not for you to decide. I own this land, and you and your friends are trespassing. I could have you arrested."

Panic widened Jody's eyes for a moment, and then she glanced at her friends. Obviously they hadn't considered that factor. The doc's wife stopped her sewing and dropped her hands into her lap. Mrs. Truesdale glanced at the woman with child.

"That's not necessary. If you'll just sell us this property, we'll gladly leave." Jody's lips turned up in a smug smile that didn't quite reach her eyes.

Aaron lowered his head and shook it. He reached in his pockets, found some coins, and started jiggling them. Perhaps the best thing would be to sell out. But he didn't like losing, and deep in his heart, he felt the orphans would be safer and better off in another location. If he gave in now, they'd most likely never get to move.

He blinked. When had Jody's mission become his?

Behind him he heard the sound of rapidly approaching hoofbeats and turned to see what was happening. People rarely charged into town unless there was an emergency. A cowboy reined his horse to a stop so fast, the poor animal practically sat on his rump. Further down the road, he could see the doctor's buggy coming their direction at a fast clip. Perhaps this little showdown would be over more quickly than he'd thought.

The cowboy leapt off his horse with an agility that left Aaron awestruck. He stomped onto the boardwalk and stopped at the blocked front door. His brow was tucked down in a severe scowl.

"India, you've done a lot of crazy things, but this one takes the prize. Get your things. We're going home." He reached down, snagged a sugar cookie, and bit it almost in half, glaring at Jody the whole time. "You ought to have more concern for your friends than to ask them to participate in such a harebrained stunt."

Jody walked up to him like a royal queen. "We're selling those cookies to raise money for the orphans. That will be two bits, please." She held out her hand.

Aaron didn't know the man but gave him credit for not punching her. He must have had a lot of self-control, although it looked as if he was at his boiling point.

He reached into his pocket, pulled out a handful of change, and dropped it on the table. Several coins spun around before falling down with a clink. Glaring at Jody, he helped himself to two more cookies, then looked across the room. India was on her feet.

"I'm sorry to jump ship, but I really do need to go. By the time I get back to the ranch and rest a little while, it will be dinnertime." She pressed her fist into her back. "Oh, I'll be so glad when this child comes."

Jody walked up to her. "You won't get in trouble, will you?"

India smiled and glanced at her husband. "Oh, you know how overprotective Joshua is. He's just worried about the baby and me. And probably a bit put out for having to ride to town when he's so busy with the ranch."

Jody leaned forward and hugged her friend around the neck. "Thank you for coming. I hope it didn't tire you out too much."

India waved a hand in the air. "No, it was wonderful to get to visit with you all, even for a short while. I've missed working at the orphanage. Come visit me soon, and let me know how all this pans out."

India glanced at Aaron with a knowing smile, and it made him wonder just what it was she knew.

The lawyer's wife removed the cookies and muffins from the planks in front of the door, while the cowboy lifted the boards and set them aside. As India stepped outside, she turned and waved.

"Where's the buggy?" her husband asked as he helped her down the steps and into the street.

Aaron didn't hear her answer because the doctor was

tramping his way inside. The older woman who'd been sewing stood up. "Uh-oh, looks like I've been found out, too."

The doctor stepped farther into the room and looked around. "Elaine, what's going on here? I was halfway back to town when I heard about this little soiree. Pete Mayberry stopped me on the road and told me about it. Said he'd bought a couple of muffins from you gals."

"It's for a good cause." The woman gathered up her sewing. "I would appreciate it if you could carry this chair back to your office. I had quite a time getting it over here."

"Of course, dear." The doctor rolled his eyes and stepped forward, his hand held out. "I'm Dan Murphy, the town doctor."

Aaron shook his hand. "Aaron Garrett. A pleasure to meet you."

"I'm sorry about this." Doc Murphy waved his hand in the air. "When these women get together, they can nearly move mountains."

They shared a chuckle that made Jody scowl. The doc hoisted up the chair and made his way out. As soon as he passed through the doorway, Jody placed a board on two crates, just inside the doorway, probably hoping to keep her last hen from fleeing the coop. Mrs. Truesdale laid out the cookies, then smiled at two men who stopped at the door.

Aaron turned to Jody. "You can't stay here. You've made your point, but now it's time to go."

As if she had more to prove, Jody glided over to a rocker

and plopped down. "I don't intend on going anywhere."

Aaron heaved a sigh and stooped down right in front of her. Jody's lovely blue-green eyes widened.

"What do you hope to accomplish by this stunt?"

Jody stared at Aaron's handsome face. She'd expected him to storm in ranting and raving, but when he gently climbed in the window and didn't even raise his voice, she'd been taken off guard. How does one fight when the other person remains so calm?

She needed to answer him, but the truth was she didn't know what she'd hoped to accomplish when she had planned this protest. The dismantling hadn't stopped, and work was still going on out back. There was banging and the squealing of nails being pulled out of wood and the clatter of boards falling to the ground.

She sighed and looked at Aaron, so patient, so close. "I don't know. I just knew I had to do something."

He laid his hand on her arm. "This isn't the way to go about it. You're getting your friends in trouble with their husbands, and you could get hurt. It's not safe to be in this building." He ran his hand through his hair. "I should have told the workers to stop."

A sliver of guilt worked its way into her conscience. Aaron was a good man, only trying to build a hotel, which the town needed. But the orphans had a greater need. Why couldn't he see that?

Jody jumped at the sound of a loud bang out back. The building gave a huge shudder and groan, and then the whole back side caved in. Aaron dove forward, shocking her as he covered her body with his. Boards clattered all around them as if an earthquake were in progress. Finally, the noise ceased, leaving behind a cloud of dust that had them all coughing.

Jody pushed Aaron off and looked for Anika. She'd been talking to the men at the door, and evidently one of them had hauled her outside when the cave-in started.

Aaron shook his head, sending a shower of dust plummeting to the ground. He hauled her to her feet, looking worried. "Are you all right?"

His concern touched a deep place in her heart. It would be so easy to love this man, if they weren't adversaries. For a fraction of a second, she wanted to lean against his chest and let the security of his strong arms make all of this go away.

A crowd had gathered outside, and Jody saw Tucker shoving his way forward. She knew he'd been out of town and was due to arrive on the train today. It looked as if she'd be losing her last ally.

"Surely you see now that this escapade of yours is unsafe." Aaron brushed off her shoulders, sending a delicious shiver charging down her spine.

Jody closed her eyes, willing herself to be strong. She couldn't give in now and let him win. "I suppose you'll just have to tell your workers to stop."

The incredulous look Aaron gave her would have melted

many a woman's resolve, but she held her ground. Keeping one hand over her nose and mouth to keep the dust out, she slid her chair closer to the front door.

"Are you all right?" Anika leaned in the doorway, her arm around her husband's waist.

The lawyer glared at Jody. "You all could have gotten badly injured. This is one of the craziest stunts you've pulled, not to mention it's illegal. Mr. Garrett is well within his rights to prosecute you for trespassing."

Ashamed for raising her friend's ire, she studied the ground where the remaining cookies lay amid a pile of debris. She sincerely hoped she hadn't gotten her friends in trouble with their husbands as Aaron had said.

But wasn't that all the more reason to stay? If she left now, it would all have been for naught.

"You go on, Anika. And thanks for being here today. I appreciate the support."

As Tucker led his wife away, Jody tugged her chair as close to the door as possible without actually going outside, then sat down.

"Jo–dy!" Aaron ground out. "You cannot stay here. I won't allow it."

She hiked her chin. "You can't make me leave."

He clenched his fist. "I could pick you up and haul you right out that door."

She glared at him and tightened her grip on the arms of the chair. "You wouldn't dare."

He looked as if he were seriously considering it. She smothered that small, rebellious part of her that wished he would and maintained her stare.

Suddenly he pivoted and fled outside, down the stairs. Jody didn't know whether to be relieved she'd won or disappointed that he'd given in so easily.

Leaning her head back, she fought the tears that stung her eyes. Or perhaps it was just all the dust. Was she doing the right thing?

When Aaron had asked what she hoped to accomplish, she had no answer to give. She just charged in, barely even asking God what to do and not taking time to listen to His answer. Why did she always do that?

Was Aaron right? Would moving the orphanage be the best thing for the children?

Now that her anger had subsided, she could see the benefit of such a move. But there were no funds for such a venture even if they had land.

Yawning, she laid her head back. The heat of the day and the stress on her emotions, not to mention their near miss, had left her tired and unsettled. A little rest would make the long day pass more quickly.

Jody jumped at the sound of someone marching up the steps and realized she must have dozed off. A shadow darkened the doorway. Aaron stood there, along with the sheriff.

"There she is, Sheriff, just like I said. I've tried to reason with her, but she's the most unreasonable female I've ever met.

I want her arrested for trespassing."

"Arrested?" Jody's heart stumbled, and her parched mouth suddenly went desert dry.

Aaron nodded, but it looked as if the sheriff was trying not to laugh.

"Are you going to come peaceably, Jody?" the sheriff asked, amusement lighting his eyes and making his thick moustache dance.

Jody clung to the arms of the chair. "I'm not going anywhere, and you can't make me." She winced, knowing how childish she sounded.

Aaron looked at the sheriff, and he nodded. Faster than greased lightning, they hoisted up her chair and carried her outside. The gathering crowd cheered and burst out in a gale of hoots and laughter.

"That's showing her who wears the pants," a man hollered.

"Git 'er, Sheriff," someone else cried out.

Jody gripped the arms of the chair and wrapped her feet around its legs, hoping she wouldn't tumble to the ground. Any other time this might have been fun, but now she was absolutely mortified. She knew her cheeks were flaming. How would she ever show her face in town after being thrown in jail?

After some jiggling around, Jody found herself in the adobe jailhouse. The thick wooden door clicked shut, and the hot, stuffy room darkened. She sat there in stunned disbelief.

How could Aaron do this, just when she was starting to care for him and even beginning to see how moving the orphanage might possibly be a good thing?

She'd been on the verge of giving in, but not now. Even though the town would benefit from a new hotel, she would fight Aaron Garrett tooth and nail.

Chapter 6

Aaron fiddled with his hat while he waited at the orphanage office to talk with Mr. Jacobson. The sheriff had suggested he'd have far better luck with the orphanage director than he ever would with Jody.

He pressed his lips together and sighed. It had been two days since Jody had spent those three hours in jail, and she still wouldn't give him the time of day. He was certain he'd agonized over the event far more than she had.

A flash of color caught his gaze. Outside the window, he saw Jody marching into view with a half dozen orphans following her like ducklings in a row. She tossed her head back and laughed at something a young boy said. Taking the boy's hands, she spun around in a circle, looking lighthearted and carefree.

The thought of that smile dimming when she saw him weighted him down. In spite of the trouble she'd caused, he couldn't help liking Jody. In fact, he much more than liked her; he was deeply attracted to the stubborn yet feisty spinster.

That in itself amazed him, since he was usually so busy he only admired most women in passing.

But Jody wasn't most women. She had ridden in and made her mark on his heart faster than a cowpoke could brand a calf, and she wasn't even aware that she had.

The front door opened, and the children hurried in on a gale of chatter and clomping feet. Aaron's heart picked up speed. Jody entered right behind the youngsters.

"No running, and you all need to get cleaned up for supper." As she passed the doorway where he stood, her head turned, and her gaze collided with his. The smile on her face wobbled, then slipped. Her brows dipped. "What are *you* doing here?"

Jody crossed her arms over her chest and leaned against the door frame. In spite of her attitude, he was glad she hadn't run off at the first sight of him, though he couldn't help wishing she were happy to see him.

"I have a meeting." He stepped closer and didn't miss the apprehension in her gaze.

"With whom?"

"Jacobson." Aaron stopped a few feet away from her, admiring her wind-tossed appearance. "I wouldn't mind having dinner with you again."

Surprise widened her eyes, and she stared at him in disbelief. "Why in the world would you want to spend time with me after what I did?" She straightened, looking as if she were ready to flee.

Aaron shrugged, then allowed a smile. "Perhaps I'm a slow learner."

Her brows dipped. "Well, I'm not. I haven't forgotten the way you embarrassed me in front of the whole town and had me thrown in jail."

She'd never forgive for him for that. Perhaps it *had* been a mistake, but it was the only thing he could think of at the time to protect her. That building could have collapsed at any moment, right on top of her.

A door behind him clicked open, and Aaron turned to see Mr. Jacobson and another man he didn't recognize. After the two shook hands, the stranger nodded as he walked past Aaron and out the door.

"Come on in." Mr. Jacobson waved his hand toward the open door of his office.

Aaron looked over his shoulder, disappointed to find Jody gone. He knew he shouldn't cling to hope that she'd ever like him.

Taking a seat, he prepared himself for another battle. Perhaps he ought to just cut his losses and leave town, but he couldn't. The image of a new orphanage, located just outside of town, had engraved itself inside his mind, and he couldn't shake it loose. The children needed a champion.

Mr. Jacobson sat down behind his old walnut desk and rested his hands on its top. "So how can I help you, Mr. Garrett?"

Aaron shot a prayer heavenward. *Lord, if You're the One who put this plan for the children's home in my head, then I need Your help to bring it to pass.*

"I won't mince words, sir. I'd like to purchase the land the orphanage is on and help you relocate."

Mr. Jacobson's brows rose, and an amused smile tugged at his lips. "Jody isn't enough of a challenge for you? Now you have to take on the whole board of directors?"

Aaron wasn't sure if the man was teasing or serious, but he wasn't going to back down. Mr. Jacobson lifted his hand in the air when Aaron pressed his lips together.

"I'm well aware of your agenda, Mr. Garrett. I've talked with Jody—several times, in fact." Jacobson tapped his fingertips together. "This might surprise you, but I've actually been praying that God would make a way for us to move."

Aaron's heart skittered, then pounded a ferocious beat. He leaned forward, his elbows on his knees.

"This town has tripled in size since copper was discovered nearby. It's not the sleepy little town it was when Jody was young." Jacobson swiveled around and stared out the side window for a moment, then turned back. "I've talked with the board already. When I heard what you were about, I suspected you wouldn't waste much time in coming here. The board has agreed that we will sell you this property under two conditions."

Aaron sat up, smelling victory—both for himself and for the orphans.

Mr. Jacobson held up a stubby finger. "One—you *and Jody* must find a piece of land priced no more than what she and her friends have already collected. And two—you must persuade

Jody that the move is in the children's best interest. Expanding the orphanage has been her dream for a long while, and she needs to be involved."

Aaron slumped back in his chair. The first item was more than reasonable, but the second? Was it possible to reason with Jody McMillan?

A smile tugged at his lips. Then again, he did love a good challenge.

"So you gonna marry me or not?" Elmer stood in front of Jody's desk, smelling like rank onions and covered in dust. His pudgy face was scrunched up, and a loud squeak sounded as he sucked on his eyetooth—a habit that never failed to irritate her.

She sighed and glared back. "Not."

Elmer's furry brows dipped. "Not what?"

How did the dense man ever run a successful business? Jody grabbed her handbag, thankful the workday was over. "I am *not* going to marry you. Why don't you ask the Widow Classen?"

Elmer stroked his chubby jaw. "Perhaps I will. That sauerkraut of hers is right special."

Jody shut the door and hurried across the street toward the boardinghouse, hoping he wouldn't follow. Her emotions had been swirling like a cyclone the past week. The board of directors had informed her that they'd told Aaron they would sell him the orphanage land if she and he could find a suitable place to relocate. Why did *she* have to help *him* find land?

She felt as if her family had betrayed her. Tears burned her eyes, and she bypassed the front door and headed down the alley to avoid questions from well-meaning folks. Fifty yards behind the boardinghouse, she stopped near a large cluster of beavertail cacti. She loved their vivid pink flowers that bloomed every spring, brightening the barren landscape, but now the prickly pear cactus was just thick, rounded pads with sharp spikes.

Like me.

As if she'd pricked her finger on the barbed bristles of the cactus, she flinched.

She wanted to argue with herself, but she knew the truth. She *was* as prickly as the beavertail around Aaron.

The man both attracted her and infuriated her. She wanted to flee his presence, and yet she longed to run into his arms. How was that possible?

She was fighting a losing battle. Tears burned her eyes and overflowed onto her cheeks. Was she upset about losing the home she'd been raised in? Or losing to Aaron?

Tilting her heard back, she looked up at the light blue sky. *Help me, Lord. Show me what to do. I don't want to be a stubborn, prickly cactus.*

The memory of Reverend McCurdy's Sunday sermon danced in her mind. He'd talked about having the faith of a tiny mustard seed. She knew the truth—ever since her parents had died, she'd had trouble trusting God. Oh, she believed in Him, but giving over control of her life and trusting Him were another thing.

Now she'd been boxed in. She had no choice but to search for property with Aaron. She loved volunteering and working with the children too much to resist the board's request and risk developing a chasm between her and them.

She picked up a rock and tossed it at a yucca, relieving some of her frustrations. A roadrunner darted out from behind the spiny plant and took off across the barren landscape as if a coyote were on its tail. Nearby, a Gila woodpecker peeked its red-capped head out of the hole it had carved in one of the old saguaros. It flitted around, then took flight.

Being around nature helped clear her mind and soothe her restlessness. Even though this part of the country was dry and desolate, God had created beautiful creatures and plants for His people to enjoy.

She had longed for this freedom during her three hours in jail. Being shut away from the sun and wind had been horrible. Still, she knew Aaron would have been every bit within his right to have her locked away for a longer time, but he hadn't. He'd only wanted to teach her a lesson.

And he was right about moving the orphanage, too, although she still didn't want to admit it. Since Aaron had come to town, she'd paid closer attention to the children playing around the train tracks. Twice, older boys had taunted the engineer and stood right on the tracks as the locomotive was approaching. Its loud, plaintive whistle had cried out a warning, and the boys jumped off the tracks only a moment before the train squealed to a stop. As if it had just happened, her heart pounded out a ferocious tempo.

She looked heavenward. "All right, Lord. I'll help Aaron search for a new site for the orphanage, but You're going to have to do something about Elmer Brody, or I'll be looking for a new job."

Chapter 7

J ody fiddled with her skirt and tried not to let her shoulder
hit Aaron's as the buggy dipped into another ridge in the
rough road. She'd had a nice time riding around with him
this afternoon, but she wouldn't admit it to anyone.

"So did you prefer any particular property over another?"
Aaron made a smacking noise that sounded like a kiss to the
horse to encourage it to keep moving.

A delicious shiver charged up Jody's spine. She shouldn't
be thinking of Aaron and kisses in the same thought. After all,
she was still upset with him, wasn't she?

She heaved a sigh. Arguing with herself could be *so*
exhausting.

Aaron nudged her shoulder. "You awake?"

Jody hiked her chin. "Of course I am. I was just thinking."
Yeah, about the wrong thing.

"So?"

Jody shrugged. "I don't know. I suppose the Nickerson farm

is the best choice. It's close to town, near the creek, and has plenty of room for the children to run and play."

"Not to mention the farm has that big, fenced-in garden."

"It's sad the Nickersons died from that influenza epidemic we had here."

Aaron nodded. "Must have been tough on the people who found them dead."

Jody glanced at Aaron. "You don't suppose there could be any disease lingering there, do you? I'd hate for any of the children to get sick."

"I seriously doubt it. Besides, the children will be getting a new dormitory. The Jacobsons could live in the old farmhouse— or perhaps use it for the office."

As they pulled into town, ideas were flying in Jody's mind. Now that she'd caught the vision, she was starting to get excited about moving the children's home.

Aaron stopped the buggy in front of the café. "Supper?"

A heat other than the sun's warmed Jody's cheeks. She probably should say no, but they'd had such a nice time that she couldn't refuse. She nodded. "Dinner would be nice."

Aaron helped her down and kept his hands on her waist far longer than necessary. His gaze penetrated hers. She loved the color of his eyes. His tempting lips turned up in an enchanting smile.

"I had a nice time today. You'll have to favor me with another buggy ride soon, Miss McMillan."

Giddy—that was the only word that described the way she

felt. When she wasn't arguing with or being mad at Aaron, she truly liked him. His impeccable dress and fine manners made him stand out in this little country town, yet it was his kind-heartedness and gentle spirit that truly attracted her. Still, it wasn't proper to stand in the road staring longingly into a man's eyes. She stepped back and bumped into the buggy.

Aaron took the hint and offered his arm. "Shall we?"

Jody returned his smile and looped her arm through his. As he reached for the café door handle, the church bell started clanging, and her heart jumped into her throat. What could be wrong?

"What's that mean?" Aaron looked down at her, his brows furrowed.

"Something must have happened." She tugged him back into the street and toward the church.

Holding up her skirt, Elaine hurried toward her. "Oh, Jody, Pedro and Ray are missing."

Jody's heart all but stopped. Pedro, ornery as he could be, was one of her favorites. "How long?"

"No one has seen them since breakfast. They didn't come in for dinner or *siesta*, so we started searching but to no avail." Elaine wrung her hands together.

"Has the train been through? Could they have hitched a ride?" Jody couldn't stand the thought of the two young boys so far from home.

"No. This is Tuesday. No train today."

Jody clenched her eyes shut. Where could those rascally

boys be? "We'll just have to search the whole town."

"Mr. Jacobson is doing that exact thing now." Elaine hurried toward the gathering crowd.

Jody sought out Mr. Jacobson and found him near the train depot. Aaron followed her, and as they drew near, she heard the orphanage director organizing a search party.

"You men"—he pointed to Elmer and two of his freight workers—"you search the north end of town. Doc, you, Parker, and Lane take the east side. Me and Truesdale will take the west." His concerned gaze fixed on Jody. "Jody, you and Mr. Garrett check south of town and be sure to check the livery well. You know how those boys love horses. The rest of you fellers pick a building and search it. Just make sure none of them get left out. All right, folks, let's find those boys."

The murmur of the crowd died down as people trotted off in different directions. Jody allowed Aaron to take her arm and guide her to the southern end of town. As they approached the weathered barn of the livery, Homer Sewell rode up on a bay mare.

"What's all the ruckus?" He dismounted and held the mare's reins in his big hand.

"Two of the orphanage children are missing." The words nearly stuck in Jody's throat. What if something happened to them before they could be found?

"I've been riding south of town, exercising my mounts, but didn't see hide nor hair of any young'uns." The big man lifted his hat and ran a dirty hand through his thin, greasy hair.

"Mind if we check in the livery?" Aaron asked.

Sewell shook his head. "No, sir. Not at all." He turned toward the livery doors, opened them, and stepped into the shadowy recesses.

A blast of heat that smelled of leather, hay, and horses slapped Jody in the face. She lifted her hand to her nose and allowed Aaron to guide her inside. As her eyes adjusted, she looked around. There were plenty of places a boy could hide, but she couldn't imagine them staying for so long somewhere this hot and stuffy.

Mr. Sewell opened the double doors at the back of the livery, allowing more air and light in. A gentle breeze drifted in, making the heat slightly more bearable.

"Pedro? Ray?" Jody slipped into the dark corners of the building, searching the shadows.

"I'll check the loft." Aaron headed for the ladder and deftly climbed upward, as if it were something he did daily.

Ten minutes later, their search unsuccessful, they stood behind the livery, watching Mr. Sewell ride off on another of his horses. He looked back over his shoulder. "I'll keep an eye out for them boys."

Aaron waved to him. Tears stung Jody's eyes. "What if we never find them? What if some mean miner kidnapped them to use as slave labor?" She sniffed.

"Hey now." Aaron took her shoulders and turned her to face him. "Don't even think that way. We'll find them."

Jody's throat burned, but Aaron's gentle massaging of her

upper arms soothed her. "How can you be so sure?"

"I've been praying for the boys ever since I heard they were missing. The Bible says that not even a sparrow can fall without God knowing. He even knows the number of hairs on our heads, so He knows where the boys are. We just need to seek His counsel on where to find them." Aaron's lips turned up in a sympathetic grin. He tucked a strand of hair that had escaped her bun behind her ear.

Jody shivered with delight at his gentle touch but also with chastisement as she realized she hadn't even thought to pray about the boys. As usual, she'd charged forth in her own power. Would she never learn? Jody ducked her head, shamed to the core.

"Hey, stop fretting. We'll find the boys. Trust me." He lifted her chin with his finger and gazed into her eyes, pleading with her.

Her rebellious heart leapt at his nearness. She wanted to absorb his strength, but she'd had to rely on herself for so long that it was hard to lean on someone else.

"Jody." Aaron pulled her into his arms, and her tears gave way.

She clung to his shirt and cried, feeling good in the release of her fear and frustration.

He gently rubbed her hair. "You don't have to be tough all the time. It's okay to lean on people who care about you."

She wiped her eyes and tilted her head up, not quite ready to step from the security of his arms. "You care for me?"

Aaron grinned so widely her heart nearly stopped beating. "Isn't it obvious?"

She sniffed, thinking that throwing her in jail surely didn't prove his affection.

"Perhaps I've been too subtle." His eyes flamed with passion, and Jody's mouth suddenly went dry. He leaned forward, gazing intently at her as if waiting for an objection. Her eyes drifted closed of their own accord. His lips were warmer and softer than she'd expected, and his kiss set every speck of her being on alert. When he pulled back, his lips looked damp and his eyes warm.

Jody suddenly realized the inappropriateness of the situation and stepped back. As much as she enjoyed her first kiss, this wasn't the time for romance. Aaron seemed to sense that, too.

"So where now?" He lifted his hat and ran his hand through his dark, curly hair.

"I don't know." They wandered back down Main Street, listening to the calls for the boys coming from all directions.

Suddenly, like a light in a fog, a memory began to take shape in Jody's mind. She grabbed hold of Aaron's sleeve, and he turned toward her.

"What is it?"

Jody kept her eyes shut as the memory came into focus. Suddenly she opened her eyes and stared at Aaron, hope blossoming. "I know where the boys may be."

She grabbed Aaron's hand and dragged him down the street.

"Where are we going?"

"The boys used to play in the root cellar at the old mercantile."

"Root cellar? I never saw one there."

Jody glanced at him as she hurried on. "It's around back, where your workers were dismantling the day I—"

A tiny smile twittered on Aaron's lips. "Ah, yes. The day of the protest."

She scowled at him for finding amusement in something she took so seriously.

"I've had the men working out front since then, but they finished and were going to resume work on the back again today."

The thought of the boys lying hurt or worse flashed across her mind like lightning. Hoisting up the front of her skirt, she hurried around the side of the old mercantile, noticing how little of it remained standing. Her heart ricocheted inside her chest. *Please, God, let them be there and not hurt.*

She skidded to a halt near the cellar, but disappointment slowed her steps when she saw the doors had been covered with aged lumber from the building. There was no chance the boys could have gotten into the cellar with all that wood covering it.

Aaron must have noted her disappointment. He put a comforting arm around her shoulder and gave it a little squeeze. "It was a good idea, Jody."

She wiped her damp eyes. "Where do we look now?"

John, Aaron's lead worker, tipped his hat and tossed another board onto the pile, making a loud clatter. Jody jumped and gazed up at Aaron.

His eyes sparked, and he turned toward the man. "How long has this pile of wood been here?"

John wiped his sweaty forehead with his sleeve. "Not long, boss. We started piling it there this morning after we started working back here."

Aaron grabbed a board and slung it aside. "Get the other men. We need to clear these boards away."

"But why?" John brushed his arm across his sweaty forehead.

"Jody suspects the missing boys could be in the root cellar." He stopped tossing boards and glanced at John. "Were the doors open when you first started work this morning?"

John peered up at the heavens as if he was thinking hard, and then he nodded. "Why, I believe they were."

Aaron glanced at Jody and smiled. She was certain once the boards were cleared, they'd find the missing scamps down there. She just hoped they weren't injured.

Half an hour later, a crowd had gathered. Aaron tossed aside the last of the boards. The cellar door creaked open with a loud groan. An echoing clatter erupted when the door dropped to the ground.

Anxious and brimming with hope, Jody hurried to the steps and cupped her hand around her mouth. "Pedro? Ray?"

The crowd waited with hushed silence. Jody's hope wavered when there was no response.

"Hand me that lantern." Aaron motioned to Clint Stevens. Clint climbed over some of the discarded boards and passed the lantern to Aaron. He struck a match and the wick flamed to life.

Aaron gave Jody a wobbly smile. "You wait here."

He made his way down the rickety stairs, holding the light in front of him. As soon as his head disappeared in the dark hole, Jody hoisted her skirt and followed. If the boys were hurt, they'd need her comfort. The stairs screeched as she made her way down.

"They're here, thank goodness, but you don't mind too well." Aaron lifted up the lantern, illuminating the two boys huddled together asleep.

Her heart soared with relief when Pedro rubbed his eyes and looked up.

"Who's there?" he called in a hoarse voice.

"It's me, Jody. And Mr. Garrett."

"I'm hungry." Pedro shoved Ray. "Wake up. We can leave now."

Ray yawned, rubbed his eyes, and glanced around in confusion. "I'm thirsty."

Jody hurried across the dirty floor and pulled the boys into her embrace. "You had us all scared."

"Ray was scared, too."

The smaller boy shoved Pedro. "Nuh-uh. I wasn't."

"They found them!" Mr. Jacobson's voice boomed, setting off a chorus of muted cheers upstairs.

"Let's get out of here." Aaron raised the lantern, illuminating the small room. Go on up, boys. I imagine you'd like some supper."

Both children cheered and charged up the stairs. Jody looked at Aaron, gratitude warming her heart, though physically she was exhausted from their long day in the sun and then their searching.

"I had a feeling they'd be all right. God was watching out for them."

Jody nodded. "You were right."

Aaron grinned. "I could get used to hearing that. I suppose this reinforces my theory that moving the orphanage is the right thing to do."

Her initial happiness turned to irritation. "Well, you don't have to gloat."

His smile dimmed, and he lowered the lantern. "I'm not gloating. Just trying to get you to see the truth."

Jody stomped toward the stairs. She was tired, hungry, and dirty and wanted only to eat and then soak in a tub of cool water. "Well, you should be happy. You're getting what you want."

He grabbed her arm. "Wait a minute. This isn't about me or what I want. It's what's best for the children."

Jody yanked her arm from his grasp. "Yes, well, you won. You will have your hotel."

Aaron sighed. "This isn't a competition, Jody. I'll admit at first I may have felt that way, but once I saw the need for a new children's home, that's what drove me."

"And what happens when your hotel is built? What then?" She didn't want to hear his answer. She'd opened her heart to Aaron Garrett, and just like everyone she'd ever loved, he'd leave her. Her parents died, leaving her scared and alone. When she was fourteen, her best friend died from a tiny scratch that became infected. The children she loved either got adopted or moved away once they were old enough to live on their own, and even her spinster friends had all found love and left her alone.

Aaron's hand made a bristly sound as he rubbed it across his chin. "It will take quite awhile to build a hotel. A lot can happen between now and then, but in the end, I suppose I'll return to Phoenix or search out another town to build in."

Jody closed her eyes against the stinging sensation. It was just as she thought. Aaron was leaving. She couldn't afford to lose her heart to a man who'd ride off someday and leave her behind. She was the only person who could protect herself.

"Well"—she hiked her chin—"it seems to me you're getting everything you want, Aaron. You ought to be quite happy." She stomped up the stairs, blinking back her tears.

"Not everything. . . ," she thought he murmured as she stepped onto the hard ground.

Chapter 8

Aaron paced his small room at the boardinghouse. Rubbing the back of his neck, he stopped at the window and stared out. His own scowling reflection glared back.

Why had Jody reacted that way after finding the boys? She should have been happy, but instead, she seemed more irritated with him than ever.

Women! Who could understand them?

He pushed away from the ledge and flopped onto the bed, lying back, staring at the ceiling. A water stain marred the whitewashed wood. He pressed his lips together as he contemplated what to do.

Jody had responded almost eagerly to his kiss, but later she was as mad as ever at him.

And he had no clue why.

He hopped off the bed and crossed to the window again. Shoving aside the curtain, he stared at the inky pane as dark as his dreams.

"Lord, why did I have to give my heart to a stubborn, fickle woman who doesn't want it? Did I miss Your guidance?"

He was fooling himself to believe Jody could ever care for him. He'd allowed himself to hope, and now his heart was aching because of it. He paced to the door, pivoted around, and strode back.

A pair of laughing green eyes teased his memory. Once before he'd dared to love a woman. Florence had turned the heads of most men in Phoenix with her unparalleled beauty and lively personality. She'd done more than just snag his attention; she'd stolen his heart when he was but seventeen, then stomped on it when she quickly married a wealthy businessman. The joke was on her when Aaron unexpectedly inherited nearly a quarter of a million dollars from his grandmother on his eighteenth birthday.

He pulled out the desk chair and dropped into it. Jody and Florence were almost complete opposites in every way. He shouldn't be comparing them, but the one thing they had in common was that both women had staked a claim on his heart.

Aaron growled and jumped up. He jerked his suitcase out from under his bed. Jody had made her feelings clear. She had no interest in him—could barely tolerate him. He couldn't spend months in Cactus Corner building a hotel and seeing her all the time. The pain would be too great.

He slapped his belongings into the case and clicked it shut. Only one more thing to do.

Aaron pulled an envelope and a sheet of company stationery

from his briefcase, then sat at the small desk and picked up the pen.

> *Dear Father,*
>
> *After careful consideration, I have decided to use the alternate location as a hotel site. I will be leaving tomorrow for Banner Ridge. I have workers here clearing the property I purchased. With the vacant land being so near the railroad, it should sell for as much as I have invested in it. The orphanage next door is interested and will most likely purchase the property to expand their facilities.*
>
> *I hope you and Mother are well.*
>
> *I remain your loving son,*
> *Aaron Garrett*

He set the pen down and blew on the ink, then stuffed the missive into the envelope. Tomorrow morning he'd catch the train to Banner Ridge, leaving his heart behind in Cactus Corner.

Jody swirled the coffee in her cup and glanced around the café, knowing she wouldn't see the man she'd come to love. She'd looked for Aaron at the boardinghouse at breakfast the day after they'd found Pedro and Ray, hoping to apologize for her appalling behavior, but he never came downstairs. That evening she learned he'd checked out and left town.

"I still can't believe Aaron is gone."

Anika gave her a pensive stare, then a sympathetic smile. "I knew you cared for him."

Jody snorted. "Lot of good it did me."

Elaine patted her arm. "At least Elmer has turned his attentions on the Widow Classen. You no longer have him pestering you to marry him."

"Yes, that's something to be thankful for." Jody toyed with her fork, doubting she'd be able to eat the plate of food Etta would soon deliver to their table. Why had she been so mean to Aaron that night when they'd found the boys?

She was a coward, that's why—frightened that Aaron would up and leave town, breaking her heart, so she had tried to keep him at arm's length. She sniffed, and her lower lip trembled. The very thing she dreaded had happened sooner rather than later.

"Stop it." Anika lowered her brows, giving Jody a stern glare.

Jody blinked, her mind swirling. "Stop what?"

"All the what-ifs and why didn't I's."

Jody glanced at Elaine, who nodded her head. "You can't rationalize everything—wondering if the situation would have turned out better if you'd done things differently."

"But I drove Aaron away."

Anika squeezed Jody's fingers. "You need to leave all this in God's hands. If you and Aaron are meant to be together, God will work it all out. Fretting won't help."

Jody sighed, feeling the tension leave as she accepted her

friend's advice. "You're right. I'll try harder to leave things in God's hands."

She took a sip of coffee, the cup clinking as she set it back in the saucer. "So are we in agreement to ask the board's permission to purchase the Nickersons' farm? It could be quite a long while before we raise enough money to build a dormitory, though."

Both Elaine and Anika nodded.

"Good. On Saturday I'll drive out to visit India and make sure she's favorable to the idea." Jody leaned back to allow Etta room to set down her meatloaf dinner. Suddenly her appetite returned. She may have lost Aaron, but he'd been right about moving the orphanage, and the children would be the real winners in the long run. Now all she needed were some creative ideas for raising some more money. . .and something to soothe her aching heart.

Monday morning, Jody grasped the arms of the wooden chair across from Tucker's desk, her heart dropping to the floor. "But I don't understand. How could the Nickerson farm be sold? Didn't Anika tell you we wanted to buy it for the orphanage?"

"Actually, no. She mentioned you all had decided on a place but never said which property. I'm terribly sorry, Jody, but there are other places that would probably work almost as well."

"But nothing as close to town that wouldn't need lots more work." Jody's hope sank as if it were trapped in quicksand. How could this be happening?

Fearing she'd burst into tears, she hurried from Tucker's office and made her way behind the building to avoid stares. Feet dragging on the ground, she wandered through the cacti, stopping in the shade of a giant saguaro. The shadow this particular cactus made reminded her of a cross with its stubby arms upturned, as if in praise to God.

Unshed tears burned her eyes, then dripped down her cheeks. Were all her dreams doomed to failure?

Aaron had been gone a week, and she missed him more than ever. Why hadn't she realized the treasure God had given her before she'd cast it away?

Leaning into her hands, she allowed her tears to flow. After a few minutes, she looked up, struggling to gather her composure. A woodpecker tapped at a nearby cactus, and the warm breeze teased her cheeks but did little to soothe her.

"I've made a mess of things, Lord. I thought I was doing what You wanted, but obviously I haven't been. Forgive me for rushing ahead with mule-headed stubbornness and not spending enough time seeking Your will. I don't know what You have planned for the orphanage, but I will continue to pray that You will direct and guide us. And if it's Your will, please bring Aaron back."

As if a cleansing rain had blanketed the parched land, Jody felt refreshed and relieved. She didn't always have to be the one to work things out. God was in control.

Chapter 9

Aaron held his breath, staring at his father. Instead of traveling to Banner Ridge as he'd planned, on a whim, he'd come home. "So what do you think?"

He'd just explained how he'd bought the Nickerson farm and donated it to the orphanage. Jody and her friends could use the money they had collected to build the new dormitory, since they wouldn't have to use it to buy land.

"I have to say I'm proud of you, son." Smiling, Phineas Garrett leaned back in his chair and laced his fingers over his midsection.

Aaron's heart leapt, and he sat numb with stunned delight. He'd finally heard the words he'd longed to hear for so many years, and they had come about not because of a successful building project, but simply from giving to someone in need.

"I know I've been hard on you, Aaron, but I didn't want you to grow up wealthy and spoiled. You're my only heir. I needed to know you would be a man of character and could run things after I'm gone." His father stared out the window for a moment, then captured Aaron's gaze again. "This whole orphanage deal proves to me that people are more important to you than money. You did a good thing."

A warmth like a steaming cup of coffee on a cool morning flowed through Aaron's being. His father was proud of him. This moment would always be one he cherished as a high point in his life.

Perhaps that was God's purpose in sending him to Cactus Corner—not to build a hotel, but to help the orphans and gain his father's respect.

If only he could get Jody out of his mind and heart.

Phineas leaned forward, a twinkling gleam in his dark eyes. "So tell me about this gal that's got you all hornswoggled."

Aaron blinked. Was it that obvious?

His father chuckled. "I may have been married thirty-five years, but I still recognize that look. Tell me what happened, son. Perhaps I can offer some advice."

Two days after his talk with his father, Aaron stepped off the train at the Cactus Corner depot. A nervous excitement surged through him at seeing Jody again. His father had said if he loved Jody so much as to mope around like he was, then he owed it to himself to make amends and see if they had a future together.

With carpetbag in hand, he crossed the street, and his gaze

automatically swerved toward the old mercantile land. His crew had done a good job of clearing away the building. Behind the orphanage were tall piles of lumber he had donated to be used for firewood.

He turned around and headed toward the freight office—and Jody. But as he passed the orphanage again, his pace slowed as he noticed the words *FOR SALE* painted on the side of the adobe building. His heart jumped. This was what he'd wanted all along. He glanced at the freight office and then across the dirt road to Tucker Truesdale's office. Perhaps a quick detour was in order.

Aaron stepped into the lawyer's office and was suddenly assailed with the scent of beeswax.

Truesdale glanced up from his shiny walnut desk and smiled. "Good to have you back in town, Mr. Garrett."

They shook hands, and Aaron took the seat the lawyer indicated.

"So what can I help you with?"

Aaron leaned back, willing his insides to settle. Just perhaps, he'd win the woman he loved and get the land he'd wanted. "I'd like to buy the orphanage property if it's still available."

Truesdale smiled. "It is."

He named a price. For a brief second, the businessman in Aaron considered dickering over the sale price, but the money was going to a good cause. He quickly signed papers, put down a deposit, and agreed to have the remaining funds forwarded.

"So what did Jody say when you told her about the

Nickerson farm?" Aaron laced his fingers to hold them steady. Had she been happy about someone buying that property and donating it to the orphanage? Had she figured out it was he?

Truesdale's brows dipped, and he sighed. "She wasn't too happy. Had her heart set on getting that property for the children."

Aaron blinked. "I don't understand. That's the whole reason I bought that land. Was there some misunderstanding?"

Truesdale leaned forward, head cocked to one side. "You may not remember, but you were rather upset and in quite a hurry to leave town that day. You purchased the land but never indicated it was to go to the orphanage. I couldn't breach confidence and simply told Jody the farm had been sold."

Aaron rubbed the back of his neck. Oh brother, what a fine mess!

A few minutes later, he stood outside Truesdale's office, staring at the Brody Freight Company window, thinking about all that had happened. He had given up on purchasing the orphanage land when he left town, but now God had turned things around and blessed him with the property. Would the same be true with Jody? Would she even be happy to see him?

Anxiety made his belly swirl. His heartbeat sped up as he stepped off the boardwalk and crossed the road. He hoped the woman he loved was in the building straight ahead.

He thought of how Jody's blue-green eyes sparked with excitement as she talked about her vision for the orphanage. He loved her fiery passion and loyalty to her cause. If only she were that passionate in her feelings toward him. His steps slowed as doubt crept in.

Before he informed Jody that he'd bought the Nickerson farm, he wanted to see her response to his presence. He wanted her to care for him, not because he was wealthy or had the means to make her dreams come true. He wanted her to love the man he was.

"Hey, clear the road!"

Aaron jumped at the gruff voice and the sound of harnesses jingling. He moved out of the road and put his foot on the first step up to the boardwalk. The freight office door jingled open, and an angel dressed in blue stepped out.

The sun shone down on Jody's golden hair, making it gleam. She squinted against the outside glare and pulled the door shut. He stepped onto the boardwalk just as she turned around. Her hand lifted and covered her brow. Suddenly her gaze shifted from questioning to surprised.

"Hello." Excitement mixed with unnatural shyness made his legs tremble.

"Aaron," she whispered. "You came back."

He flashed her a soft smile. "I couldn't leave things the way they were. You need to know how I feel."

Jody glanced around. Two scruffy miners passed by, giving them quick, curious stares. "Not here."

She grabbed his hand and pulled him behind the freight office and out onto the desert floor. Cacti of various sorts littered the barren land, along with a stubby tree or two. Closer to the creek, greenery grew in abundance. At the sight of Jody and him, a lizard darted under cover of a yucca.

Jody dropped his hand and turned to face him, looking as shy and anxious as he felt. "So what was it you wanted to say?"

Sweat trickled down his back as he stared into the eyes he loved so much, hoping to see affection staring back. "I couldn't just leave things as they were. I've been miserable since I left here. You have to know I care for you. Love you."

Something flickered in Jody's eyes, and she started crying. "Oh, Aaron. I'm so sorry for driving you off. I tried to find you to apologize for my irrational behavior, but you were already gone. Can you forgive me?"

"All is forgiven, sweetheart." He took his beloved's hands. Jody's warm smile took his breath away. "I love you, Jody. I know we haven't known each other long, so I won't mention marriage yet, but could I court you? Should I ask Mr. Jacobson's permission?"

Hope soared in his heart at her expression.

"I'm a twenty-six-year-old spinster, Mr. Garrett. *My* permission is all you need." Jody squeezed his hands and smiled. "You may come courting—and you may also talk marriage, if you're so inclined."

Aaron was sure his smile nearly reached his earlobes. "I'll have you know I aim to retire your spinsterhood status."

"That's perfectly fine with me." Jody laughed and fell into his arms.

Aaron wrapped his arms around her, holding her tight

against his chest. His heart surged with love for Jody and gratitude to God. He gently set her back a little and leaned down, and their lips met. For a few too-short minutes, Aaron was in heaven on earth.

With regret, but knowing it was necessary, he pulled back. "I have a surprise."

"Another one?" Jody grinned, her pretty lips looking puffy and thoroughly kissed.

Aaron nodded. "I bought the Nickerson farm. Truesdale was supposed to notify the orphanage board that I purchased the land as a donation, but obviously I failed to make that clear to him."

He didn't think Jody's smile could get any bigger, but it did. "Oh, Aaron. That's so kind of you. We can use the money we've collected to start a dormitory right away."

He nodded. "I thought we could also buy a place in town to live when we're not traveling. That way you can still help out at the orphanage and visit your friends."

"Oh yes. That sounds perfect." Tears gleamed in her eyes, and she lunged back into his arms, but Aaron didn't mind one bit.

VICKIE MCDONOUGH

Vickie is an award-winning inspirational romance author. She has written four Heartsong Presents novels and five novellas. Her second Heartsong book, *Spinning Out of Control,* placed in the Top Ten Favorite Historical Romance category in Heartsong's 2006 annual contest. Her stories have also placed first in several prestigious contests, such as the ACFW Noble Theme, the Inspirational Readers Choice Contest, and the Texas Gold contest. She has also written book reviews for over five years and enjoys mentoring new writers. Vickie is a wife of thirty-one years, mother to four sons, and a new grandma. When she's not writing, Vickie enjoys reading, gardening, watching movies, and traveling. Vickie loves hearing from her readers at vickie@vickiemcdonough.com.

A Letter to Our Readers

Dear Readers:

In order that we might better contribute to your reading enjoyment, we would appreciate your taking a few minutes to respond to the following questions. When completed, please return to the following: Fiction Editor, Barbour Publishing, Inc., P.O. Box 719, Uhrichsville, OH 44683.

1. Did you enjoy reading *The Spinster Brides of Cactus Corner*?
   ❑ Very much—I would like to see more books like this.
   ❑ Moderately—I would have enjoyed it more if _____
   _____
   _____

2. What influenced your decision to purchase this book?
   (Check those that apply.)
   ❑ Cover   ❑ Back cover copy   ❑ Title   ❑ Price
   ❑ Friends   ❑ Publicity   ❑ Other

3. Which story was your favorite?
   ❑ *The Spinster and the Cowboy*   ❑ *The Spinster and the Doctor*
   ❑ *The Spinster and the Lawyer*   ❑ *The Spinster and the Tycoon*

4. Please check your age range:
   ❑ Under 18   ❑ 18–24   ❑ 25–34
   ❑ 35–45   ❑ 46–55   ❑ Over 55

5. How many hours per week do you read? _____

Name _____

Occupation _____

Address _____

City_____ State_____ Zip _____

E-mail_____

If you enjoyed

The Spinster Brides
OF CACTUS CORNER

then read

LOVE LETTERS

*Four Generations of Couples
Changed by Expressions of the Heart*

Love Notes by Mary Davis
Cookie Schemes by Kathleen E. Kovach
Posted Dreams by Sally Laity
eBay Encounter by Jeri Odell

If you enjoyed

The Spinster Brides
OF CACTUS CORNER

then read

KISS

THE

Bride

~~COOK~~

FOUR CONTEMPORARY ROMANCES ARE
STRENGTHENED BY THE SAME LASTING INGREDIENT

Angel Food by Kristy Dykes
Just Desserts by Aisha Ford
A Recipe for Romance by Vickie McDonough
Tea for Two by Carrie Turansky

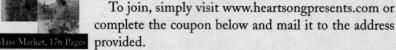